I0728143

DARKER DEPTHS

by

K.M. Robinson

DARKER DEPTHS: Book Two of The Siren Wars Saga.
Copyright © 2018 by K.M. Robinson.

Published by Crescent Sea Publishing.
www.crescentseapublishing.com

Cover designed by Reading Transforms.
Image copyright © K.M. Robinson Photography.

This is a work of fiction. Names, characters, brands, trademarks, places, and incidents either are the product of the author's imagination or are used fictitiously. Any resemblance to actual events, locales, organizations, or persons, living or dead, is entirely coincidental and beyond the intent of either the author or the publisher.

All rights reserved, which includes the right to reproduce
this book or portions thereof in any form whatsoever
except as provided by the U.S. Copyright Law.

Antaire
Hontan
Waterfalll
The Ropes
Abandoned
Dwelling
Brine
Pool

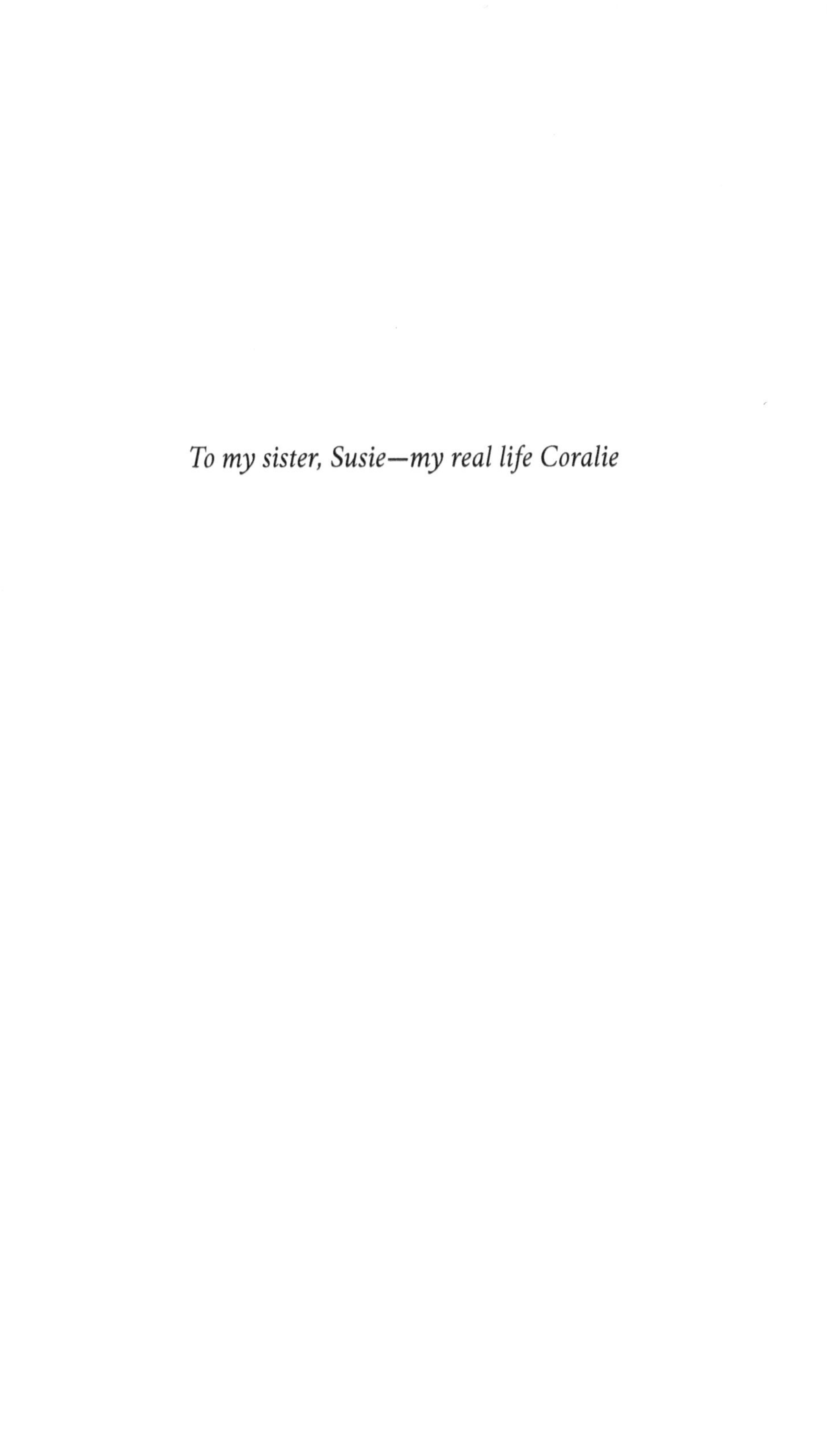

To my sister, Susie—my real life Coralie

CHAPTER 1

EVEN THE BEST INTENTIONS—THOSE WELL THOUGHT OUT
and planned—have the potential to end in disaster.

This is one of those disasters.

Then again, this was *hardly* thought out.

"Just stay quiet, Coralie," I instruct, her head on my
lap. I pet her hair as if our life depends on it.

My finger grazes over the shell I tucked away in her
hair while we were still in the palace in Scylla—*it's still
there*. When Murdoch turns away to face the love of his
miserable little life, I dart my fingers toward my *iluse* and
pray no one notices.

I dig a small hole in the sand beside me—once they
realize I have a weapon, they're going to look for an
explanation. They swept the area before letting us sit, but
if I can convince them that I found it under the sand,
maybe they'll let me keep my *iluse*. I wouldn't put it past

them to take my covering and make me swim around without one.

The light filters down through the water, giving everything a muted look, but at least we can see again—the moonlight hardly gives enough light to swim by under the waves.

"Sit up!" one of the sirens demands, holding a trident out toward my little sister. I grab her shoulders before she can move and drag her to a sitting position.

"She's up," I inform the siren.

"Don't touch," he snarls, turning back away.

"What are we going to do?" Coralie asks quietly. "It's been two days."

"You heard Caspian and Merrick—they're coming to get us," I remind her. "At least they're letting us talk now."

The sirens had spent the last two days dragging us through the water. It's a miracle I can move my tail at all after being bound together backward.

"You're not getting any ideas in that pretty little head of yours, now are you?" Tarni asks, feigning innocence as she floats over to me. She drops down onto the sand, leaning back on one arm to support herself.

If only mermaids could be drowned.

She eyes the gash on my neck and shoulder. I nearly reach up to rub it but that's likely exactly what she wants—to see that it bothers me. My captor sighs, sweeping her gaze over to my sister.

Drown her—yes, that's *exactly* what I want to do.

"I suppose it's time I learn a little bit about you, don't you think, tiny one?" She swims over to Coralie and lifts a lock of her blonde hair. "Are you one of Aila's descendants too?"

Tarni smiles, looking back over her shoulder at me menacingly.

"Good thing you're older, Celena," she taunts. "We'll offer you up to the humans before we send your sister to the surface."

Coralie bleaches whiter than coral.

"You still need us, Tarni," I retort.

"Oh? Why is that?" she asks. "It seems to me that we've accomplished what we wanted—to get away from Scylla. We're safe now, and your friends aren't close enough to catch us, so we could siren you out of our lives and into the hands of the sailors, and it would actually speed our trip up—*and* get rid of the witnesses."

"There are three mermen coming after you. They're more powerful than any of you here and they're smart enough to bring reinforcements. They're going to catch you, and the only leverage that you're going to have is being able to trade the two of us."

"Fine," Tarni sighs. "I'll keep you around for now, just in case your merman shows up, but don't forget that at any time, I can drag either of you to the surface and destroy you."

She tugs harshly on Coralie's hair, jerking her entire body forward. Coralie tries not to gasp, closing her eyes to focus herself.

"Time to move, mer children," Tarni says motioning for the other sirens to pick us up off the ocean floor.

The siren that stopped me from rescuing Coralie outside of the palace two days ago swims over to me. He's slightly bigger than Merrick and Caspian, but not so much so that it will throw me off balance when we inevitably fight. I've practiced with Merrick so many times that it's become second nature to me—I know right where to hit this siren merman.

"Let's move," he says gruffly. He picks up the chain attached to the shackles on my wrist. I'm loosely bound between my hands and my tail. A secondary chain runs from the middle of those links to my captor's hands, allowing me to swim—difficult as it is to move with heavy chains around my tail—and if I try to escape, he can pull the chain and restrict the use of my tail.

I could curse the seven seas that the sirens got us far enough into their territory that they could find supplies they had hidden in the cave.

I glare at Murdoch. He almost looks apologetic for dragging us into this disaster, but he's following the lead of his partner, and Tarni controls it all. Murdoch sucks in a breath and brushes back his hair—it's a deep red with a purple sheen to it—and narrows his eyes at me.

I swim slightly behind Phorcys, keeping a careful eye on Roni as she oversees my little sister. Thankfully, they didn't chain her up the way they've constricted me, though Roni is much stronger than Coralie and could easily hold her back by the chains on her wrist, even with her tail free. I, on the other hand, might be a tough match for Phorcys.

Tarni brushes her hand over Murdoch's shoulder, reinforcing her manipulation. She's brilliant really—sirening a merman is as easy as making him fall in love.

"Where are we going?" I ask loudly. It's been two days of them dodging my questions—I've had enough.

"Does it matter?" Murdoch mumbles.

The rest refuse to speak, though Roni snickers at me, looking back over her shoulder as she dangles my sister's chain from her fingers for my benefit. I use the silence to look around.

I keep a careful eye on the route ahead of me, but my eyes bounce over the sea floor, looking for anything that might help me. I try memorizing what I see in case Coralie and I can escape—I'll need it to guide us home.

We swim over a seaweed garden that hasn't been maintained in years. It looks like this used to be a dwelling place for sirens at one point, but they've since moved on. I wonder if all the sirens stayed together after they left the mer collection or if they branched off and formed smaller groups.

We're close to the seaweed, hovering just far enough above it that I can't reach down and touch it. The further we swim, the more something nags at my brain. We nearly reach the end of the garden before I realize what it is—a message.

Swimming so close, it's hard to tell, but I'm nearly certain the gaps between the seaweed aren't random. It looks like a path has been cut into it.

Caspian has been here.

I perk up the second the thought crashes over me like the waves on the side of the human ship I sirened not long ago. Phorcys notices my shoulders jolt and glances at me out of the side of his eye. I wiggle, trying to make it look as though I'm attempting to adjust the shackle around the bottom of my tail.

"Couldn't have picked a lighter cuff, could you?" I snip.

He rolls his eyes at me, tugging just enough for me to feel it through my chains. I risk a look back, pretending once again to fuss over my tail. In the distance, I can vaguely see part of a division in the seaweed—definitely a path.

If my twin has been here, that means the others are here too. There's a chance that Caspian, Merrick, and Llyr out-swam us, going the long way around.

But do they know where we are or are they searching for us and just went too far?

I glance around, looking for more clues.

If I can find them—or if they can find me—Coralie and I might be able to survive this. I just have to make sure to position Coralie correctly so that they can ensure her safety.

A fever of stingrays glides by effortlessly in front of our path. Tarni hesitates for a moment, allowing them to cut us off. Several have their wing-like fins up in the water, not moving them at all as they propel themselves forward. I wish swimming were that easy for me.

Coralie catches my eye, looking pitiful. Her blonde hair hangs down over her face. I haven't been able to slip the necklace off of her neck yet, but she miraculously wore our grandmother's jewelry to the palace during my trial—the one with the secret weapons in it that I used when we chased the sirens the first time. If I can transfer it to my own neck, I'll have at least a few resources on my side. It's a shame Coralie doesn't know what hides inside the necklace, nor does she know how to use them.

We swim to the left, avoiding a wall of coral that stretches halfway to the surface. The collection of sirens and mer could have easily gone over it, but it seems that Tarni likes to keep us low in the water.

"Princess," one of the other sirens says. "Would you like me to—"

"Yes," she cuts the merman off. "Go."

I watch his movements as he swims ahead of the

collection, likely to scout the next place we'll stop. It would be nice if Merrick could take him out before we arrive, but I know the mermen won't hurt the scout until they're certain that they know where we are.

A sign. I need another sign.

The sirens haven't left us alone long enough for me to leave a conch shell message for anyone—even if I *did* have the time, which one would I leave it for? The message can only be listened to by one mer and I have no idea which of my friends would find it or if they'd even be together. It's practically pointless to leave a message like that.

Coralie sighs ahead, dropping her head down slightly in the water. The poor thing has been through so much.

"Can I swim with her?" I ask quietly, hoping Phorcys has some kind of heart.

He grumbles but knows it will make it easier if I calm Coralie down. We position ourselves so that I can swim next to my sister.

"Hey," I say, announcing my presence.

She sucks in a breath and sighs, turning with a small smile.

"This is the worst," she responds.

"Yeah, I know," I say ruefully. "Let's play a game."

Roni and Phorcys both lecture me, but I don't care—Coralie needs a distraction, and *I* need another set of eyes to help me look for clues.

Cor just doesn't know what the stakes are yet.

"Do you remember that spy game we used to play with Casp when we were little? Let's try that," I encourage her, hoping she remembers the real reason we played that game—Caspian had hidden a baby sea turtle, and we had to sneak it in without our mother looking, and the clues he left were the only way to find where he had hidden it before returning home that day.

"Which one?" she asks.

"The one where we had to find the baby sea turtle and other things."

She frowns for a moment and I pray she wasn't too young to remember.

"Oh, I remember," she adds. "I'm Thinking Of…"

"Yes! That one," I cheer. "I'll go first."

She nods, but I'm not sure she fully understands.

"I'm thinking of…something red," I say, spotting a school of red fish swimming at us.

"The fish," Coralie replies.

"Yes," I chuckle. "They remind me of Caspian."

"Isn't your brother's tail teal?" Roni criticizes.

"Yes, that's not why they remind me of him." I keep my words pointed, hoping Coralie starts to process all my clues and pieces this together.

"I'm thinking of something dark," Coralie says, doing a terrible job of hiding where she was looking.

"The cave," I reply.

"It reminds me of Merrick's tail," Coralie responds

with a smirk. It reminds *me* of Merrick too, but for an entirely different reason.

"So this whole game is about your pathetic little friends?" Roni asks, flicking her tail impatiently.

"Oh, well excuse us," I retort. "We just won't say why things remind us of them anymore."

Good, now we have a focus, but we don't have to discuss the connections out loud.

Coralie glances at me from under her hair, nodding so briefly that I can barely tell. I think she understands.

We continue to play for a while, pointing out rocks and jellyfish. Phorcys starts to pay attention, glancing around to see if he can spot the items before the guesser does. Roni continues to frown.

"I'm thinking of something green and long," Coralie says, sounding more excited than she has the entire game.

"Seaweed?"

"Kind of," she replies. "But not from the bed over there."

I keep looking around, trying to see what my little sister noticed.

"The fish?"

"Nope, better hurry," she informs me.

I look straight down, swinging my gaze up just a little to see what is in our direct path that we might be leaving behind soon.

There, on a rock a dozen lengths away, is what appears to be a *sarasa*.

Merrick.

Coralie tips her head at me when she knows I've seen it.

"Too late," she pretends to gloat. "It was a dead jellyfish tentacle floating over there."

She points in the opposite direction.

"Do I get to go again?" she continues.

My sister might be brilliant.

"Yes, Cor, you can go again," I say dramatically.

She makes a show about searching for something else to point out while I desperately look for another clue. I spot a second *sarasa* draped over another rock on the left. Not long after, another appears, though none of the sirens take notice of them.

"We're here," Tarni finally announces.

Ahead, a cave looms in the water, dark and dangerous. I have no doubt if the scout hadn't gone ahead, they'd shove me into the darkness of the cave first to test for sharks or other dangerous creatures lurking in the depths of the shelter.

The scout hovers outside of the rocks, nodding to the siren princess. Tarni takes Murdoch's arm as she smiles at him like he's the whole sea to her—I'm positive she'd leave him for dead if he ever becomes unuseful to her.

Murdoch wraps an arm around Tarni's waist and

guides her into the cave. Phorcys pulls on my chains, moving me away from Coralie. For a moment, I panic, thinking they're going to separate us, but Roni follows, allowing us to swim into the cave first.

Phorcys moves me to the back of the cave and lets me settle on sand against the wall. Roni swims away before Coralie curls into me on the ground.

"They're here," I whisper into her ear around her hair as she adjusts her position, moving enough to cover my words.

She ducks her head slightly, indicating that she understands.

"Follow my lead and do whatever I tell you to do. No questions."

She nods, settling her head on my shoulder. Roni looks over, rolling her eyes at us, but she lets us stay curled up together.

Murdoch eventually brings us some oysters to eat. I take them hungrily, helping Coralie to hold them.

The midwater squids light up the cave as they swim slowly around the room. The light entering from the doorway adds some visibility as well, though it will be significantly less within the next hour as the sun vanishes entirely from the sky above us. I stare at the space, waiting for a dark figure to conceal the light, but Merrick never arrives to block the sunlight.

"How long?" Coralie whispers while the sirens are distracted with their meals.

"Probably morning," I reply. "Just try to rest."

I touch the necklace clasp on the back of her neck as I stroke her hair. I'm sure my hair is a disaster too after days of not being able to brush it.

"Can I brush her hair?" I ask loudly, making all of the sirens look at me. "I just want to brush her hair out."

The sirens scoff at me, but not Murdoch.

"Murdoch, please. You can sit here and make sure I'm not doing anything, but let me fix her hair. Don't let her turn into—"

"Fine," he cuts me off before I can bring up the old mermaid in town that hasn't taken care of her hair in three years.

He swims to Roni's belongings and digs a comb out of her pouch. She protests, but Murdoch can apparently get away with things now given his connection to the siren princess.

Handing it to me, he sinks down to the sand.

"It was nothing personal," he says.

"I get it," I reply, starting to brush through Coralie's hair. I'm careful to avoid knocking into the shell I have hidden there.

"Ow," Coralie complains when I hit a knot in her hair.

"Sorry," I murmur.

"I kind of wish you two had stayed out of the way," Murdoch informs me.

"Well, I'd love to get out of the way *now*," I reply, pretending to be sweet.

His face goes slack before his eyes narrow.

"Hurry up," he snaps.

"Love to," I reply, brushing Coralie's hair a little faster. I work my way through her locks. She sinks back into my hands as I work.

I intentionally clip her necklace with the comb, making her flinch.

"That looks heavy, starfish," I say just loud enough for Murdoch to hear. "Do you want me to take it?"

I unclip it without waiting for a response and Murdoch stirs from where he watches us.

"It was our grandmothers," I explain softly. "It's the only necklace we have from her."

He reaches a hand out, and I drop the necklace into his waiting palm. Murdoch inspects it, flipping it over, but Grandma Tama had concealed her secrets perfectly. My sad story proves effective when he reaches around my neck and clasps it on for me, instructing me to hurry with Coralie's hair.

When I finish, I look to Murdoch to see if Coralie can help with my hair. He frowns, taking the comb from me. He shifts so that he's sitting behind me and quickly rips through my hair with the brush. Unlike Merrick and Caspian, this does not relax me. Every moment is filled with as much tension as Murdoch is putting on my hair.

"Thanks," I mumble as he swims away, taking the comb with him.

"That looked painful," Coralie says with wide eyes.

"It was," I glance down at the necklace.

Coralie quirks an eyebrow up, but doesn't ask questions.

We take turns sleeping, one keeping watch while the other rests. So far, I've been able to make sure Coralie has had the majority of the sleep—she'll need it on this journey to wherever we're going—but my body needs to rest soon. It's a miracle I haven't turned to foam already.

I wake with a start as Roni screams in the cave.

My eyes blink quickly as the mermaid swims directly at me. She rips Coralie away from me—Cor's nails dig into my tail as she panics.

"You signaled them!" Roni accuses.

"Who?" I shriek, trying to get to my sister as Phorcys holds me back.

"Your mermen!" she shouts. "They're here."

Swordfish, they found them.

"How would I have signaled them?" I screech. "You've been watching me this entire time—we haven't been out of your sight!"

"I don't know how you did it, but you did." She

attempts to slap me, but I dart out of the way, leaning into the merman holding me.

"It doesn't matter," Tarni interrupts. "We have to move."

"Good thing we know how to avoid the mer," Phorcys says harshly into my ear as he digs his nails into my upper arm, pulling me roughly toward the door.

CHAPTER 2

ONCE AGAIN, I'M RELEGATED TO STARING AT THE PATH behind us as Phorcys carries me over his shoulder. My hands are attached to my tail behind me, bending me uncomfortably in the wrong direction.

Murdoch has taken Coralie from Roni's oversight, carrying her on his back. Thankfully, he bound her in the front, so she's not in much pain.

I bounce against Phorcys' back each time he flicks his tail to move us forward—the merman has muscles for days.

I look for any signs of Merrick or Caspian in the dark. I'd even be grateful for a sign of Morgen, but there's no way he will be involved in this rescue mission with the injuries he suffered in the palace when Nir attacked.

I wonder what's happened to Nir. Merrick damaged his tail badly during the battle, but he *is* three times the size of a normal merman, and he *did* manage to escape the palace somehow.

I hope Tarni isn't taking us as a gift to her cousin.

We travel quickly through the water—faster than we have the entire escape from the palace. Tarni has a plan to avoid Merrick's wrath, and whatever it is, it can't be good.

Despite the sun starting to come up, we find ourselves swimming into darker and more dangerous waters. A boat passes overhead, casting a dim shadow on the sea floor. Instinct tells me to hide, but siren hands tell me not to move as Phorcys readjusts how I'm sitting over his shoulder.

I wish on every starfish in the sea that Merrick and Caspian are hovering just beyond the light behind us where I can't see them.

Yet, they don't appear.

"Are you sure this is a good idea?" Murdoch asks, still carrying Coralie.

"It's our only option," Tarni says. "We have to lose them, and they'll never suspect we'd risk going in there."

My head jerks toward the sound of her voice. I wish I could see her around Phorcys' body, but I have as much luck as I did seeing around Nir the last time he moved me this way.

"Is it safe?" Murdoch continues, setting me on alert. Whatever we're swimming into, it must be bad.

"We've done it before," Tarni replies.

"Successfully?" Murdoch sounds nervous.

As a mer who has never been outside the kingdom of Scylla, I imagine this is even more terrifying for him than it is for me—at least *I* have some experience.

"I'm *here,* aren't I?" Tarni chastises him.

I wonder if Tarni really *has* done what she's claiming though. If Nir's mother trained her to be a secret weapon in hiding, then would she have gone out on her own to face the terrors of the ocean?

I realize that Tarni has been trained to fool everyone —*including the other sirens*—but she's played the part of being fragile and weak her entire life. Would she really have gone into the darker depths of the ocean at any point?

"You've been out here before?" Murdoch whispers, clearly concerned over his girlfriend.

"*I* have," Roni interrupts. "Now get over yourself, *mer,* before I tie you up with the other *mermaids.*"

Murdoch huffs, angry over being called out.

The light around me brightens just enough that I can see a few lengths behind us—still no sign of my friends.

I pull a piece of driftwood from my *iluse,* hoping I can pick the lock on my shackles. It attached itself to my attire last night in the cave, but I made sure it didn't slip away, looping it in the netting until it was wrapped securely in back of me. As the last in the line up of sirens, no one can see me working at the lock.

We swim into a kelp forest, debris dancing in the water all around us. There's something eerie about a kelp forest in the dark. Once, I thought kelp forests were beautiful, but that was before the sirens tried to take over Scylla.

The water changes around us, getting cooler. The kelp whips back and forth and I wonder if perhaps there is a storm on the surface causing the change in the water below. It would explain the darkness as well, but I can't see through the kelp to tell what's happening above us.

A flash of blue above me gets my attention, though.

It moves so quickly, I wonder if I'm seeing things.

A shell floats down through the water, getting tossed in the waving kelp, but I catch just enough of it to be certain—there is a merman overhead.

The sirens don't notice Caspian's tail high above us in the water. He holds back, letting us swim away. I imagine it's harder than when he had to let us go outside of the palace in Scylla.

If I can see him, we can figure out a plan—there will be some way to communicate—but he's too far away and out of reach.

But if Caspian is here, so are Merrick and Llyr. I imagine some of the others are as well. It wouldn't surprise me if Keone and Natale had raced after us with them.

They had to wait until we were far enough away that the sirens couldn't spot them. *I* had been watching the entire journey and hadn't seen my friends, so the mermen had to have had enough time to form a plan. The king had been with them when we were taken from Scylla—it's possible he went to Marilla and secured some of her guards to come with them to rescue us.

Regardless, it doesn't matter—they're here. They know where we are. Even with Tarni's plan, they can't escape my collection.

Working on the lock, we swim further into the kelp forest. I stop searching for my brother as I try to pop my shackles open while resting on Phorcys' back—Caspian wouldn't have backed off if he planned on setting us free inside the kelp forest. Whatever he, Merrick, and Llyr are planning, it will happen on the other side of the massive strands of kelp.

It takes time, but I manage to break the lock inside the shackles, popping it open. I'll have to move quickly when the time comes to free Coralie, but even if we just get her away from Tarni and her collection, we can free her of her chains after.

"This way," Tarni suddenly announces, darting sideways out of the kelp forest.

We race after her, out into the open waters still

consumed with dim light and shadows. Phorcys is struggling to catch his breath by the time we slow—I might have maneuvered myself to slam into his back extra hard while he was swimming to keep up with the siren princess.

I'm not sure what Merrick's plan is, but I assume I should probably help to distract the sirens so they can sneak up on them and help free us. I consider my topics of choice, wondering which will get the best reaction from Tarni.

"Where are we going?" I ask, leading into my line of questioning.

"It doesn't matter," Tarni replies, swimming low to the ground. Everyone sinks down, following her lead.

"Are you taking us to your brother?" I ask. She cringes as she uses the connection her uncle gave her to their family when he took her in. Tarni is really the former siren king's niece by his brother, but she was raised by the siren king and queen as their own, effectively making Nir her brother.

She turns to look back at me.

"Do you think he's still alive?" I ask casually. "If he's dead, does that make *you* their queen? Or does that title fall to the one who stabbed him after we did and ended it for real?"

Tarni launches herself at me, knocking me away from Phorcys. She grapples with me, trying to hurt me. I use the metal still wrapped around my wrists as protection. Miraculously, I manage to angle them, so they stay on despite having popped the lock.

She yelps as her knuckles collide with the heavy metal. Tarni reels back, arm over her shoulder as she prepared to scratch my face with her nails.

I use the metal clasped over the end of my tail just above my fins to injure her again, crashing into her tail with mine.

"Enough, Celena!" Murdoch shouts, dropping Coralie and rushing to push me away from Tarni.

One of the other mermen grabs Coralie as she floats toward the ground, keeping her from crashing into the sand. She holds her feelings in, bravely facing our captors as I provoke them.

"What if we're swimming into a trap," I protest. "What if there's a new siren king already and he's going to dispose of you as soon as you return? What then?"

"Nir is fine," Tarni hisses at me. "They barely touched him."

"They stabbed his tail," I reply in horror before switching to sarcasm. "Didn't you see it? Oh, no, maybe you *didn't*—you *were* knocked unconscious, after all."

If Merrick weren't nearby, I wouldn't risk taunting Tarni so soon, but if this is my last chance to terrorize her, I'm going to do all I can to destroy this siren.

"Move," Murdoch directs, forcing everyone into action.

Phorcys scoops me up, tossing me over his shoulder again. Murdoch takes Coralie from the siren and leads us forward, swimming quickly once again.

"He could barely move the last time I saw him," I call out, making the situation worse. "He *pulled* the trident out of his tail. They must have had to carry him out."

"Enough!" Tarni shouts, racing toward me. She rips her hands through my hair, pulling my head violently to the side.

I barely hold back my scream, knowing that if I make a sound, Merrick will descend on us so quickly that it will ruin whatever plan he and our friends have created to save us.

Bits of pink hair pull out of my scalp, remaining tangled with Tarni's fingers as she pulls them away. She drops my hair in the water, and the pieces float away.

"Nir is *alive*," she hisses at me, seething. "You couldn't kill him if you tried. Who was it that hurt him—that little boyfriend of yours? I'll see to it that he *dies* before all this is over."

"You can't touch him," I whisper fiercely. I try not to grin too smugly.

Even if for some reason Tarni beats me, she'll never be able to hurt Merrick—he's too smart for her.

"No, but I can hurt *you*," she sneers. "You're being

awfully bold for someone who is trying to protect her little sister."

Her face begins to shift, realizing that I *wouldn't* be this bold unless I knew something was coming. I over-played my hand, and she's caught on.

"To the pool," she shouts in horror. "Go, go!"

We dart once again through the water, pummeling our bodies forward in the expansive dark ocean.

"I don't know where they are, but you *will* tell them to stay back," Tarni growls.

"I don't know what you're talking about?" I reply innocently. "The only mer here are you and us."

"I doubt that," she mutters. "You *will* play by my rules, Celena, or your sister pays the price. Remember that."

Threatening my sister is nothing new, but I should probably be careful.

"I still don't know what you're talking about."

"You will," she promises.

As we continue to swim, strange things start happening. In our wake, a trail of dead shellfish litter the ocean floor, their tones a mixture of dark blues, grays, yellows, and tans.

It's like something swept through the ocean floor, killing everything in its path, and left the carcasses to rot —only they haven't. It's almost like they've been perfectly preserved.

Trails etch their way through the ocean floor, leaving swirling designs covered in—crystals?

A large crab body sits at an odd angle. Underneath it, an extra leg sticks out, noticeably a different color. It's like the creature was trying to eat the dead crab and died on top of it. It's a horrifying color—both of them.

More tiny crystals sit on top of the shells and dead creatures that lie in a strange pool. It almost looks like the pools of water sitting on the deck of the fishing vessel I was trapped on when the sirens coerced the fishermen into killing the mer they caught in their nets.

I try to get a good look at the crystals in the pool sitting on the ocean floor. They aren't like the ones we wear on our crowns or *ilueses*. These are short and strangely shaped. They cover everything.

"Remember what I said, Celena," Tarni sings.

An eel dips into the pool, diving into the strange-colored water. When it comes back up, it twitches, diving back into the darker water. Suddenly, the creature spasms, twitching and rolling in on itself. It jerks mercilessly, bending and twisting its shape.

"It's a brine pool," Tarni explains viciously. "It's four times as salty as the ocean. If a creature swims in there, it goes into toxic shock. It convulses, and if it can't escape, it dies."

She grins as she swims close to my face.

"All those crab bodies you see in there…they're probably older than either of us."

I look away, eyeing the muscles forming walls to contain the brine pool. I've never seen anything like it. It's haunting in all the wrong ways.

The eel continues to twitch, convulsing violently as it bends around its own body in unnatural ways. Suddenly, it stops moving, sinking down to the bottom of the brine pool.

"Get back!" Tarni screams to something beyond us, drawing my attention away from the brine pool. She holds a trident out toward the darkness. "*Get back!*"

From the shadows, a figure emerges—our savior.

I don't know where the others are, but Merrick's shape fills my vision. He's backlit, and I can't see his expression, but I'm sure it's murderous.

"I said, *get back*," Tarni punctuates her words. "Or else."

Coralie is shifted off to Roni so that the merman can take a place beside Murdoch for the impending fight. She holds Coralie in front of her, letting her dangle in the water.

"Or else *what?*" Merrick's voice is threatening and still the most lovely thing I've ever heard in my life. He swims slowly toward us.

His moves are precise as he closes the distance between us. I adjust myself so that I'm ready to break free of my shackles—my hands will be free, but my tail will not be. I'll have seconds to pop the lock before I'm out of time and they use it against me to pull me back.

Control a mer's tail and you control the mer.

"Or this," Tarni says, flicking her hand in the water toward Roni.

With horrific force, the siren throws Coralie into the brine pool, submerging her in the toxic saline.

CHAPTER 3

"GET BACK!" I SCREAM, KNOWING MY JOB IS TO REMOVE Merrick.

Coralie fights under the water, twitching under the influence of the toxic shock to her system. Roni hovers above her, ready to pull her chain up when Tarni approves.

"Merrick, get back!" I scream, sobbing. "Tarni, pull her up."

"No," she says in a voice so quiet, only I can hear her.

"Tarni, please!" I plead, body shaking with tears that leak out into the water.

"What's happening?" Merrick shouts, swimming a few lengths toward us, losing all bravado in his concern for my reaction.

Caspian rushes toward us from the side, trident in

hand. He swims straight toward Tarni, ready to take the siren out.

I use the opportunity to pop the shackles off of my tail. It sinks to the sea floor, but I hold the ones around my wrists in place, knowing any movement away from Tarni would earn me a trident in my side and then I'd never be able to pull Coralie up.

Tarni barely has time to react to Caspian's movements.

"Merrick, stop him!" I shriek.

Without knowing why—knowing it's against everything we're trying to accomplish—Merrick listens to me, swimming straight at my twin. The mermen collide as Merrick knocks Caspian off course.

"Pull her up," I beg, dropping the rest of my shackles. I race toward Roni, attempting to pull my sister out of the pool as she convulses.

Surprised, Roni can't withstand my assault and accidentally relinquishes the chain to me. I pull as hard as I can, swimming toward the surface.

Coralie coughs, popping out of the brine pool. Murdoch catches her, pulling her back from me. He panics as the saline touches him, but it barely has an effect as it brushes off my sister.

I swim down to them, slapping at my sister's skin to remove the toxins. My system tingles but I ignore it as I try to help Coralie recover.

All of the sirens surround us, tridents poised to force us back into the brine.

"Get back," I shriek at Merrick and Caspian. "Go!"

Both mermen are breathing heavily, shoulders visibly moving. I pray Llyr is here and staying hidden—if they don't know he's here, maybe he can come after us even if Merrick and Caspian can't.

Coralie shudders against me, sobbing as she attempts to catch her breath. I brush her hair back to ensure it's not hindering her recovery.

"Are you okay?" I ask quietly. "Coralie, look at me. Are you okay?"

She continues to choke against me, and I pull her closer. It's probably not helping her ability to breathe, but I would wrap myself entirely around my little sister if it would protect her from the sirens who are obviously willing to kill us if it comes to that.

Murdoch looks horrified, but he sides with Tarni—he will not help us escape. He clutches at the chain around Coralie's wrists and tail.

"Take it off her tail," I demand. "She's in trouble, Murdoch, and whatever happens next is your fault."

"No," he growls, eyes fixed on Tarni as she holds a trident out in the direction of my friends who are slowly backing away at my insistence.

"Murdoch, please, I need her free," I plead, still trying to clean her tail off as she sporadically spasms.

He finally relents, unshackling Coralie's tail. I drop in the water, using the entire length of my arms to hug around her waist, sliding down her tail to clean her off. Coralie clings to Murdoch's shoulders, curling into him. I don't even care if it means she's safe. Mercifully, he holds her up while I work.

Tarni challenges Merrick and Caspian in the background, but I don't have time to listen. I will do whatever I have to do to protect my sister, and if that means staying as a hostage to the siren princess, I'll do it.

I take Coralie back from Murdoch, holding her against my body. Her convulsions turn to shivering as she slowly recovers.

"Deep breaths," I murmur, willing her system to cooperate.

"Celena?" Merrick yells in the distance.

"She's alive!" I call back, trying not to shake Coralie as I yell.

"Get back," Tarni roars. She drops her voice so that I can't hear but I assume it's a threat.

The mermen start to retreat.

"Actually," Tarni adds. "Stay there."

She nods to Phorcys. He bends down, scooping up the shackles I left on the sea floor when I escaped. She trades with him, taking the chains herself as the two of them approach Merrick and Caspian. Roni joins her with another set of shackles—they must have brought a spare in case I broke mine.

"Turn," she demands, eying my boyfriend and brother as they slowly spin. Her eyes linger over them as she appreciates what she sees. My nostrils flare and I'm sure Coralie can hear my heart beating furiously in my chest.

They comply for the sake of our safety. Phorcys holds them in place with the trident while Tarni runs her hands down Merrick's arm slowly. I cringe as she slips the shackles into place. Just as the sirens did to me, she binds the mermen with their hands behind them attached to their tails.

Caspian and Merrick rest on the ocean floor, struggling to free themselves. Tarni leans forward and says something that makes both mermen snarl at her.

Spinning, she and the others swim back to us.

"They're hot when they're mad," she taunts me. "Let's go."

Leaving Merrick and Caspian is heartbreaking. I'm no longer in shackles since they gave mine away, but keeping Coralie bound is enough to keep me in line now that I know what they're willing to do.

My vision bounces between Coralie ahead of me, and

Merrick and Caspian behind me until I can no longer see them.

I force myself to stay quiet and forbid my shoulders from shaking as I cry into the ocean—at least the sirens can't see.

After a few hours, they finally let us rest. Coralie hasn't been able to swim on her own since we left the brine pool, but she huddles on the sea floor anyway as if she had raced all the way here.

"Cor," I'm nearly in tears again as I pull her against me.

"It's not as bad as it looks," she croaks. She looks up and winks.

My eyes grow wide. Coralie may not have ever been trained by my parents, but the mermaid catches on quickly, faking worse symptoms than she actually has.

I squeeze her shoulder to let her know how proud I am of her and try not to snort.

A shark starts to swim by—it's small enough that we don't have to worry about it—but one of the sirens pulls out a bottle from their bag. Inside it must be parts of a dead shark because the creature swims out of range so quickly you'd think it had been stabbed as we continue our journey, swimming away.

It's several more hours before we're able to stop and rest again.

"Can you swim?" I murmur into Coralie's hair as I hold her.

"I think so," she replies. "Are Caspian and Merrick okay?"

"I'm sure they're fine. They're probably free by now."

If Llyr was around—and I'm sure he was—he probably had them free within minutes of us leaving. Unless, of course, they split up. Then it might have taken longer to find them.

"Can we do that?" Murdoch mumbles from across the cavern where we stopped for the rest of the day. The sirens' plan was to stay hidden until well after dark and swim through the night, hoping to catch anyone else who might come to free us when they swim by in the light. Darkness will be our companion now, I suppose, as will the midwater squids be if they insist on traveling under the cover of night.

"Try to rest, Cor. I'm going to listen."

She puts her head down, desperately needing sleep to recover.

"But can we really go there?" Murdoch takes Tarni's hand in his.

"We'll be safe, darling," Tarni hums. "I'll keep you safe like you kept me safe. We'll just siren them into doing what we need them to do. They can't harm us if they're under our control."

If Tarni is talking about sirening, she must be planning to take us near the humans. My fingers still as I pet Coralie's hair.

I can't let her near the humans.

"It will be easy. I'll teach you how to do it too, so you'll always be safe," Tarni says, leaning her head to rest on Murdoch's shoulder. She wraps herself around his arm, tail twitching in the light streaming in from the cave entrance.

Phorcys turns around from the gaping hole in the rock.

"Still clear," he murmurs before turning back around. He makes a face when he sees Tarni latched on to the merman under her spell.

"Can we make it that far that quickly?" Roni asks, leaning forward to wrap her arms around the bend in her tail. I still have the urge to claw some of her scales off, and after what she did to Coralie, I'd happily hand her over to the humans and watch them skin her.

"As long as we don't have any other setbacks, we can make it," Phorcys assures them. "I've been there enough times to know."

"They wouldn't dare come after us up there, would they?" one of the others asks, looking to Murdoch.

"They'll do anything to get Celena and her sister back." My former collection mate sighs, "but if we use them to leverage the situation, I think we can control it."

He points up when he mentions *them.*

"And they can remove us from the situation anyway," Tarni chimes in, looking relaxed as she nestles closer to Murdoch.

Roni looks disapprovingly at Murdoch before turning to stare out the entrance of the cave. At least I know I can play Murdoch against them if I need to later.

"What, the big tough merman is afraid of a few humans?" Roni says without looking back. "Haven't been to the surface yet, guppy?"

The muscles in Murdoch's back tighten at the sound of her words. Tarni sits up, still keeping her fingers wrapped around her boyfriend's arm.

"He'll be fine, Roni," Tarni addresses her friend. "He'll probably end up being the best siren of us all. You saw how good Celena was and she hasn't done it until just now."

She drops her voice when she speaks my name, not wanting me to overhear. It's amazing that she doesn't think I can hear any of her conversations at this point.

"But the others didn't, from what I hear."

"Murdoch is better than those other mermen anyway. You saw the way he deceived them. He's skilled at this." Tarni tucks a lock of her hair behind her. "We should rest. We need to leave soon."

"Tell me about it?" Murdoch asks, changing the subject.

Tarni pulls back to look at him. She sighs before answering.

"There's an inlet. It's almost like a bay. The deeper ships can't get in, and most of the sea life stays out. We can hide under their docks and in the underwater caverns there. There are even waterways that take us into land.

"If we need, the humans can move us from one location to another. It's something we've only tried once, but it works. We'll be able to survive."

"The mer will have no idea where we are if the humans take us to the other side of the peninsula—and they wouldn't have time to reach us even if they *did* know," Phorcys calls in over his shoulder.

"It's flawless…as long as you don't screw it up, *mer*," Roni adds.

"How will they move us?"

"Ships? Carry us? Does it matter?" Tarni asks. "They'll be under our control. We can command them to kill the mer brats and then we can return to Shadare."

"Do we have a plan if something has happened to Nir?" Murdoch asks Tarni as if they were alone.

"He's fine," she insists.

I open my mouth to harass her and suddenly realize that's a bad idea while trapped in a cavern. An octopus crawls against the wall, looking for a new place to nestle in—if only I could be like that—I could flatten myself out and slip along the edge of the cave, sneaking out without Tarni noticing. It's amazing what an octopus can do to survive.

Without warning, Tarni turns around to look at me. Her eyes grow wild when she sees me staring back at her —too late to look away.

She swims up off her seat on the ground and moves toward me.

"How much did you hear?"

I consider my options but know I'll only pay for it if I lie. If I confront her with what I know, maybe I can get more information.

"Everything...*mostly*," I inform her. "Where is it that we're going to deal with the humans?"

I wait for her to give the name—any name—of a human kingdom, as I try to figure out where we're going. Over the course of our travels, I've figured out the general direction, but it would be so easy to move to different kingdoms with the change of the current here— we could be headed to anywhere.

Mer have always had an innate sense of direction, but predicting the future isn't in our skill set.

"So many questions, so little cares," Tarni croons at me, but it's her grin that terrifies me. "Good night."

She raises her hand, bringing a rock down on my head.

CHAPTER 4

When I wake up, it's nearly dark. Coralie is across the room, looking at me with seaweed wrapped around her mouth as a gag. She tries to swim up when she sees me stir, but Roni forces her back down to the sand.

"Next time, I suggest you mind your own business," Murdoch hisses in my ear, scaring me. "Keep your mouth shut, Celena, or you'll pay."

He was willing to label me as a siren to the collection, but suddenly he wants to help? If I could bite him, I would.

"Time to go!" Tarni announces, swimming into the cave. "Our ride is arriving."

Murdoch drags me outside.

"Behave, or your sister will be making this trip by being dragged by her chains, understood?"

I nod as the dolphins approach. Phorcys signals them

over, grabbing on to one's dorsal fin. We all catch a dolphin, allowing them to swim with us as passengers. Phorcys oversees Coralie, nestling her between him and the dolphin. He uses his powerful tail to assist in the swim so the dolphin doesn't have to do all of the work on its own.

My fingers on one hand quietly pet the dolphin, allowing myself small strokes that won't be seen by the others as I try to make friends with the creature in case I need her later.

Unlike the mer, the sirens don't let go when the dolphins need to surface to breathe.

"Cor, it's okay," I call as I realize her dolphin is about to surface. She tries to turn to see me, but Phorcys tightens his grip as he says something into her ear.

"Up," I whisper, urging my dolphin to follow.

She does, crashing out of the surface of the water as the moon glitters down on us.

Coralie catches sight of me over the dolphin's back.

"It's okay," I promise her before she sinks back down into the water. After a moment, we follow.

We continue to swim through the night, bouncing over the waves in the moonlight every so often as the dolphins carry us away. By morning, I discover that we're in a part of the ocean so deep that I can't see the bottom no matter how low we swim.

"You don't want to go down there," Phorcys says,

glancing over at me. He turns to Coralie. "You either, little mer. Remind your sister you don't want to find out what's in the depths."

Coralie's eyes grow wide, but she stays quiet. I can see she wants to make a biting remark—wisely, she holds it in.

Partway through the day, we find a coral reef to hide behind. I'm careful not to touch the edges of the coral as we sit. At some point, we swerved away from the unknown depths of the ocean, coming to a place where colorful fish once again grace the waters.

We don't rest long before continuing on, the dolphins leaving us to our own fins.

My tail hurts less now, thankfully, as we pick up our journey, though the first few days on a split fin were merciless. The sirens allow Coralie to swim on her own, still forcing her hands together at the wrists. If I could take the shackles for her, I would—I'd even accept being cuffed at my tail if it meant she wouldn't have to wear the metal around her wrists, but in order to control *me*, they need to control *her*.

We travel through the night again, putting another day between Merrick and me. The bioluminescent squid help light our way through the waters.

In the distance, other creatures glow, calling their prey to them. It's eerie as we swim through the water. Coralie is close by, though I wish I could tuck her under my arm for safekeeping. I may not trust Murdoch, but I think he is looking out for my young sister as much as he can. He stays close by in the dark.

"Ow!" one of the siren yelps. "What—?"

A second yell cuts him off as another siren is disturbed in the water.

"What's happening?" I ask, swimming to Coralie.

A piercing scream frightens us all into action. I wrap myself around Coralie, pulling her away from Murdoch. He pulls out a knife, ready to defend himself. Tarni and Roni lift their tridents, having carried them in their hands instead of on their backs.

When the screaming merman turns, something is sticking out of his arm. It's long and slender with a nose like a knife. It twitches, still embedded in the siren.

"What is that?" Tarni gasps.

Roni screams as a similar creature attacks her. In the glow of the midwater squid, I see an entire school of the creatures with long bodies and noses.

They crash into the sirens, accidentally inflicting wounds. The creatures swim wildly in the water, swarming around the squid.

"The light!" I shout. "They're drawn to the light."

The creatures race toward me, drawn in by the nearby squid.

With all the force I can muster, I shove Coralie down in the water, pushing her into darkness.

"Get down," I command, pulling the shell from my *iluse.*

So much for saving it.

I slash at the creatures, narrowly missing being struck by two of them. They look like Morgen's swords in the palace in Scylla.

The school looks like a storm raging in a kelp forest, throwing everything around wildly as they twist and turn in the water in a horrifying blanket of reflective scales picking up the color of the bioluminescent glow.

I bat my hair back as it floats in my face, wishing I could braid it back for battle with the creatures of the night.

Everything happens so quickly as the fish huddle together, following their instincts. They don't mean to attack us—it's not their intent—we're just in the way.

Coralie screams as one of the creatures comes toward me, but Murdoch's trident knocks it out of the way, spearing it. He turns without acknowledging me.

"It's the light," I say again. "They're drawn to the light."

I drop down into the darkness, away from the squids floating in the water. The sirens follow, cradling their injuries. The merman whose name I still haven't learned isn't quiet about his pain.

We swim lower in the water, trying to put distance between us and the needlefish still swarming the squids.

"You're hurt," Coralie whispers. She touches my arm, and I reel back—I hadn't realized I'd been injured.

"I'll be okay," I assure her.

Swimming in the dark is difficult. The collection stays close together to avoid losing each other. Once we're safely away from the needlefish, we move closer to the surface to see by moonlight.

I hope Merrick, Caspian, and Llyr don't run into those things on their way to find us.

The siren merman has suffered a number of wounds. I can tell even in the dark that he should have them looked at soon. Inside my necklace, I have something that could help him heal but I'm reserving that for Coralie if she needs it.

"You should look at that," I inform them. "That's only going to get worse if you don't take care of it."

"And what makes you the expert on that?" Tarni snaps.

I don't say anything.

"She's right, it should be bandaged," Murdoch informs them. "I've seen injuries like that before, and you don't want to know what happens when it's not taken care of."

The injured siren looks horrified, thinking about all the possible scenarios he might face. He won't die, of course, but the scars won't be pretty if they don't take care of it.

Sirens often use their looks to manipulate humans,

drawing them in before they use their voices. I can't imagine that scars would help his case.

"Fine, then you handle it, *mer*," Tarni replies, annoyed. She leads the group to the sea floor as the water brightens a bit. I look up, noticing that the sun is starting to lighten the sky, even though we can't see it yet.

I tug Coralie along behind me, keeping her against my back as I examine the siren's cuts.

"I need seaweed," I inform Murdoch, giving him a list of items I need to help repair the merman resting on the sand. He glares at me as I lift his arm to get a better look.

Murdoch returns after a few minutes, dropping my supplies on the ocean floor near my tail. I twitch as his hand brushes against my fin.

"I saw that little trick you pulled back there," Murdoch whispers in my ear. "The next time I see you, your *iluse* had better be cleaned off or we'll do it *for* you."

There it is—the threat of taking my *iluse* away.

I pick a few pieces of driftwood out of my *iluse* as I work on the siren's arm. Knowing he'll be looking, I take away the tiny decorative shells as well, leaving only the netting in place.

I wrap the siren's wounds, covering them as best I can. The cut in his abdomen is subtle, but I wrap it to be safe. By the time I'm done, he looks like Merrick and I did before we entered the palace in Metten the first time we met Nir.

"We should go," I push, knowing if I add greater strain to the sirens now, it will work in my favor later.

The sea starts to come to life again as we swim, the sun now clearly in the sky above us. Schools of fish glide by in an array of colors.

"It's cooler here," Coralie murmurs as we swim beside each other.

"It is," I answer, noticing a stingray swimming by, the debris in the water near it glittering fiercely in the sunlight streaming through the ocean.

"We're going to Antaire, aren't we?" she asks miserably.

"I'm not sure, starfish, but we're definitely headed in the direction."

"You don't think they've moved back yet, do you?"

"The queen moved Prince Jarek out of the palace when Persephone and Chantay tried to drown him a century ago. From the sounds of it, I doubt the royal line will *ever* return to the palace by the sea."

"But there will be others, won't there?" she asks nervously.

"Yes, I'm sure there will be."

I keep my arm around Coralie as if I'm helping her swim, still acting like she's recovering from the brine pool.

"I've always wanted to see the human palace, but not like this," she murmurs.

"I know, starfish, so have I." I never *actually* thought I'd see it though.

My heart half tugs on me, wanting desperately to hope we're actually going to Antaire. The other half chides me for wanting to see where the fall of the human-mer agreement came to take place.

The surface is dangerous. I shouldn't want to go, no matter *what* is up there.

Yet, I do. *I desperately do.*

If I didn't have Coralie with me, I might not even protest until I had seen it—I'd have to destroy the sirens at that point, but at least I would have seen the steps Aila sat on over a century ago with Persephone and Prince Jarek.

I wonder what it would be like to see the things my great-great-grandmother saw over a century ago. To be fair, I've seen the palace at Metten where she spent her entire life until the war, but I haven't seen the human world through her eyes.

What must it have been like to sit on the palace steps with the human prince, her tail half in the water, half resting with him on the steps?

Was it easy to talk to him? It must have been—they were friends—at least until Persephone tried to drown him.

Aila used to watch the sunrises and sunsets from the

steps that were built down into the water. My scales itch to sit on the steps and watch the world from there.

Her time was when worlds overlapped. Mer and humans respected each other. King Gaspar and the human queen intentionally worked together to preserve both mer and human lives.

Now we all live in fear of the known.

"We'll find out soon, I suppose. We'll have to turn at some point if we're not."

We swim for hours, keeping up a grueling pace as Tarni leads us forward. I wonder how often she's been in this area, and if the sirens ever resided near here that she's so confident with where we're going.

Coralie and I are both exhausted by the time we reach the next resting place. At this point, I give up keeping watch, letting us both sleep tangled in each other's arms so we'll know if the other moves.

Darkness is our guide once again. While we were resting, one of the sirens acquired more midwater squid to see by, though this time, we try to keep our distance to avoid any more attacks. We swim near the surface, using the moonlight to guide us.

As the sun rises again, we slow our pace. Just before I

swim into the mouth of the cavern we will be resting in, Tarni pulls me back by my hair.

"Mission time."

"What?" I reply, pulling at my hair to get her to release me.

"Let's go, mermaid," Tarni tugs harder on my locks.

"I'm not leaving her," I proclaim as Phorcys tries to push Coralie inside the cavern.

"She'll be fine as long as you cooperate," Tarni assures me. "Now, let's move."

I struggle against her.

"I'm not leaving her," I yell loudly, disrupting a school of fish. They swim away quickly, changing directions.

"You are. You don't have a choice." Tarni nods to Murdoch. He lifts a knife and swims toward Coralie.

"Murdoch, *don't!*"

Coralie holds her space, not flinching as he moves toward her.

"You're coming with us, princess," Tarni decrees. Murdoch and the others will stay here and watch her, and you can have her when we return. The faster we swim, the faster you get back to your sister."

"Where are we going?" I growl reluctantly.

Coralie bites down, clenching her jaw. She watches me intently as I glare at the siren next to me.

"I'll be back," I look to Coralie. As I turn, I tap the back of my head as if I'm adjusting my hair where the siren had pulled it, hiding my message to my sister—use the weapon I hid in your hair if you need to, and be merciless if you must.

I don't know if Coralie can, but if it comes down to her safety, I hope she can do what needs to be done to survive.

Tarni and Phorcys guide me away. I wait until we're out of sight and they can't easily swim back to warn the others if I become problematic for them before I speak.

"Where are we going?" I demand.

Phorcys' fingers wrap around the trident when he hears my voice. His shoulder shrugs up just enough to indicate that he's displeased with me.

"We're running a little mission for my brother," she says referring to her cousin. "There is something of his mother's that we need to retrieve. You're going to help us."

"And what is that?"

Tarni smiles but doesn't answer. When I open my mouth to speak, Phorcys holds the trident up to my arm, threatening to knick me if I don't stay quiet.

I let them guide me through the waters, around a kelp forest, directly into the heart of a decaying city.

"What is this?" I ask.

"Dwellings, you foolish mermaid," Tarni snips at me.

Siren dwellings look like a convoluted version of mer dwellings, though these appear to have been haphazardly put together—perhaps the others are better. It looks like the sirens aren't ones for long-term locations, meaning my guess was right—they travel, wandering the seas.

"When did you live here?" I inquire.

"*We* didn't. This was before our time," she corrects me. "My aunt moved us closer to Scylla before Nir and I were born. We've been moving for years, scouting our revenge on the mer and finding the best locations to control the humans."

"I see you've done so well for yourselves," I murmur as we swim up to the coral reef blocking most of the temporary siren city from view.

Phorcys uses the opportunity to scratch his trident along my upper arm, leaving a line that's anything but straight. I grit my teeth to avoid grimacing, though my nostrils flare, giving him the satisfaction of a reaction anyway.

"You, Celena, get to go retrieve a necklace for us," Tarni replies. She quickly describes which of the dwellings I'm going to be looking for inside. "Bring it back and we'll let your sister keep all of her fingers."

Tarni holds her trident in the crook of her elbow, balancing the end in the sand below us. She holds a knife in her hand, spinning it so the tip rests against her left pointer finger. When she looks up, she smiles.

"Good luck."

Phorcys forces me around the coral reef's edge toward

the main part of the city. Instead of seeing the same dwellings that rested on the other side of the reef, I find that the entire city has been overtaken with jellyfish.

They dangle everywhere in the water, their long tentacles flowing in all directions. I've never seen anything like this. Some are so large, they could likely eat me.

"What is that?"

"It's not a monster, if that's what you think," Tarni replies. "They just get really big out here. Swim along now. We have to be back within the hour."

"If we're not," Phorcys adds, "you don't want to know what Roni will do to your sister."

That's all the incentive I need.

I swallow hard as I swim forward. The first bloom of jellyfish is easy to swim under. I hover over the sand as I lightly flick my tail in the water to propel myself forward. They're floating high enough their tentacles rest at window level on the homes I swim by as I make my way through the abandoned city.

When I make it several lengths into the city, the blooms seem to sink lower in the water. I take a deep breath and hold it as I attempt to swim under them. One tentacle touches the back of my tail for a moment, sparking against my scales.

I try not to cry out.

I make my way through them, finding an opening

between two dwellings. Flipping over in the water, I sit on the sand, looking up to get my bearings.

If I'm careful, I can swim up in the water at full height to try to determine where I am.

"Better hurry," Tarni calls from her place by the coral. When I turn to look at her, she's backing up in the water, avoiding a jellyfish that is swimming at her. She makes a face as it darts up in the water, over her head.

Without waiting, I swim up, turning my head quickly to see what is around me. A jellyfish moves and I dart back down.

Two dwellings over, I see the monstrous jellyfish that I saw from the reef. It's so large that it could practically be a dwelling. Making a note to avoid that, I chose to go the longer way around it.

Of course, Tarni had to pick the home in the middle of the small city, making me work incredibly hard to retrieve a stupid necklace.

Necklace.

My hand darts to Grandma Tama's necklace around my throat.

Is there anything that can help me here?

A weapon or two may be of use, but I doubt there will be any reason for me to get it out. Shells litter the ground, and I can easily use one of those to defend myself if I need to.

Phorcys will probably search me when I return, so I

don't even have any hope of smuggling the broken shells back with me when this is all over. I risk a glance over my shoulder and find them both trying to see me.

The jellyfish pulse around me, moving slightly in the water. They dip up and down in a massive cloud of toxic tentacles.

I round the corner, hoping to remove myself from view of the sirens so I can think more clearly. Another clearing allows me to see the central dwelling place I'm looking for—the home where Nir's mother left her belongings once when the sirens left in a hurry.

Unfortunately, to get there, I'm going to have to swim directly through a bloom of jellyfish. There's no way around it.

I drop to the sand, hoping to crawl as much as I can under the tentacles floating in the water. It stings as I brush by the first few, tingling fiercely against my back.

Using my arms, I dig the sand out in front of me, trying to create a deeper trench to drag myself through. My fin stings as I flick it in the water to help me move forward—I stop instantly, opting instead to drag my body through the sand.

Like a crab scurrying under the ocean floor, I pull myself through the bloom, crying out when the stings are too much.

"Still alive?" Tarni yells in the distance.

I'm sure this is payback for Caspian and Morgen dropping a net full of jellyfish on Nir's head in Metten.

"Ow," I moan quietly, hoping the sirens can't hear me. I don't take the time to look back.

The water moves around me—my first hint that I should look up. Above me, a jellyfish approaches, it's bell longer than any merman I've ever known. Its tentacles could stretch to the coral reef, and I'm sure beyond it.

It quietly makes its way to me.

CHAPTER 5

MY BODY RADIATES WITH PAIN AS ITS TENTACLES TOUCH MY body. I scream, unable to help myself.

My hand digs helplessly in the sand, trying to cover my body to avoid the pain. I'm sure Tarni is torn between panicking that I won't succeed in retaining her gift to her cousin and being thrilled that I'm suffering.

I can feel where every mark and every line will stretch across my skin. If I survive this, I'll end up looking like Nir for weeks, covered in red welts. At least my face and stomach are somewhat protected against the sand.

Picking up a shell, I slice at the tentacles, trying to force the giant creature away. Another scream escapes my lips as it catches my forearm as I move.

Tears leak out into the ocean as I swat at the jellyfish.

I'm doing this for Coralie, I remind myself. *Her safety is at risk—don't mess this up. You can handle this.*

The sand feels gritty against my stomach as my *iluse* shifts below me. I push myself forward, trying to gain ground on the creature.

I know I'm just making things up, but it seems like the jellyfish is descending on me even further. Glancing up, I see it's giant bell still hovering over the dwelling, not moving since I last saw it.

Tentacles wave in the water over me, dancing along the skin on my back and tail. They tangle with my hair. Occasionally my locks offer me protections—and occasionally they trap the tentacles against me, forcing me to endure more stinging.

I reach up, brushing my hair back toward my tail, cringing as another tentacle moves along with it. I have no choice but to remove myself from this situation.

I gather my strength, forcing myself to do what I know needs to be done.

"Go!" I instruct myself, knowing the only way *out* is *through* this mess. I push myself off the sand, flipping my tail as powerfully as I can. I dart through the large jellyfish tentacles and the surrounding bloom, refusing to stop until I'm away from the monstrous creature.

I try not to cry out as pain slips through my entire body. Darting inside a dwelling, I find it free of jellyfish. I sink to the ground, trying to assess my injuries.

"Celena?" Tarni shouts, almost sounding worried. After a moment, Phorcys lends his voice to the inquiry.

"I'm here," I finally respond, still not moving. I didn't mean to sound so pitiful, but it's all I can manage in my current state.

Remarkably, the stings aren't as bad as they felt, though I can only see a few on my arms and hands—those should heal in a few days. Even more miraculously, I appear to have found the dwelling I was searching for—the former home of Nir's mother during her travels.

I drag myself the first few lengths until I can swim again. I twitch in pain with every flip of my tail, but I keep going—I have to get back to the sirens immediately, and then we all have to get back to the cave or Roni will hurt Coralie.

"I'm in the right place," I scream to let them know I'm coming and not to leave without me.

I hurry through the small dwelling, tipping crates and boxes, dumping their contents out onto the floor. Most of the pieces look like they had been collected from sunken ships or lost during storms.

The dwelling appears to not have any furniture, though if they were just passing through, that makes sense. I have a vague idea of where she slept in the small dwelling, but with the amount of possessions she left behind, who can really tell.

I look for anything that could be of use getting back to the sirens as I search for the necklace, hoping for something to make the return trip easier—I don't know if I can survive the toxic sea creatures again.

Tarni screams for me to hurry up, earning a nasty reply from me.

A strange device is tucked away in the corner of the room, barely sticking out from under a pile of useless trinkets. It appears to be a tool of some kind. Two bars, almost like oars, connect at a curved metal piece at the top. When one of them shifts, I realize they're similar to the scissors we use to cut fabric for our *iluses*—my cousin, Dylana has the most beautiful golden pair in her room that she lets me borrow when I'm in the palace.

Thinking of her prompts me to look down at my *iluse*. I'm a complete disaster and would be ashamed to let other mer see me in such disarray, but I don't have time to do anything about it now.

I pull my hair back again, wondering if I should quickly braid it to avoid having it tangle with the jellyfish again. Finding a small piece of rope, I reach back, nearly fainting from the pain of moving my arms and shifting my injuries, and quickly braid my hair just enough to keep it close to me as I swim.

I look back to the device I found on the floor of the dwelling. The metal snaps together powerfully when I move the two ends—this will be coming with me.

I tuck it under my arm as I continue my reckless search of the room. Inside a bag meant to be strung over a mermaid's chest, I find the necklace. I grab a few other useless items that can't be used against me and cram them into the bag, hoping it will earn me a little grace with Tarni if I deliver extra.

Taking the tool I found, I slowly slip out of the dwelling.

Not knowing how the creatures will react, I quietly lift the tool, making sure the end is open. Slipping it around a small tentacle on the first jellyfish I see, I close the device around it as quickly as I can. It recoils, moving away from the pain of losing an appendage.

The tentacle floats in the water, drifting away as gracefully as a large stingray. Nodding, I move forward.

I snip away, clearing a path for myself as the blooms scatter around me, lifting higher in the water when they sense danger. It's slow going to get around them, but I manage to swim under a number of the creatures, cutting off a bit of the time...along with a few tentacles.

In the distance, Tarni looks shocked. I wish on all the starfish that I could hold up the bag around my chest and see her reaction, but that will have to wait until I survive my current trial.

My body aches, still stinging from the jellyfish, but I eventually find myself clear of the vicious creatures. Tarni looks like she wants to rush to me to claim her prize, but she's smart enough not to get too close as the lionmane's tentacles continue to float nearby—the giant jellyfish continues to hover over the dwellings, unaffected by my assault.

"You did it," Phorcys sounds impressed.

Sagging in the water, I try to lift the bag from my shoulder. I drop the bladed tool to the sand, knowing I couldn't wield it against the merman even if I tried. The last thing I need is for him to take it and turn it on me—or worse, Coralie's fingers.

Phorcys eyes it curiously in the sand but lets it sit as Tarni rips the bag away from me. My fingers trail after it, pulled with the force of her movements.

Phorcys notices me slipping and swims over to me, ripping the end of my braid out so that my hair hangs loose once more. His face is hard and unrelenting, but he slips under my arm, supporting me with his shoulder. We float in the water together.

Never have I been so grateful for a siren in my life.

I wrap one arm around him, refusing to give him the satisfaction of knowing I need him by curling around him like I want to.

If Merrick were here, he'd take me in his arms and carry me all the way back to the cave.

I want his safety.

"We need to get back," I croak quietly, concerned about what Roni might do to Coralie.

"Come on," Phorcys instructs Tarni. She looks euphoric when she pulls the necklace out of the bag.

Surprisingly, it looks exactly the way she described it to look.

As we swim, she fishes around inside the cloth pouch, looking to see what else I retrieved from her aunt's former dwelling.

I barely remember what I shoved in the bag—mostly trinkets—but she considers each piece carefully before returning them to the pouch. Tarni slips the strap of the cloth pouch over her head, pulling her lavender hair free after settling the bag across her *iluse,* down to her hip.

The sirens leave the metal tool behind, deciding it's too heavy to bring with us. I don't bother helping Phorcys swim—he carries me under his arm back to the cave.

Yellow fish swim by us, reminding me strangely of the rays of sun cascading down through the ocean's surface. A turtle glides by in the water, curiously turning toward us for a moment before veering away.

Phorcys is warm under my touch. His long hair trails out behind us as we move through the open waters. He holds his trident at his side, keeping it as far away from me as possible, though I pose no threat in my current state.

I want desperately to lean my head against the merman's shoulder to rest. I allow myself enough grace to let my head hover halfway between his shoulder and where it should be if I straightened my back while being carried.

A stingray swims close, nearly colliding with us. I don't have the energy to avoid it, so I duck my head against Phorcys. At the last second, it pulls up, gliding over our heads. It's tail bumps against me in the process.

Phorcys swallows, jerking my head as it rests against the side of his neck. I pull away, trying to untangle our hair without him noticing. He shifts his grip on me, and I gasp as he brushes against the stings on my back. The merman releases me slightly, loosening his grip. He drops his hand down to my hip from my waist to support me without hitting my injuries.

Tarni looks at me when I gasp, and I quickly tip my head up, looking at the stingray swimming away. She rolls her eyes and continues toward the cave where we left Coralie.

"Is she going to be okay?" I whisper, hoping Phorcys will swim faster.

He refuses to answer.

"Tarni, is Coralie going to be okay?" I repeat louder.

"We should make it back in time," she replies carelessly. "You kind of took forever in there."

"Knowing I was walking into the valley of the jellyfish, why did you schedule such a short amount of time?" I attempt to growl.

"You needed the proper motivation," Tarni replies.

"Just be glad I gave Roni strict instruction not to touch her while we were gone before the time ran out—she's still incredibly mad that we left without Tiko."

"I'm sure he's rotting in the cells in Scylla with Persephone's bones."

Phorcys cringes against me. Tarni turns to glare.

"I can still cut her fingers off and feed them to a shark if I want, Celena," she offers. "Don't tempt me."

I take a deep breath, stretching the skin across my back. I blink back my tears. If mermaid tears really were pearls like the books the sailors dropped in the sea said, our collection wouldn't have to worry about finding new pearls for the next two Pearl Festivals just from the tears Coralie and I have cried since leaving Scylla.

"I'm really tired of listening to you, *mer*," Tarni adds. "Keep talking, and I'll start pulling scales up again."

"I had a feeling you enjoyed that," I murmur.

"Had to keep up the act," she replies. I can hear the grin in her voice.

As we continue, I try to figure out a way to get enough strength to steal the trident from Phorcys and take Tarni out. If I pin her tail to the sand, she'll never recover enough to swim on her own again. If I miss, it could cost Coralie.

I'd have a lot more confidence in my plan if it were Caspian being held hostage with me—at least my twin has been trained to protect himself. Mother and father did us all a disservice by keeping our training quiet from each other.

If only we'd all been aware, the three of us could have been trained to a more advanced level. Instead, Mother trained me as passed down by Grandma Mara and her mother before that all the way back to princess Aila. Father had quietly trained Caspian, keeping it hidden from the rest of us—something all of the men in our line have apparently done.

I wonder if the king has suffered Marilla's wrath yet for quietly training the prince, or if she, Morgen, and Dylana are still recovering from the injuries they suffered at the hands of the sirens.

My parents must be beside themselves—all three of their mer children out in the darkest, most dangerous depths of the seas, far out of their reach. I imagine it would be terrifying for any parent, but even worse for them since Caspian, Coralie, and I come from Aila's line —the only one the sirens hate worse than the reigning royals because Aila was the one that interrupted Persephone and Chantay's plan to control the humans.

I'm sure my parents found out shortly after Caspian and the others left to find us. There's no way Casp, Merrick, or Llyr would ever wait around to come and find us. There must be a whole team looking for us though—my mother and Marilla would never let it stand if the best mer weren't out looking for us.

With any luck, the rest of the collection is on their way to Metten to bring back the royal mer children after we helped them escape the palace during the siren attack. I hope they made it safely through the dark—though, the more I travel at night, the easier it has become. I almost don't mind it now except for the terrifying things that come out at night that you can't see in the dark waters.

In the distance, I spot the cave. Afternoon is shifting into evening and the rays of light dance in the open waters, shifting and crashing into each other as they overlap. A few starfish crawl across the sea floor below us, catching the light as they move.

Anemone wave in the current, tiny fish darting in and out, using them for safety. I've always wanted to wear an anemone in my hair, but I know better. Instead, I mimic their look in other ways.

I watch the cave carefully, looking for any sign of the sirens or Coralie. The mouth of the structure is wide and dark, preventing me from seeing inside.

Phorcys notices me taking a breath to yell to the sirens, and he squeezes me against his hip.

"Don't," he warns quietly enough that Tarni doesn't hear him. My breath catches as I still against him, tensing my muscles.

"I can swim," I whisper.

"No, you can't," Phorcys objects.

"I can do it," I defy him. "Let me go, I'm fine."

"She's going to know when she sees you anyway, so there's no need to make it worse," he replies. "That will just make it more difficult for us to transfer you anyway."

"She doesn't need to know how bad it is, now let me go, and you go tell Roni to get away from my sister. Tarni can guard me."

He's shaped similarly to Merrick, though slightly taller. This reminds me of swimming backward with my partner, checking for dangers following behind us, though the siren isn't nearly as comforting.

I wiggle, trying to get him to release me, but he holds fast. I purse my lips, defeated.

"What—?" Tarni mumbles, jolting up in the water to see better.

I follow her gaze as I see someone shoot out of the cave.

Coralie turns around, screaming at the sirens that follow her out.

My sister is free from her shackles and holding the shell from her hair. She spots us and screams my name.

I don't have time to think, I only have time to act.

Coralie is free and defending herself, and I need to swim.

This is our only chance at escape and if they stop us, they'll kill us.

CHAPTER 6

Coralie screams again, slashing the shell at Roni. She connects with the merman whose name I don't know, slicing across his arm and chest. He reels back, knocking into Tarni.

I squeeze Phorcys' neck, pinching tightly enough to knock him out after cringing in pain. I catch his trident as it floats down in the water and attempt to race to Coralie's side.

On my way, I slam the trident against Tarni's head— she didn't see me coming from behind while she was busy trying to figure out how Coralie escaped.

Roni pushes the merman off of her and charges at us.

"Go!" I instruct, trying to swim while looking over my shoulder to see where Roni and the others are.

My world spins a little between the pain of the jellyfish stings and the loss of my equilibrium as I continually turn around to look while I'm swimming.

"What happened?" Coralie shouts.

"Jellyfish, keep going," I answer.

"I used the shell," she informs me, swimming as fast as she can.

The water streams over my body as we move and I can't tell if it's soothing my injuries or making them worse.

"I saw," I reply. "Cor, I need you to guide me."

"What?" she yells, glancing back at me.

"I'm hurt, and I can't swim backward to protect us like this. I need you to be Merrick."

"I don't understand," she shouts as we whip through the water. Roni is quickly gaining on us, two of the other sirens right on her tail.

"Grab my arm," I instruct her. "You swim forward and guide us while I swim as fast as I can backward and protect our tails."

Coralie slows, letting me catch her. She loops her arm through mine, ready to follow orders.

"Your only job is to swim as hard as you can and get us out of here. I'll help as much as I can, but my job is to keep us safe—I'll have no idea where we're swimming to."

"I can't do this," she cries. She lowers her head and swims faster anyway.

"You can, Cor, just don't stop," I shout above the rushing water. "And if anything happens, keep going. If we get separated, I'll find you. Just swim until you physically can't swim anymore and then find a place to hide. I'll find you."

She doesn't answer but hesitates slightly before pushing ahead even stronger, attempting to be Merrick for the moment. I flick my tail up and down, desperately trying to help my sister swim faster—I don't think we have any hope.

Now would be an incredible time for our mermen to show up and save the day. Instead, we'll have to save ourselves.

"Sharp turn right, Cor," I call, directing her. The wise choice would be to go left—toward mer territory, but turning left puts her directly in between the sirens and me, meaning I can't protect her. If we go right, I'll be wedged between them and able to defend her—we can find our way back later.

I turn my tail, using it to steer us hard to the right as Coralie angles her body to turn us as well. We pull quickly away from the path we were on, shocking Roni and the others for a moment.

Realizing I can easily steer us with my tail, I use the opportunity to take control of the situation.

"Is it clear?" I ask, hoping the path is open for us.

"Coral ahead," she shouts.

"How far?"

"Twenty lengths," she replies, still pushing her tail as hard as she can go.

"Tell me when we're one length away," I yell back to her. I flip my tail, trying to help as Roni begins to catch up to us. "We're going down and then back around."

"Are you sure we can do that?" Coralie sounds like she's struggling.

Focusing on escape is giving me temporary relief from the jellyfish stings—I wonder if that's how Nir still had the ability to nearly kill me in the palace in Metten after Caspian and Morgen's plan slowed him down.

"Now," Coralie gasps, clearly in pain from the strain this is putting on her body.

I flip my tail, sending us into a hard dive. Coralie shrieks, indicating it's time to swerve. I move my tail again, turning us to the left sharply. I look straight ahead and see the end of the coral ahead of us. I dive around it just as Roni pops over the edge.

"Did she see us?" Coralie gasps quietly.

"Probably, I don't know," I reply. "I couldn't tell that quickly. I only saw her for a moment."

"Where do we go?"

"Around and back toward Metten," I say. Our best hope is to hide in Metten and pray that all of Scylla is there to back us up. If they aren't, we could be risking the royal family. If nothing else, I hope Marilla has sent people to recover her mer children and bring them home before we arrive.

At least in Metten, I'd have the advantage of knowing where to hide and where our ancestors might have hidden supplies for us over a century ago should they ever return. I have no clue out here.

The light is nearly blinding as I look up, pumping my tail to aid our escape. When I look back down, I see the end of everything.

The collision knocks us down in the water. I lose my grip on Coralie as the siren slams into us. Using the stolen trident, I attempt to fend them off, but I'm too weak to do any damage.

My world spins like a whirlpool. Colorful fish form a beautiful blur. The water makes me wavy. I sink, unable to control myself.

"Nice try," Roni remarks, knocking the trident from my hands so that it snaps my wrists. "Too bad you weren't fast enough. That's the brilliant part about trying to escape while injured—it never works, does it?"

Coralie looks miserable when I regain the ability to comprehend my world again. Her idea was good, but her timing was off, and she knows it.

"She was going to take my finger," Coralie announces. I'm the only one that cares.

"Still might, *mer baby*," Roni reaches toward the pouch

on her hip, ready to pull out Caspian's knife again.

Tarni swims up, arm around Phorcys. Murdoch stares in obvious discomfort.

"We have to go," Tarni announces. "You'll pay for this tomorrow. I'm not sure how yet, but we have the entire rest of the night to figure it out. Now let's swim."

By the time the sun drifts down in the water, we find ourselves staring at the underside of a small kingdom in the distance. Boats fill the inlet far ahead of us, and even Phorcys seems nervous of the number of humans that must be nearby.

Murdoch attempts to hold a brave face, but I can tell he's shaken by the way his eyes pull back to his ears further than usual. He stays close to Tarni as we turn to the left, swimming away from the human world.

A boat seems to be following us as we swim parallel to the land. The vessel is long and dark and doesn't appear to made for fishing.

"What's that?" I ask, hoping to get a better idea of the types of humans we might be facing here.

"A boat," Phorcys answers.

"What kind?" I try again.

"We *siren* humans, we don't *talk* to them." He bristles, brushing his hair back as it floats between us. He keeps a firm grip on his trident—I didn't do myself any favors by knocking him out.

The water grows shallower as we swim adjacent to where the humans walk on the land far above our heads. Being in such a shallow depth makes me nervous. Finding places to hide isn't as easy as Tarni made it sound while we were traveling.

We swim closer to wooden columns in the water, drawing dangerously close to the ships in the water in the quieter part of the inlet. Rounding a piece of land that sticks out into the ocean, we come to what appears to be a quiet bay. Three ships bob in the water, tied to the docks.

"Tarni?" Murdoch asks.

"It's fine, Murdoch," she encourages him. "You'll learn quickly enough. All mer have the power to siren—we just need to wake it up in you, that's all."

"Don't you think we should do this slowly?" he replies. "Maybe practice first?"

Something bad is coming—I can feel it in the waters.

"I see that you need proof." She puts her finger on Murdoch's lips before he can speak. "I'll show you."

She swims a length away before turning around to face us. Tarni latches eyes with me.

"Hold her." Her words come out dark.

Phorcys and one of the other sirens grab onto my arms, prohibiting me from moving. Tarni and Roni grab Coralie and drag her toward a large wooden column in the water.

She says something to Coralie before they pull her to the surface.

"Murdoch!" I scream at him, knowing he's my best hope at stopping this.

He turns to me, shocked at the turn of events. Tarni's tail twitches happily as she holds Coralie above the surface.

"She can't siren," I shout, pulling viciously against my captors—it hurts me more than it hurts them.

In the water above us, the sirens move closer to the dock until they're right against the wooden column supporting the structure blocking all the light. When they dip back down into the water, Coralie isn't with them.

"Where is she?" I scream as Coralie's tail flicks back and forth, barely in the water.

"She's proving a point," Tarni calls down. "She'll figure it out."

"Maybe," Roni adds.

"They'll kill her," I shout in horror. I turn to Phorcys, hoping he'll listen. "Please, they'll kill her, let me save her."

He holds his expression, staring straight ahead.

"Phorcys, please, she's a little mer girl, don't do this." I turn to Murdoch. "Please, you might have turned your back on the collection, but please don't do this. She's only thirteen."

Murdoch shifts to look at me. When he does, Phorcys loosens his grip. I take it as a sign to move and beat my tail as hard as I can, ripping my arm away from him.

My movements surprise the other siren, and I escape his grasp as well, racing toward the surface despite the pain crawling over my back.

Coralie screams, begging for the humans to leave her alone as they reach for her chains with a hook. Tarni and Roni managed to lift my sister out of the water enough to string her up on a metal hook sticking out of the column holding up the dock.

The bottom of her tail is still in the water, but she's out far enough that the sailors have taken notice. They call down to her as they attempt to catch the chains binding her wrists over the hook and pull her up.

I swim for her on the surface, the waves crashing around my chest and abdomen as I move. Singing, I try to ensnare the men in my melody. Coralie quiets, eyes round with shock—she doesn't know the extent of my skills with sireny.

The men drop their hook into the water, and I let it sink to the ocean floor as I continue to sing. I try to think things through as I lure the men into my trap—do I kill them or let them live?

Holding them still, I swim to Coralie and struggle to free her. I have to stop several times to continue my song, leaving my sister hanging in the air longer than she should be.

I position myself under her tail so that she can sit on my shoulder. Gathering my strength, I push myself out of the water with everything I have, lifting her high enough that she can use her tail to push off of me and extend her hands over the end of the hook suspending her.

We crash down into the water, Coralie dunking me under the waves. I pop back up over the surface immediately, singing so that the humans don't fall out of my sireny and attack before we can escape.

My hair is plastered against my face, and I rush to move it back enough that it doesn't hinder my words as I lull the humans into my sireny again, keeping them at a distance.

If I make them jump into the sea, they could fight off the sirens for me, or at least get in their way and prevent them from stopping our escape. Tarni once said that the humans could move us if necessary—I consider letting them lift us into their boats and allowing them to sail us out of Tarni's reach, but I don't trust my voice to hold out that long, nor do I trust what will happen to our bodies if we remain out of the ocean for more than an hour or two.

I look around, trying to find Coralie. She's not on the surface with me, nor is she below me in the water near my tail as I expect her to be. Panic rises in my chest as I use my hands to try to clear a path in the water to see her —an impossible task.

I look back at the humans, not wanting to release them from my sireny, but also knowing I have to find Coralie immediately.

I dip under the water, finding Tarni once again holding my sister.

"Come back down," she directs in a casual manner, holding a knife to Coralie's throat.

"But—"

"Now." Coralie rolls her eyes as Tarni speaks.

Ducking all the way under the water, tail flipping up into the air as I maneuver myself back down into the sea. I hear the humans already starting to come out of my sireny as I make my way below the waves.

The hook that the humans dropped into the sea sits on the ocean floor, too far out of reach to be of any use to me. Tarni and Murdoch are arguing when I arrive.

"She didn't though, did she?" he protests. "Her sister did it for her."

"Oh, but she will," Tarni retorts. "She'll learn just like

her sister did, because there will come a day when Celena can't save the little princess."

She glares at me as I approach.

"What's the matter? Grandma Aila didn't teach you mermaids how to defend yourself?"

"Aila didn't have to. She took down sirens without even trying—it's in our blood," I growl.

"Unlike you, though, Aila didn't siren," Tarni challenges me.

"Maybe not like *you* siren," I approach her threateningly. "*She* sirened to help the humans, but she most assuredly did siren."

"You wouldn't be caught dead helping the humans, though, would you?" Tarni releases Coralie to me.

"No."

"Then why not side with us?" Tarni replies with a knowing smile. "Not that we'd ever trust *you*, but I see no reason why the mer and sirens can't work together. We already command the humans when we need to. With all of us, we could control them all of the time, not just when we come across them."

"We're in Hontan, not Antaire," I remind her. "Just what do you plan on doing?"

"We're going to end them all, Celena. Don't you see? Nir is on his way with the entire siren army. We're going to destroy the humans and rid the ocean of them once and for all, and you're going to help."

"The royals have always been better at sirening than the rest of the collection," Phorcys adds.

"That's why you were able to siren the humans away from us outside of Scylla." Murdoch swims into the conversation, earning glares from Roni and Tarni.

As a royal, my sirening skills are stronger than the others'—which is why Merrick couldn't control them outside the reef barrier in Scylla but I could.

It *also* explains why Nir didn't kill Marilla and Dylana when he had the chance—he needs us.

But as the descendant of Chantay, Nir should have the same skills we have. Maybe one royal voice isn't enough for whatever they have planned.

"You *want* them to follow us," I murmur, realizing there was a reason behind leaving Merrick and Caspian alive. "You want the royals."

"We'll let the others join us if they cooperate, but we don't really need them if they don't want to do as they're told," Tarni replies.

"This was always your back up plan if taking over Scylla failed," I point out as a fish swims between us.

"It was. *Smart* mermaid," Tarni taunts. "We just had to accelerate our plan, that's all. We'll get the humans to help us get the mer royals and then we'll use them to destroy the humans—if the royals happen to come to us, that just makes it easier.

"Nir should be here soon," she concludes, pulling her

hair over her shoulder as she turns to bat her eyelashes at Murdoch. "If *we* can siren, *you* can siren. You'll see."

"I'll go check for Nir," Roni announces, swimming off without waiting for permission.

"We have a few things to check on before they arrive," Tarni tells Murdoch. "Want to see the most magical place you've ever seen in your life?"

She takes him by the hand, leading him away. I watch them swim through the water until I can no longer make out their details.

"We have things to do too," Phorcys says, grabbing my arm.

Having no choice, I swim alongside of him in his slip-stream. My body aches, battling between the pain from the jellyfish and from what I did to save my sister.

He guides us in the opposite direction, swimming away from the humans, still parallel to the land. We keep a safe distance between us and our tail-less enemies, but we could easily spy on them if we rose to the surface.

"We're going to scout the area," Phorcys informs us, glancing back at Coralie as she follows. "We won't go near the humans though, don't worry."

On occasion, it's like Phorcys actually has a heart.

A few sirens swim behind Coralie, watching us to ensure we don't attempt to escape—even if I wasn't so broken, now would not be the time to attempt an escape.

Coralie swims under my arm, helping to make sure I

swim straight without veering off course or crashing into anything.

"Casp will have something to say about all this," she murmurs so no one else can hear her.

The ocean is still and unmoving around us, not even a hint of light dancing through the water as if everything above us is perfectly calm. An octopus sits on the ocean floor, slowly moving one tentacle across the sand and rocks below. Fish swim by as if nothing were wrong in their lives.

I note several caverns as we pass, but Phorcys guides us forward. Soon, we find ourselves nearing the surface again, though the sea floor is still just as far below us— the shallows. Coralie doesn't say anything, but I feel her tense up under my arm when she realizes where we are. It makes my skin prickle.

"We need to fix her injuries," Coralie suddenly protests. "She won't be able to make it much longer if she doesn't rest."

"She'll be fine," the siren merman answers.

I glance at him, worried that he'll try to carry me again.

"You're on your own this time, *mermaid*," he mutters, realizing what I'm thinking. "I have too much to do to haul your tail around."

He darts ahead of us, letting Coralie guide me. The sirens behind us perk up, knowing Cor and I are their responsibility now as the merman swims away.

Ahead, Phorcys darts low in the water, gaining speed. A cold terror washes over me as he launches himself out of the water, jumping like a dolphin. Coralie's fingers bite into me where her arm is wrapped around my waist to help me, and I cry out softly.

She darts her head toward me, eyes wide from the sight. My sister releases her grip on the edge of my scales before looking back to where Phorcys is crashing down in the water.

He dives low, flipping over so that his back barely misses the sand on the ocean floor as he races toward us. The merman pulls up at the last second, twisting to face us. The rush of water sends our hair floating above our heads.

"You're going to want to see this," he grins, eyes narrow.

Turning, Phorcys grabs my hand, dragging me along. I yelp, but he doesn't stop. Coralie tries desperately to keep up while I let the merman drag me, refusing to help swim.

I take a deep breath right before we break the surface of the water. We bob on the waves together as Coralie and the others join us.

Most land that I've seen has been covered with sand and rocks. There have been some plants, but the majority of the colors were tans and grays. This is like an explosion of color.

Green fills the hill, rolling all the way down to the rocks at the edge of the water. The cliff is raised high above the waves, overlooking it dangerously. I imagine if any human stood on the edge of it, they might be perilously close to falling off it.

"You're going to need to remember this," Phorcys murmurs just loud enough for me to hear.

Sea urchins speckle the side of the cliff, swaying in the breeze in a multitude of colors—I think they call them flowers. In the sky above, the blue is miraculously bright, etched with white clouds in the distance. Looking straight up, I can't find a single one.

A single line of water makes its way down the cliff, cascading into the ocean at the base of the land. I'm sure it's bigger up close, but it looks so tiny from our distance.

Birds fly overhead, crying out in obvious pain. Over and over, they shriek. A few land in the distance, picking at things on the sandy shore next to the cliff.

A stingray brushes against my hip, scaring me. I look into the water and notice him gliding to one of the sirens to check for food, which makes no sense since mer don't live this close to the shores—unless they do.

"There are more sirens here, aren't there?" I ask Phorcys quietly while Coralie is distracted by the sights.

"Once, not anymore." The muscles in his arms tighten. "Speaking of, it's time to go home."

He dives under the water.

"Time to go, Cor," I say, tugging at her hand.

We slip under the water, diving to the sand below. A crab scurries across the ocean floor, guiding our path for a moment until we overtake it, leaving it angrily in our wake.

Swimming further, we find ourselves back in an area covered in ships again—another harbor. The collection stays low to the ocean floor, moving under the danger-ous-looking boats.

An anchor drops in front of us, surprising even Phor-cys. He reels back, pausing in the water.

"Around," he announces, moving us out of the path of the boats.

Swimming through the harbor is as terrifying as entering the shark barrier without anything to scare them off. Even when scouting for the queen, if I left mer territory, I always went around the reef barriers instead of daring to venture into the feeding areas.

"Scared?" I taunt the siren. "I thought you could just siren them into doing your bidding…"

He glares to me from under his brow.

"You'll see," he mutters.

Flipping his tail, he directs us around the boats and humans, keeping enough distance that he doesn't bother to watch their every move. I, on the other hand, mind them very carefully.

We swim into a cavern that looks like a giant shelf. The rock stretches above the surface, forming part of a new cliff. The dark rock moves down into the water deeper than the human boat's sit, hiding the entrance from sight.

Surrounded by darkness, our only guide is Phorcys' voice as he instructs us to continue straight ahead. I hold my arms out, looking for any obstacles in the way as we swim slowly into the shelter.

When we venture back into the light again, the cavern is bathed in a bioluminescent glow. The cave rises up overhead, opening into a grotto that rises out of the water.

We surface. A long ledge sits just above water level—the perfect place for a human to sit by the water. I wonder if this is what the cave looked like where Persephone sirened Prince Jarek a century ago.

Glowing algae covers the bumpy rocks. I've never seen a cave like this before, with its strange angles and smooth edges.

"Stunning, no?" Phorcys asks coyly. He swims so close that he could reach out and touch my face. "Look closer."

His words have an icy edge, and the spark in his eye sets my scales prickling. I swim back, not taking my eyes off of the terrifying siren. His skin is tinged blue in the bioluminescent glow of the cave, making him look even more menacing.

I bump into the wall of the cave before I turn.

Phorcys moves toward me again, and I turn, quickly trying to follow his command. Examining the rock, I find that the legends are true—the sirens built their kingdom with the skulls of their victims.

CHAPTER 7

BONES LITTER THE GROUND BELOW US AND OVER THE water's edge. Skulls piled on top of each other form walls and barriers, strengthening the rocks already in place.

Some blend with the rocks, old from age, while others look only a generation old. Sediment has filled in the gaps over time, covering the secrets the skulls once held, allowing only their hollow eyes to communicate now. They watch us, judging our every move.

"You see, mermaid, the thing about sirens is that we always do exactly as we say we're going to do. We built our kingdoms on the deaths of our enemies. We took over Scylla. We're going to use the mer royals to control the remainder of the humans, and when we're done, you'll either be useful to us or you won't. Time to make up your mind."

Phorcys motions for me to swim to the ledge.

"Now is a great time to start." He grabs my hips and forces me into the air. I land heavily on the ledge, rock biting into my scales. "Crawl over there."

He points across the ledge to the back of the cavern. In the corners, I can see where two doorways lead out of the cavern—a human entrance.

"Against the back wall is a hidden partition. Find it and open it." The merman points to the right side.

I steel myself and crawl away from the water, grateful he didn't put Coralie through anything else.

"Be careful," Cor warns. "Don't catch your scales on the rocks."

I look down, realizing I should be more mindful.

Hand-over-hand, I pull my entire body weight across the flat rock, wishing I had the water to keep me warm. Despite the cooler temperatures, the water was much more agreeable than the cool chill of open air.

Skulls clutter the higher rock formations on the mainly flat surface. My finger accidentally reaches inside an empty eye socket when I reach forward. Knowing I can't recoil, I keep my cringe to myself and use the skull to pull myself forward.

Old and fragile, it breaks, dropping a cheekbone into my hand.

There's something more horrific about finding skulls

on the *surface* than there is when finding them under the sea.

I worry I've gone soft in the presence of the sirens—a few days ago, I never would have hesitated or been squeamish about any of the things I've faced since being dragged away from the palace in Scylla.

For a moment, I consider ripping the skulls out of their places in the ground and using them as weapons against Phorcys and the others, but Coralie is still in the water. The sirens were the ones that did this to the owners of the skulls—I'm sure the people they came from wouldn't mind getting one last word in as my weapon of choice.

"Move it along, mermaid," one of the sirens calls.

A few more arm lengths and I reach the back wall. Hidden partially behind a rock formation, I use the opportunity to look at the doorway near me. It appears to be a tunnel, and though dark, I can see that it takes at least one turn. Faintly, I can hear more water—perhaps another room? It doesn't sound like the ocean waves though, it's more of a consistent noise instead of the pulsing waves.

"Did you find it?" Phorcys interrupts my thoughts.

"Not yet," I call back, running my fingers along the wall. An indentation so small that I can barely feel it appears under my touch. "I found it! How do I open it?"

"If I knew that, I would have told you," he calls back.

"Are you okay?" Coralie calls.

"I'm fine, Cor, I'll be back in a minute."

I trace the outline, carefully gliding my fingers over the thin line. When I can't reach the top, I drop my hands to the ledge and push myself into a sitting position. Once up, I can barely see over the rock formation between the sirens and me, but I have just enough visibility to see that Coralie is surrounded by sirens.

Reaching back up, I continue my way around the outline of the hidden partition of the cave.

"I think I need to pry it open," I shout. "I can't find any other way in."

I hear a loud smash, turning to discover pieces of bone skidding toward me.

"Try that," Phorcys calls, expecting me to pick up the shattered skull he just threw at me.

"Lovely," I mutter, picking up the cracked bones.

I wedge it between the wall and the small door. The bone starts to crumble in my hand—age mixed with the pressure I'm putting on it—but the majority of it holds while I work to pry open the panel.

When it finally pops open, I set the bone down and use my fingers to open it the rest of the way. Air moves quickly through the tunnel leading into the cave, rushing past me. My hair moves over my shoulder and I realize that I probably look ridiculous with my wet hair plastered down my back and the sides of my arms—I'm sure Merrick would have a snarky comment if he were here.

It opens silently, swinging to the side away from me. I scoot my tail over to avoid colliding with it, making me twist at an odd angle to reach back into the dark space.

I give myself a moment for the light to fill the recess—it's so dark inside that the glow of the cave barely helps.

"Well?"

"I letting my eyes adjust, just a minute," I shout angrily.

"There should be a box inside," Phorcys shouts back. "Bring it back."

I deftly reach in and scoop the box out, setting it next to me. Chances are that the sirens know exactly what is inside the box, so snooping won't help me. Instead, I use the few precious moments I can steal from them to search the rest of the hidden compartment.

Knowing I don't have time to be cautious, I scrape my hands along every bit of the inside of the partition until I find another hidden panel. Inside sits weapons. One slices the end of my finger like a piece of coral. I retract my hand, wiping the blood away quickly—blood on land isn't like blood in the water—it smears on the rock.

I can't sneak a weapon by Phorcys. There's no way he wouldn't see it tucked in my hair and I have nowhere else to hide it. I shut the door quietly, hiding it back in the dark recesses of the compartment. A second hidden door reveals a set of shoulder armor—also helpful, yet unavailable to me.

I pick up the box again, dropping it heavily to the ledge so that the sirens can hear it. Pushing it forward, I move away from the hidden compartment and close it again.

"I'll be back for you," I whisper to the contents locked safely inside.

I ensure that it's closed firmly so that no one else can access it easily and then push the box forward again as if it's heavy—the sirens won't lift it outside of the water, so they won't know it was light enough for me to move without much struggle.

The box drags across the ground as I push it, then pull my tail to join it, only to mimic the movement all over again. Moving this way requires much more effort than merely dragging myself to the back wall had, but between the split fin and the jellyfish stings, this doesn't seem nearly as bad.

When I reach the edge, Phorcys rises up in the water to help move the box. I intentionally push it past him, knocking it into the water.

By the time I sink into the ocean again, relief washes over me with the water, calming my scales. I hadn't realized how on fire they felt from dragging myself over the sand and rocks.

"What's in the box?" I demand.

"Maps," he answers truthfully. One of the sirens holds the box under the water for him while he opens it, proving his point. "You've just uncovered all of the details we need for fighting the humans. Time to go back."

We make our way out of the cave, back to open waters as the sirens carry the box with maps. Phorcys pages through a few of them, attempting to organize them before we reach Tarni and whoever might be with her—I hate to think what she's been doing this whole time.

A plan starts forming as we swim now that I know where weapons are hidden. I'll need to know as much as I can about the area when Coralie and I try to escape. I assume by the time I'm well enough to fight in a day or so, Merrick, Llyr, and Caspian will be nearby, but they won't have the layout of the ocean here—I'll need to do some intelligence gathering for us.

I swim alongside Phorcys, glancing over his shoulder at the maps.

"Is that where we are?" I ask bluntly, pointing to the sketches.

"What do you care?" he challenges.

"If I'm going to be swimming around helping you, you're better off letting me know how to avoid the humans, *you eel*," I counter.

He looks amused at my resorting to name-calling.

"So the princess wants to learn her way around, huh?" He grins. "What are you willing to do for it?"

He's flirting with me, I realize in shock.

Fine. If Persephone could siren a human and Tarni could siren a merman, I'll do what I have to in order to siren a siren.

"I won't kill you when this is all over, how about that?" I say in a low voice.

"You honestly think you're going to win?" he counters.

A stingray swims by, cutting through the water between us. I pull back to avoid it.

"I think there's only one way this ends and it's with most of your sirens' skulls being added to your little collection back there."

"If you thought *that* was bad, wait until you see Shadare." He shrugs. "I'm sure we'll take you back when it's all over—assuming I can save you during the battle, that is."

"Like you saved me from the jellyfish?" I bat my eyelashes innocently at him.

Coralie pokes my stomach as I swim. When I turn to her, she looks horrified. I smile and turn back to the siren.

"So you *did* want me to save you from them. Here I thought you'd rather be eaten by that monstrosity than spend more time with us."

I sniff at his words, trying to be mysterious. After a moment, I point back to the map.

"Where are we? There, right?"

"We're here." He uses his finger to trace a route from where we left to where we're going.

"What's that?" I scrunch my nose as I lean closer, trying to decipher what the picture means.

Phorcys follows suit, pulling the map closer to his face.

"Oh." He lowers the map, looking at his companions. "Around, mermen—to the left."

We change course slightly, following his directions, though he doesn't take us far before correcting our path. Eventually, we swim upon what I saw in the drawing—a dark, terrifying stretch of ocean covered in all the waste the humans have left to the ocean's devices for a century or more.

Anchors lay on the ground, kelp growing quietly around them. Ropes twist in the current, caught on anchors and rocks. Chains litter the ground, much as the skulls had inside the cave. Light filters down, finally dancing again in the water—this time adding a dangerous edge to the dark, isolated place.

"Remember this sight, mermaids," Phorcys insists. "I have no problem chaining you up in there if you don't cooperate. I doubt you'll ever make it out, even if your friends *do* show up to help you.

"Swimming over the top would be easy," he continues, motioning to a bit of open water over the stretch of destroyed sea. "Dropping you into the middle of that mess wouldn't be difficult. Good luck surviving *that*."

The loose ropes sway in the water. Some lay coiled on the sand below. A few chains snake out like jellyfish tentacles, quietly resting on the outskirts of the area.

Bones of creatures long since dead rest mixed in the middle of the disaster. Most of them are fish skeletons that got caught while floating through the water, but some are from larger creatures that got trapped in the ropes and floating netting.

One catches my eye as we skirt around the dangerous area—mer.

"Is that—?"

"I told you, princess, it wouldn't be hard to drop you in there. We know this from experience." He glances at me before shifting the map to the next in the pile. "She didn't want to cooperate."

If there were mer bones entangled in there, that meant the sirens had sentenced one of their own this way. A siren had died there at the hands of her collection.

"Don't worry, that was two generations ago," he says loudly. "But if you think you'll need help remembering this little lesson, I can assist with that."

Phorcys swims away, diving down to the sand. He

crawls toward the edge of the ropes and chains, fishing out something before returning.

"Obviously I couldn't reach her, but this will serve as a reminder for you." He holds up a fish skeleton between his fingers. Breaking off the bone, he lets the rest fall. "Now, just in case you get any ideas, I want you to think about this moment."

He swims dangerously close to me.

"Turn around," he whispers, growling at me.

The siren reaches under my hair, tangling the bone in the underside of my locks as I had done with the broken shell in Coralie's hair.

"This stays," he reminds me, giving me a warning look. "And when you think about doing something stupid, remember this and be glad it's in *your* hair and not your sister's."

Beyond him, on the far side of the ropes and broken pieces from ships and cargo, a bit of blue flashes in the distance. I try to keep my focus locked on Phorcys as he floats in front of me, but it catches my eye again.

"Are we going to go?" Coralie is quick to ask.

Phorcys turns to face her, angry at the interruption.

"Yes, little mermaid, we are," he sneers. "No need to waste any more time at The Ropes."

Behind him, Merrick ducks behind the debris in the water.

Coralie nods to me as we swim away.

Our mermen have arrived.

"Come with me," Tarni grabs on to Coralie's arm the moment we swim into the cave where we're supposed to be meeting them.

"Tarni," Phorcys says forcefully. "A word."

Tarni scowls but swims out of the cave with him to talk in private. Murdoch takes Tarni's place by Coralie, guiding her outside to join Tarni and Phorcys.

"Murdoch, let her go," I warn him as he tries to take her away. My skin stings again as I move in the water.

"Tarni needs her," he replies.

"Murdoch," I growl.

"No, Celena. You don't get a say in this."

I glower as he takes my sister to the entrance of the cave. He pauses while the others hold their tridents on me to keep me in place.

If the fishbone in my hair were stronger, I'd slice their throats open with it and start the battle early—Merrick and Caspian could catch up.

Perhaps it was my decorations that made me brave— my shells and knives, and things I wound into my *iluses* to protect myself. Suddenly a single hidden accessory is making me ready to destroy my enemies again instead of just survive them.

Tarni and Phorcys swim back into the cave. Roni follows behind them, forcing Coralie and Murdoch back into the shelter.

"They'll be here tomorrow," Roni sings enthusiastically. All of the sirens smile.

She clings to a siren merman who looks like he's been racing here for days. Their collection must have sent him ahead to scout for them.

"They're in Rochay now, but they'll be here before the tide tomorrow."

"Which means we have work to do," Tarni announces. "You all have your assignments—go."

Several of them swim away quickly.

"Behave, Celena," the siren calls to me as her counterpart takes a place by my side, "Or Nir will do a lot worse to you tomorrow than I will."

"Where are they going?" I demand once she's gone with my sister and Murdoch.

"Celena," Phorcys says with a sigh. He shakes his head. "I have a mission. That means you have to stay here so that you don't interfere."

He rushes toward me, strong arms grabbing my shoulders as he propels me back into the wall of the cave. I can't breathe for a moment after slamming into the rock, the pain worse because of the jellyfish stings.

He pins me, dropping down to the floor to pick up a shackle. He attaches it to my tail while I'm crumpled over on myself, unable to deflect his hands from chaining me inside the cave.

"You won't be alone," he informs me.

I consider taking the fishbone to his eye just to make a point.

"You're leaving?" I ask in a sad voice.

The merman immediately perks up, straightening to face me for a moment with a blank stare.

"Behave," he instructs, repeating Tarni's words.

The moment he leaves the cave, another siren swims in front of it. He looks in, only to turn and hover outside, leaving me somewhat alone inside the cave. After a moment, he moves over so I can only occasionally see his tail as he floats to the side of the entrance.

I turn, trying to examine the shackle. The fishbone is too thick to do any good picking the lock, but a piece of driftwood nearby might be up to the job.

Unfortunately, it's out of reach. I tug relentlessly at the shackle, trying to claw my way to the driftwood.

If I can escape, I can knock the guard out and find Merrick or my brother to help me locate Coralie—I'm terrified Tarni might take her back to the humans.

The sand collects under my nails as I attempt to scrape my way to the driftwood. No matter how far I stretch, I can't get close enough. Nothing in the sand is close enough for me to reach to extend how far I can stretch.

A gasp sounds outside. I reel back, shooting straight up in the water, worried the siren might see what I'm attempting to do to free myself.

The siren guard struggles with something, clearly panicking.

"What's happening?" I call.

More strangled sounds filter into the cave.

"Hey!" I shout. "What's happening?"

The siren grunts and I press myself against the back wall, unable to escape whatever is lurking outside. My eyes dart around, begging for something to float close enough for me to escape the shackles with to escape..

All goes quiet.

A minute goes by...

Then another.

Finally, the siren turns, hovering in the entrance of the cave, backlit so that I can't see any of his features, just his outline against the strong light of the open waters.

"It was a shark—a small one—but I had to get rid of it."

"You killed it?" I ask in horror. I didn't want any more baby shark deaths in my presence.

"No, you stupid mermaid, I scared it away. We always carry the scent with us. Now clam up! I don't want to hear you until Phorcys gets back."

He turns, floating out of the entrance, back to his post.

As he does, someone else slips in.

The siren hurries toward me, taking up the light again. I press myself against the wall once more as he rushes foward.

"Quiet," he hisses.

No, *not* a siren—*Merrick*.

CHAPTER 8

"How did you—?"

"Shh," he hisses. Merrick leans in, pressing his lips against my ear. "He didn't see me swim up beside him. I gambled that he would turn back to his post without looking and I slipped in. He's still out there listening."

His lips are warm against my skin. Merrick quickly risks kissing me behind my ear, nearly sending me into the sporadic twists the brine pools cause. I clench my body in place, hoping he doesn't notice, but my insides twist and writhe under his gaze as he pulls back.

Without thinking, I reach up and tangle my hands in the very ends of his hair, scooping up his jaw in the process. Smiling, he quickly grabs my waist, pulling me toward him as he kisses me properly on the lips.

Merrick reaches around, running his hands from my hips up my back. I yelp in pain, mumbling into his lips, as he comes into contact with the welts striped across my back.

He pulls back, shocked.

"Celena?" he gasps, hoping he didn't go too far by kissing me—he should have known he *wasn't* by the way I was kissing him back.

I gape, not wanting to explain.

He looks at me cautiously before moving closer to me and running his hands over my sides again, fingers brushing the edges of my back. I wince, and he immediately swims behind me, moving my hair out of the way.

"*Len!*"

When he swims in front of me, his narrowed eyes demand an answer. My jaw opens and closes, trying to figure out how to explain.

"Celena," he says harshly, "what is this? What did they do to you?"

"They needed something from an old siren dwelling," I whisper, hoping the siren outside can't hear me. "It's been overtaken by hundreds of jellyfish—the biggest ones I've ever seen. Tarni wanted me to collect something from Nir's mother—"

"The siren queen?" Merrick murmurs. "Anything that could help us?"

"A necklace," I inform him. "I don't think so."

I pause for a moment, suddenly remembering the revelation that Nir's still alive.

"Nir is on his way—he'll be here tomorrow."

"How did *this* happen?" Merrick punctuates his words, motioning to my injuries.

"I had to swim through the jellyfish to get the necklace for Tarni."

"When?"

"Yesterday," I admit.

"Len, how are you even functioning?"

"I'll be fine." I rest a hand on his chest just below his shoulder.

"We have to get you out of here." He looks like his wants to shatter every jellyfish and siren in the sea.

"Tarni has Coralie."

"I know, Caspian and Llyr are following them, but she took half the collection with her."

"So you came to rescue me?" I whisper against his cheek, making him shudder.

"You're shackled," he surmises, looking down.

"Driftwood." I nod. "Over there."

He darts back, scooping up the possible pick that is still just out of my reach. Expertly, Merrick works to free me, attempting to break the lock from around my fin.

If Caspian and Llyr can save Coralie, and Merrick and I can escape, we can bring the collection back to stop the sirens once and for all—and keep the royals far, far away from them.

I twitch as he works—both anxious to be free and

nervous to be near him for the first time since we changed our relationship.

A small gasp escapes his lips as the driftwood breaks.

"I don't know where they got this, but I've never seen a lock so small," he mutters as he tries to find something else to break my bindings with before we're caught.

We both freeze when a second voice approaches the siren outside. They murmur together, only a few words drifting in.

"They're going to move you," Merrick looks up at me.

"You have to go," I tug at his hair—the only part of him I can reach as he fumbles with the lock around my fins. He hesitates, but I pull harder on his tresses and force him to swim up to me. Merrick buries his hands in my hair protectively.

"What is this?" he asks as his fingers find the fishbone in the back of my hair.

"A lesson from Phorcys."

"Who?" Merrick's brow furrows.

"One of the sirens," I say hurriedly. "Oh, I might try to siren him, just ignore anything you see."

"*Excuse me?*" Merrick's voice rises.

"You need to *go*," I push at him as the siren's squabble grows louder.

"I'm not leaving you," he hisses, shocked.

"Then we'll both be trapped inside this cave, Merrick," I respond, thinking practically. "Go help them save

Coralie. Once she's safe, I can fight back and we'll get me away from the sirens."

He sighs, annoyed at my point.

The two sirens get into a heated debate outside, my guard not wanting to release me until Tarni or Phorcys return, the other wanting to take me…*somewhere.*

"Promise me, no matter what," I say in a rush of words, "Promise me that you'll get Cor out of here, no matter what happens to me. She is priority."

He grimaces, but I grab his neck, demanding his attention. Merrick will do as I ask though, if it comes to that. He will always protect my sister and let me take care of myself if the choice is between helping me or protecting someone that can't protect themselves—as it should be.

"Promise me she comes first."

"I promise," he whispers but looks like he wants to argue.

"I have my orders," one of the sirens shouts.

"Please, Merrick. We'll handle my escape later, just don't get caught or we'll be in an even bigger mess," I beg.

His hair looks especially blue in the light filtering into the cave, making his eyes pop fiercely. Merrick wraps his arms around me.

"Merrick, please, you have to go," I repeat, attempting to push his arms back even though that's the last thing I want to do.

The corners of his lips tug down as he studies me, taking the corners of his eyes down with them. I'm sure his face matches my own as I wrap myself around him quickly, clutching the muscles in his back under my hands.

"This isn't fair."

"You need to go, Merrick," I insist. "You'll get caught."

"I'll risk it," he replies, slowly leaning into me to catch my lips in his.

Merrick's kiss is slow and deep—nothing like the frenzied, passion-driven kisses we've shared before. Every movement is painfully slow and perfect.

He pulls me closer to his chest, running his hands through my hair while he avoids bumping my injuries. Somehow he works a hand between us, cradling my chin before tipping my face up to look at him.

"I will come back for you," he promises.

I pull on his seaweed *sarasa,* dragging him back to me for one more kiss a moment before the sirens turn to enter the cave, still arguing.

Horror washes over me—they're about to find Merrick.

I push him, forcing him away from me. His hand reaches out, clutching mine as long as he can as he flings himself toward the wall of the cave and slides along it quickly.

Without any other choice, I start screaming, hoping to

distract the sirens. I wail as loudly as I can, bending down to claw at the shackle around my tail as if it's hurting me.

The two stare at me, unsure if they should rush to me or if I'm tricking them and will kill them the instant they get too close like the human books claim. I consider playing into that delusion for a moment, bending my fingers enough that I could use them like claws against my captors, but instead, I still.

"Please," I whine. "It hurts."

They approach me cautiously as Merrick slowly slips around the wall of the cavern, watching my performance. One of the sirens moves as if he might turn around or back away so I gasp, recovering his attention.

"I'm injured—this is too heavy," I whimper.

"Then sit down," the second siren sneers.

I pause for a moment as if the thought had just occurred to me. Sinking to the sand, I keep my focus on them.

"It's still too heavy," I complain. "You *do* realize I just swam through a jellyfish bloom for your princess, right?"

"The chain stays on," my guard snips.

Merrick pauses in the entryway—a final goodbye— then he's gone, lost to the open waters outside the cave.

"I thought I was supposed to leave," I comment flippantly.

"You are—"

"You aren't—"

They glare while they talk over each other.

"We're going to move her," the second objects.

"Tarni didn't say to move her."

"But Phorcys *did.*"

If Phorcys sent for me, that can't be good. I consider my options—Merrick can't be too far away—if he hears them screaming when I attack them, he could easily come back to assist. I need to know what the siren's plan is though, and I can't do that while swimming for my life —I need to play along.

"I'll go."

They both turn to look at me.

"Well?" I look down at my tail, indicating that they should hurry up. "I've learned it's best not to keep you eels waiting, so let's hurry up, shall we?"

The second siren looks triumphant as the first unshackles me. I'm thrilled when none of Merrick's attempts at freeing me caught inside the lock. The siren merman pops it open, freeing me, while the other cuffs my wrists together.

I follow them out of the cave like a queen would— head in the air, shoulders back, unyielding even in capture.

Marilla and my mother would have been proud.

The swim is longer than I expect, but we eventually reach Phorcys.

"Our job is to move the humans toward one central

area," he explains. "Once your friends arrive, we need to make the transition as easy as possible."

"And I am to *sing* them into submission?" I ask dubiously.

"You are to sing them to the west side of Hontan."

Near Antaire, where the remnants of Prince Jarek's former kingdom still sits on the cliff next to the sea.

"You can't do that on your own, *siren?*" I question, running my fingers through my hair.

"Why should I? We have *you*. Your voice holds more power than ours—it will be faster this way. We might even beat Tarni and your sister back if you hurry up."

I open my mouth to ask where they are but he silences me with a hand in the air.

"You belong up there." He points to surface. "There are a hundred men out on the docks. Get them to the west side or we'll kill them all. I know you don't like humans, but I also know you don't want their blood on your hands, so handle it or I will."

The way he looks at me with a sharp glint in his eye tells me he's more than willing to siren the sailors into the sea. He'll probably use their skulls to build his new dwelling when this is all over too.

Reluctantly, I swim up.

Perhaps I'll siren the men into the sea myself and allow them to kill Phorcys and the other two mermen with us. If my voice really is as powerful as the sirens believe, even if the three of them work against me, I still have a chance at winning.

Phorcys stays right by my side.

"See those sailors over there? Start with them." He puts a hand on my forearm as he points with his other hand.

His hair drips down his back, much as I assume mine is doing as well. I was conscientious about how I exited the water this time, brushing my long bangs back as I surfaced.

I look to the west where the sun sits low in the sky. It glares off the surface of the water with harsh orange tones.

"They need to go there?" I confirm, nodding to the distant shores.

"Beyond," he replies. "They need to bring their royals back."

I whip around to face him, regretting it the instant my muscles scream in pain as I move.

"What?"

"They need to go and bring their king back. He needs to be here when we siren them all."

"How do you expect me to get them there—follow them?"

"You're creative, Celena. Find a way. Suggest they do it and make it so compelling that even once you're gone, they'll follow through because they believe there is no other choice. Make them follow your commands."

"That won't work—"

Phorcys opens his mouth to sing. Though not as lovely as mer voices, Phorcys quickly produces a sound that makes the sailors near the shore turn to us.

I panic as they lay eyes on me, but Phorcys holds me in place at his side while the other sirens hover below us in the water. He tightens his grip on me and propels us closer to the shore. My instinct is to whimper in the presence of the humans, but I choke it down, summoning the strength my mother has trained into me.

Phorcys glances at me as if it's my cue to take over. I hesitate, and he turns cruelly away. As his voice rises, the sailors walk quickly toward the dock. After a moment, they start to run toward the end, keeping in step with the siren's voice.

"Stop."

I pry at his fingers around my arm.

"Stop, I'll do it. Stop."

"You had your chance," he pauses long enough to say. He doesn't bother to face me.

The men reach the end of the dock as more clamber over the terrain to rush onto the wood planks that rest quietly above the water.

My voice surprises me, though it shouldn't—I have to prevent the men from jumping to their deaths.

The siren doesn't stop, attempting to overpower my voice. My fists clench at my sides, but I won't give him the satisfaction of a reaction. I close my eyes for a moment, focusing on my song. When I open them, I raise myself out of the water to be higher than Phorcys and sing as loud as I can.

It takes a moment, but some of the men fall under my command. They reach forward, lashing their hands out to rescue their fellow sailors as they attempt to walk off the dock, plummeting perilously to the water below.

I pitch my voice higher, hoping to project my words louder than Phorcys, though if what he says is true really is, I should be able to siren them away from him without too much effort.

I will the humans away from him, instructing them to force back the men that they can on the dock until every last man standing above the water is under my control. Manipulating them back, they slowly start to turn as they listen to my guidance.

A few men splash in the water, unsure of whose command to follow. The rest turn on the dock, walking back toward the land.

Phorcys continues to sing, miraculously still controlling a few of the men left in the water. He instructs them to dive under the surface to meet their fate.

I work harder, changing the song so that my words have more of an impact on the humans. I command them away from the siren next to me, lowering myself to his tactics to gain control.

Still, a few remain under Phorcys' power. Willing to risk the lives of the men in the water under my control, I send them after their counterparts below the surface, instructing them to return them to the air above the water.

Several dive below, pulling the other sailors up with them. The men come up choking—coughing and spitting until their lungs are clear enough to breathe again—still under Phorcys' siren song.

Frustrated that the men in the water are so torn between us, I push down on Phorcys' shoulder, submerging him as far as my chains will allow me.

With the men's attention, I sing them back to shore and command them to rush toward the western shores to retrieve their royals.

The siren stays under the water, but his anger is unfurled in the form of nails piercing into my tail. I cry out, disrupting my song, but my own nails in his shoulder encourages him to release me.

Desperately, I issue my final orders and drop back under the water before my captor can do anything else to injure me.

"Happy?"

"I would have been if you'd done what I told you to immediately," he huffs.

"At least they're going," I snap. "I doubt *you* could have made them do that."

"And look at you, little mer princess, you saved the humans. I bet you'll regret that in a few days," he counters.

He swims back up to the surface. I join him to ensure he doesn't try to undo my work—I'd rather have the sailors walking to the western shore to eventually return with a king with the *hope* of surviving whatever will be coming along with the sirens' wrath rather than to have them drown today.

The thought makes another resound in my head—I sent the men to retrieve a royal.

Any *royal* must be a descendant of Jarek's, must they?

Soon, I may be face-to-face with a man tangled in this war because our great-great-grandparents broke an alliance together. The lines of Aila, Chantay, and Jarek will all be present for another battle, and I will be at the center of it, commanding fates and changing lines.

"What did you tell them to do?"

"I instructed them to go to the western shores and to return with their royals."

"That's it? You think *that* will work?" He blinks at me, hair flowing out behind him majestically. Phorcys would make an attractive mer if he hadn't made such bad life choices.

"I think if the royal mer have any chance of doing as

you asked and controlling the humans even while not in their presence, that was your best shot. If it doesn't work, it never will."

What he doesn't know is that I added in a little instruction of my own to the song while he was underwater—the humans will do as the sirens want, but they'll also hopefully be activated to do my bidding as well when the time comes. Now I'm left to wish on all the starfish that my song really *does* work.

"It will work," I insist, taking the lead. The sirens quickly follow behind me as I swim away.

I instantly regret my burst of speed, slowing to prevent the welts on my skin from crinkling as I move.

I hadn't realized as I was singing that the sun had set and a dingy gray color filled the world around us while on the surface. Now, under the water, everything was growing dark.

A large fish swims by us, swaying its body back and forth until it veers off from us, abandoning our shared path. For a moment, I want to follow it as it swims into the darkening water.

"You're not so lucky," Phorcys mutters, seeing my gaze traveling away. "At least you've got your sister to go back to."

I cast a look at him, asking without words. He sighs.

"Tarni is teaching her to siren." His words cut into me. "Don't object. If she doesn't learn now and we throw her into the fray with the rest of you to command the humans, she could die because she doesn't know how to manipulate her voice yet. Tarni knows what she's doing."

As much as I hate it, he has a valid point. Coralie needs to learn how to protect herself for the battle to come.

We dive deeper, following the ocean floor as we make our way back. I don't have long until Nir arrives with his sirens. I can't even begin to surmise what condition I'll find the monstrous merman in when he graces us with his dark presence.

Ahead, several squid—or possibly jellyfish—glow in the water in the distance. The sirens around me frown, squinting to see what creatures lay ahead of us.

The sea life twinkles in front of us in group formation long enough to distract us—the same trick most biolumi-nescent fish use to capture their prey—and we're drawn to the mysteries that they hold.

Our careless stares betray our safety and we find ourselves surrounded, an attack eminent as a vicious cry fills the water.

CHAPTER 9

I MOVE QUICKLY, THRUSTING MY HANDS IN FRONT OF ME TO protect myself. The chains dangle around my wrists, swooping in front of me as I launch myself toward the merman.

With the chain wrapped around Phorcys' neck, I pull back. Caspian and Llyr rush to assist me.

The siren struggles against me, but I'm at the advantage having caught him off guard. I pull back forcefully on my restraints, attempting to subdue him.

He pulls against the chain, trying to slip his fingers between it and his neck. He grimaces, twitching against me as he attempts to overtake me. A strangled laugh escapes his lips as if this amuses him.

"You can't—" he grunts out before Llyr slams his trident into the siren's skull. He falls limp in my arms.

"Coralie?" I demand, attempting to keep the siren from sinking to the ocean floor.

"Not now, Celena," Caspian yelps as he turns to collide with my guard.

The second siren rests on the ocean floor nearby—Merrick took him out. His face is hollow as he stares at me.

"Celena, are you okay?" Llyr asks. I turn to face him.

"What happened?" Caspian shrieks, noticing the injuries on my back. "*Merrick?*"

When I twist around, my twin is glaring at Merrick, demanding an answer as to whether he knew about my injuries or not.

"There wasn't time." Merrick holds up his hands.

"Where is Coralie?" I demand again, eyeing the sirens at the bottom of the moonlit sea.

"We have to get you unchained," Llyr interrupts, darting down to the sirens to look for a key to release me.

"*Caspian!*" I shout, ready to loop my chain around *his* neck until he answers me.

"We couldn't get her," Merrick answers quietly. My body stills, only my eyes turn to him.

"What?" My whisper comes out as a growl.

"Tarni and Murdoch were teaching her to siren. We couldn't reach them without risking Coralie's life, Celena," Caspian sounds heartbroken as he swims slowly toward me.

Merrick darts up in front of me, making the water rush up my tail uncomfortably. He reaches for my hands, trying to stay low enough in the water to not obstruct my view.

"Merrick?" I can feel a bubbly sensation crawl it's way up the inside of my tail, working its way through my stomach until it flushes in my cheeks, making me dizzy.

"I promise we'll get her back, Len."

"We'll rescue her, Celena," Caspian adds. "But we couldn't get to her, so we got to you instead."

"But I can protect myself," I argue. "She can't. You should have stayed with her."

"Well, we didn't," Caspian snaps, making me drag my accusatory gaze away from my partner. "Stop fighting against us and start fighting with us."

The moonlight flickers in the water as the surface grows stormy. I look up, noting the rough waters overhead.

"What do you think they'll do to her when they discover I'm gone?" I ask. "And what happens when the sirens wake up?"

"We could take them with us," Caspian suggests. "Make a trade, maybe?"

"They won't do it," I sigh. "They wouldn't trade Cor for their entire collection—it's our voices, Casp. Royals have stronger sirening abilities than other mer. They didn't just want Scylla—they wanted the royals. We aren't the reigning royals, but we still come from the same line. That's why I sang those sailors away from the blue-tailed siren outside of the reef barrier when they dragged Marilla out.

"Fine, then we take them so they can't cause any more trouble," Caspian declares.

Llyr breaks the lock and the shackles slide off my wrist. I grab my wrist, rubbing it with my thumb.

"Been a while, huh?" Llyr mumbles quietly enough that the others don't hear.

I let out a soft snort.

"Where are we taking them?" I ask, louder.

"We can probably get away with having you disappear for the night." Merrick brushes his hair back. "I'm sure Tarni will be worried, but a few hours will probably be tolerated before she does something irrational. The mermen will be with us, so for all she knows, you're still under their control."

"We'll incapacitate the sirens, and then we'll get in place to rescue Coralie at first light. Dylana and the others should be here tomorrow—they weren't far behind us," Caspian adds. "They won't see us coming."

"They already know you're coming, Casp—they've been waiting for us to arrive. They made sure you were never too far behind."

"And Nir is set to arrive tomorrow as well," Merrick reminds us.

We swim down to the sirens, using rope that Llyr was carrying on his belt to tie their hands to their fins. I glare at Phorcys as Caspian restrains him.

"Do we have any intelligence on what state Nir is in?"

"Nothing," Llyr replies, tightening the rope around my guard. "We came straight after you. Dylana only stayed long enough so she and her father could plan the rescue and get the collection together."

"Everyone else moved to Metten because they thought it would be safer for the time being."

"*Perfect*," I mumble. "Now they're closer to this war."

"We'll send someone to warn them when they arrive tomorrow," Llyr assures me.

The mermen lift the sirens off the sand, letting them dangle in the water as they guide me to wherever we're dropping them off. Silver light flashes off Phorcys' long hair as we swim through the sea.

The water grows darker as the storm intensifies overhead. I'm grateful we don't have to deal with the storm aside from our loss of moonlight below the waves.

"We're close," Merrick says, eying me as my body sags under the intensity of my jellyfish stings. All three of the mermen look like they want to scoop me up and carry me back to whatever cave we'll be residing in for the night, but none of them say anything, knowing I'm likely to have a biting remark.

"Up ahead," Caspian murmurs, floating closer to me as the cave's mouth comes into focus in the dull water.

"Keone and Natale came with us, but we separated yesterday, trying to find you faster. They'll join us soon, but don't be surprised if they show up tonight."

I nod, tired.

Llyr hands off the siren he's carrying to Merrick and swims inside to make sure we still have control of the location. After a moment, he exits, glowing squid in tow. He waves us in.

The floor of the cave looks so inviting that I nearly tumble onto it the moment I make it to the center of the small cave. The boys let me sprawl out, hair flipped over my head and arms as I stretch them above my head on the sand, my back facing up to protect my wounds.

"Len." Merrick breathes, seeing my injuries better in the blue glow of the cave.

"Celena," Caspian sounds like he might cry. He lowers himself to the ground next to me and brushes the under-side of my hair with his hands. I arch into his touch, tears springing to my eyes.

"It hurts," I whisper.

"More or less than the pried-up scale?" he asks with a small, sad chuckle.

"She's endured a lot in the last two weeks."

Looking at how far I've come, I realize that less than a month ago, we weren't even sure sirens were in our midst, and now we are so far into siren territory that we were practically on land.

The water moves slightly along the sand as Merrick settles down on my other side. He hesitates before touching my skin, tracing the welts with his fingers. I suck a breath in, hissing at the pain.

Through strands of my hair, I see Llyr turn to look at the sound I made. He sits near the sirens, trident in hand as he wraps his arms around his tail, waiting for one of them to wake and challenge him. I have no doubt he will take an eye out and *then* ask questions.

My eyes are too heavy to keep open any longer. I let them flutter shut under the cover of my long locks while the mermen talk. I interject occasionally, telling them what I've learned over the last few days. I explain the cave made of skulls and how we were attacked by needlefish in the night. I can practically feel them cringe as I recount the jellyfish to them.

Caspian flips over next to me, staring up at the top of the cave.

"I'm sorry, Celena. I should have been here."

"Don't be silly, Casp," I say sleepily. "One of us needed to be here to free Cor. I clearly can't do it in this state.

Merrick's hand quietly finds its way to mine, surprising me. I nearly yelp as his skin touches mine, but I manage to hold it in. His thumb rubs circles around the fleshy part of my hand, soothing me as much as my brother combing my hair had.

"Rest now, Celena," Merrick encourages as I finish my harrowing tale of surviving the jellyfish bloom.

"What, you don't want to hear about how Phorcys had to carry me back, and Coralie tried to escape just as we arrived?"

"*What?*" all three mermen demand. One of the sirens stirs—Llyr takes care of it before I can even lift myself up to see which one.

"Coralie decided to try to break out. She used a shell I gave her." I smirk as I tell them the story, occasionally yawning. I want to curl into Merrick, even though I'm still furious with him for returning for me instead of staying with my baby sister.

"Sounds like something *you* would have done," Caspian says in a smug voice.

"Except *I* was trained. *I* would have incapacitated at least one of them and escaped."

"And likely would have found a dolphin somewhere," Casp adds. "You have an affinity for finding those right when you need them most."

"There's something else," I add reluctantly, telling them about how Tarni strung Coralie up and offered her to the humans, and what I had to do to save her.

"You're becoming a natural at this sirening thing," Llyr

tries to joke. "Looks like we may have to change some rules in Scylla and Metten so you can come back to us."

"Who says I want to do that?" I try to tease back. "Maybe I'll move into the skull cave and spend my days there."

Merrick squeezes my hand, making me jump out of my scales.

"Somehow a dwelling built out of the skulls of your enemies makes you even more fearsome, Len," he laughs. "Now, rest. We have to go save Coralie soon, and you need sleep."

"Yes, partner," I sigh, nestling my head against my arm, trying to get comfortable.

Merrick releases my other hand so I can pull it under my head to rest on it. One finger runs over the curve of my side from my *iluse* down to my scales before he swims over to Llyr to help keep watch. Caspian stays by my side as I fall asleep, allowing them to watch over us until morning.

"*There* she is," a merman's voice interrupts my thoughts as I wake.

I take in a deep breath as the world floods in around me, filling my senses once again. It's like everything inside of me wakes up at once, jolting me into consciousness.

"Stop speaking," Caspian growls at the siren.

I lift my head, still surrounded by blue light.

"It's time to go," Caspian says, swimming over to me and lowering his face to mine. "It's almost first light and we need to get in position before they can see us approaching."

"What are we doing with *them?*" I motion to the siren that just crooned at me. "I vote we stab their tails and take them out of the picture."

Momentary horror washes over Phorcys' face, but then he grins, knowing I wouldn't subject him to a fate like that. Pushing myself up, I swim over to him, getting dangerously close to his face. His eyes widen in surprise.

"Behave, Phorcys." I level a cold gaze at him before allowing the smallest smile to transform my face as I bat my eyelashes.

His breath comes in a short gasp, pulling back from me slightly. The other two sirens turn to him, evaluating his response. They snarl at me, looking every bit like the deadly sea creatures the human books describe our kind to be.

One of them hisses at me, jerking toward me in the water. Merrick and Caspian dart toward us, but Phorcys' glare stops the siren. Phorcys angles his shoulder to block him from me, but his stare is enough to end his short-lived tirade.

"Control them," I whisper. His pupils dilate—maybe this sirening thing really is working.

"He won't have to," Llyr announces. "The advanced team is here."

Several mermen—Marilla's personal guards—swim into the still-dim cave. They nod sharply to me, respecting my title, even though I'm not a reigning royal.

Three of the mermen float over to the sirens, taking a place where they can watch over them, while the remaining two prepare to join us in the rescue mission.

I turn to leave. Warm skin caresses mine, but the fingers are foreign.

Phorcys smirks as I whip back around to him. I dart toward the door, pulling away. My body says to destroy him, while my brain reminds me that I might need to keep him under my influence.

I swim past the mermen, refusing to make eye contact. Caspian leads the way to where the sirens have Coralie.

"Want to explain that?" Merrick attaches himself to my side.

My hand floats back to tap the knife on the makeshift belt we created out of seaweed—the boys didn't have time to bring me armor in their race to find us. The weapon brings me security as I touch the blade.

"You know as much as I know," I remind him. "Just trying to use every advantage we have."

"Look!" Llyr's voice interrupts. He points up and behind us where a pod of dolphins swims our way.

My breath exits my lips as a loud sigh that I instantly regret. I clamp my lips shut, cutting off Merrick's snide comment about my current condition. He closes his mouth, and suddenly I wish I could press my lips against it.

"Here we go," Caspian warns us as they approach.

I swim with them, refusing to show any weakness despite the pain in my back.

Like the ones from Scylla, the dolphins seem thrilled to see us, allowing us to latch on to their dorsal fins as they race through the water. I suck in the human air as we surface, releasing it when we dive back under the water.

It's still dark when we arrive at the cave where I had been held.

"You think she's still here, right?" I murmur.

"I'd say so," Merrick mutters as something catches the light by the cave entrance. "Is that Murdoch?"

"I think," I reply, squinting to see through the dark waters.

"That means they're here. Time to stage a rescue." Merrick grins at me as he releases the dolphin carrying him. Reluctantly, I do the same and drop down in the water next to him as the pod continues forward.

Quietly, we swim through the water, coming at the cave at an angle so the watch mer can't see our approach.

"Your job is to get Coralie," Merrick directs. "We'll take care of the others."

"Once you get her out, swim as far as you can—we'll catch up," Caspian promises.

"You sure that's a good idea? Nir is set to arrive today —what if we run into him?"

The group gets quiet for a moment.

"Don't go too far, then. Just hide nearby and we'll find you," Caspian corrects.

They quickly form a plan that involves me waiting at the mouth of the cave until they engage with the sirens. The plan is for me to slip in and free Coralie—assuming she is chained—and escape while they hold the enemies off. As we approach, I fall back, allowing the mermen to sneak up first.

Tarni has joined Murdoch outside the cave. I can't see her around the rock formation, but I assume she's clinging to his arm as she speaks to him.

"But where are they?" she pouts. "Even if they *had* trouble, they should be back by now."

"Do you want to send some of them out to look?" Murdoch counters with a sigh.

"No, they couldn't do anything in the dark anyway.

Phorcys can take care of himself, even against that stupid *mer princess.*"

"They probably met up with Nir and are on their way here."

"I suppose," Tarni replies. I can picture her pursing her lips in annoyance as she speaks.

Merrick darts forward around the rock while Llyr holds his trident. He drags Murdoch back so fast by his tail, I'm sure Tarni is left to believe he disappeared with only the water rushing by her as evidence. Caspian quickly holds a knife to our former collection member's throat, threatening him to stay quiet.

His terrified eyes meet mine, and I see a flash of concern for Tarni's wellbeing before hatred fills them. I hold a finger to my lips, reminding him we're in charge, and if he gives us away, he will pay, and so will his girlfriend.

"Murdoch?" she screeches.

Sirens stir inside the cave at the sound of her panic.

When she rounds the corner, she's clutching at her trident. In the dark, it's hard for Tarni to see, though the storm above seems to have cleared enough to allow the muted gray light of morning to start filtering through the water. She's greeted by the tridents of Llyr and Marilla's guards while Caspian and Merrick hold her lover in place.

Merrick expertly uses the shackles that were once on

my wrists to bind one of Murdoch's wrists to his tail, preventing him from swimming. A piece of rope ties his hands together behind his back as he struggles.

"Tarni, go!" he shouts, earning a knick in his neck.

"Get the girl!" Tarni shouts into the cave. My head jerks up, knowing she means Coralie.

The others surge forward as Merrick and Caspian drop Murdoch. He sinks, still bound.

"Cooperate," I hiss at him. "Marilla might just let you spend your days in the cells instead of tied out for the sharks."

He struggles to free himself, but quickly realizes it's pointless, settling himself on the sand below the cavern.

I move around the rock, hovering in the entrance.

The siren with the injured arm from the needlefish attack holds Coralie by her throat, knife raised. Her eyes are locked on Caspian as he grapples with Tarni.

"Cor!" I call, trying to get her attention so she can assist me in freeing her.

The siren whips around to face the entrance.

"Don't even think about it," he cautions.

"Kill her!" Tarni instructs. "We don't have time for this. We need you to help us!"

"No!" Coralie screams.

"Don't!" I caution from the entrance.

Darting down in the water, I pull on Murdoch with everything I have. He grunts as I pull his arms backward, separating them from the sockets enough to cause discomfort.

"Tarni!" I challenge from the open waters.

Light spills down through the water—morning has arrived. Fish come alive, filling the ocean with dark flashes of color.

Llyr's arm pulls back viciously as one of the siren blooms pink. A vicious gash runs from one shoulder, across part of his neck, down to his armpit on the other side. His head lolls forward, lifeless.

"So, what—you want to trade? Is *that* it?" Tarni growls, slashing her weapon at my twin. Caspian twists, attempting to roll her wrist. She moves, avoiding his maneuver.

"That's exactly what I propose."

"Len!" Merrick warns as one of the sirens pulls away from him, darting toward me.

I push Murdoch down in the water. He grunts as his face scrapes along the side of the cave accidentally, but I don't have time to correct my course. I duck just before a trident is thrust at me. Dropping Murdoch, I fling my hands above my head to twist the trident away from the siren.

I cry in pain as I rip it away from him, pulling tightly on my injuries. He loses his grip and the trident slams into me, crashing into my side.

"*Celena?*" Llyr yells, terror in his voice as he realizes

what happened.

I look down, checking to see if I had skewered myself. A little blood escapes a small scrape, but on the whole, I'm fine. The pointed weapon had missed me, much to the chagrin of the siren merman.

"I'm fine!" I shout, rushing to get Murdoch before I accidentally lose control of him to a siren—it's not like he doesn't have enough of them in power over him.

I drop him on the floor of the cave and pull his head up to expose his neck.

"Celena," Murdoch gasps as my knife pokes into the side of his throat.

It's adorable that he doesn't think I'll slit him open right now.

"You made your choice, Murdoch. I even gave you the opportunity to make a different choice, and you didn't," I murmur dangerously into his ear. I realize how much I'm looking forward to do the same thing to Phorcys at some point—threatening sirens might become a new hobby of mine.

I raise my voice, ready to take on Tarni.

"How much do you really care, siren?" I taunt, quickly realizing that that question might not work in my favor.

Tarni moves to Coralie, relieving her siren of his duty. He slinks back, still cradling his injured arm. Based on the injuries I'm pushing through, I come up with several names to throw at the *baby octopus* that looks like he's about to ink.

The siren's knife drags down over Coralie's shoulder and back, leaving a trail of blood bubbling up from the thin cut.

"Please, don't," Murdoch begs as Tarni squares off with me.

"She won't have to," Tarni calls, looking over my shoulder.

"No, she won't," a new voice booms behind me outside the cavern.

CHAPTER 10

SOMEONE HOVERS IN THE WATER BEHIND ME SO CLOSE that I can feel the water pulsing as he moves his tail to stay in place.

I throw my elbow back, colliding with the merman's chest, refusing to relinquish my hold on Murdoch.

"You better hope I save you and they don't get their hands on you," I hiss at him.

Turning, I discover a siren mermaid floats next to the merman behind me. She has long, elegant hair in a soft white color. It dips gracefully down to her waist, curling softly in the water. Her tail is a dazzling blue that matches her eyes. Gentle pink lips are the biggest feature on her face— they pick up some of the colors from the objects she wears in her hair.

Holding her face calm, she looks serene enough to be a royal portrait from Aila's journals. Her expression doesn't change when I lock eyes with her, recognizing her as the siren that killed all of those sailors outside of Scylla.

The merman wraps his hands around my waist harshly as Coralie screams for me. He pulls my hips back toward him, forcing a collision between us.

The blue siren silently lifts her hand toward Murdoch, curiously tipping her head at him. The knife lays silent in her fingers making him shudder when he realizes it.

"Nir!" Tarni calls, seeing the scene unfold.

"Fine," a voice responds from outside.

He's here.

The blue siren lowers her weapon, instead, raising her other hand to cup Murdoch's chin in her fingers. He looks at her uneasily as I drive my knife into my captor's tail.

He shrieks in pain, releasing me.

I push the blue siren out of the way, knocking her into the open waters as I drag Murdoch out with me. I hear Caspian grunting inside the cave as he fights to get to our sister.

The blue siren retreats to hover by her king.

Nir sits on the upper part of what was once a chair, lost from some ship into the ocean. Several sirens hold onto poles that have been placed under the seat to help move him across the open waters of the ocean. He looks like a king making his servants carry him around.

His tail is badly damaged, though its dark color hides many of the blemishes on his scales. When the light catches them at just the right angle, they glint off his twisted scales, showing the injuries he suffered at Merrick's hands.

The siren prince—now king—glares up at me from where his sirens hold him in position. His shoulder armor glares in the early morning light.

"I see you survived," I break the silence.

"No thanks to you," he yells back. "Why don't you come down here so we can even the score?"

He sits up on his makeshift throne, trident teetering to the side in his hand. He looks vicious enough to attack from where he sits.

"I don't think that's how this is going to work," Natale says from behind me.

Relief floods through me as she swims around in front of me, Keone right behind her.

"Bring me the princess," Nir commands.

Caspian bursts through the entrance behind me.

"Here," he gasps. Something collides with me, nearly making me release my hold on Murdoch. Arms wrap around me, dissolving into sobs.

"Celena," Coralie cries, burying her face into my hair and the welts underneath it.

Tarni rushes out of the cave past us so quickly that Keone can't catch her.

An invisible line is drawn between mer and siren, and neither side dares cross it yet. Only a few of Nir's sirens are with him—just enough to keep the king safe while coming to find his cousin. The rest must be nearby.

I stare down the siren king as he broods, watching us. Tarni reaches him and whips around to face us. Her pouch sits on her hip, and I imagine she's dying to give Nir his mother's necklace.

In my peripheral vision, something catches my eye below us. Nir sucks in a breath from his seat far enough away that I can't hear him unless he yells to us, but his chest swells with the movement.

Looking down, I discover several corpses floating to the ground, Murdoch's entire body shakes as he notices them.

"They didn't make it," Merrick says softly as he approaches.

Caspian throws himself at Coralie, prying her off of me as he wraps her protectively in his arms. He brushes our sister's hair back, murmuring to her to keep her calm.

Llyr forces two sirens out of the cave, handing one off to Merrick now that his arms are free of bodies.

"Perfect timing, looks like our rides are here," he

murmurs as dolphins show up at the perfect time once again.

Natale and Keone growl viciously at the sirens, holding their tridents menacingly toward them, though none of the sirens move—most are busy holding Nir's throne. The two mermaids wait by his side, poised to follow his commands, though neither holds any power over other mer.

Nir watches us as we swim up to the pod of dolphins, captives in hand. Tarni looks ready to murder us, but there's something different in Nir's eyes—this wasn't his battle, and he knows it—his time will come.

His face morphs into a one-sided smile as he watches us dart across the ocean with our dolphin rescuers, chilling me to my fins.

"Let me take that, Celena," Keone says, leaning over from the dolphin he's swimming with to me.

I stretch my arm out, handing Murdoch off to our friend. With a flourish, he moves Murdoch away from me, looping his arm through the shackles between Murdoch's wrist and tail. He winks at me as he *acciden-tally* digs his nails into Murdoch's flesh.

"Oh, I'm sorry, buddy. Did I inconvenience you? I'm usually so good about protecting mer...oh, that's right.

You're not mer—you're a traitor. I forgot." He smirks. "We don't take kindly to those, you know."

Natale takes the opportunity to poke at the siren Merrick is holding.

"That goes for you too." Her voice is terrifying. She recoils her hand, pulling it to her chest.

I'm going to have to take some serious time to find out just how much my cousin knows about interrogations and terror tactics—she might be able to teach me something my mother and the queen haven't already taught me.

Once we're far enough away from the sirens that they can't reach us, we release the dolphins, swimming the rest of the way to the cave. We pause far enough away for Llyr and Keone to check to ensure Nir's other sirens haven't found the rest of our collection.

They return after a few minutes, waving us in.

"Miss me?" I swim up to Phorcys. I can feel the entire room stop to stare.

He grins wickedly, enjoying the game.

"You can't stay away too long, can you?"

"I brought you a little present," I bat my eyelashes. Turning, I glance to the boys. They take that as their signal to drop the captured sirens on the cave floor.

Phorcys' face falters just enough for me to notice as I turn back.

"I saw your king," I address him as if I cared about

Nir's title. "He didn't look so good—they're carrying him around on a makeshift throne. He'll probably be thrilled to get you back so you can carry him around—well, he will be *if* he doesn't find out how helpful you've been to us."

"I'm sure he'll love hearing how you betrayed him," Merrick adds, flicking one of the sirens with his tail to make sure he's listening.

They all snap their heads up, stretching to see Phorcys.

"I did no such thing." His voice is gravelly.

"How else did we know where to find Tarni?" Caspian asks. "You clearly have a thing for my sister, it wouldn't be that difficult to get information from you."

Casp shrugs as he swims away from the sirens bound on the sandy cave floor. They swing their heads from Caspian back to Phorcys, considering our well-placed accusation.

Coralie swims behind Caspian, holding her head high. They sit in the corner as Caspian examines her injury. I want desperately to join them and take care of my sister, but I know my place is with the sirens, sewing the seeds of discourse among the mermen.

I sink down in the water to be on eye level with Phorcys, smiling sweetly, thinking of what Tarni would do. I reach out, brushing the tips of my finger under his chin, lifting his jaw just enough to be noticed before I pull away. Swimming away, I exit the cave followed by Merrick and Llyr.

Once we're around the side of the cave, I turn back to them. Llyr looks shocked.

"Perimeter," he commands Merrick. Llyr doesn't give him a chance to argue, pushing him away from us.

Merrick complies begrudgingly, swimming around the cave.

"What is going on?" Llyr demands. "I thought you were with Merrick?"

My heart crashes into my tail as I realize it's not a secret.

"Don't give me that look, Celena, of course, he told me. It's all he and Caspian talked about while we were chasing after you. I'm pretty sure the only reason Merrick is still alive is because Caspian knew we needed his muscle to get you back."

My brother and my boyfriend discussed my relationship. Lovely.

"I am," I frown, contemplating my relationship. "I think. We haven't really talked…"

"Yeah, too busy kissing," Llyr cuts me off. If my eyes weren't wide enough to freeze my entire face, I might have warned him before I slapped him. Fortunately, my hand missed the memo too and instead of hitting him like my head told me to do, I hover there, gaping at him.

"He didn't tell your brother, *but don't worry*, I heard

you're a great kisser." He looks at me with a blank face, trying not to make his comment worse as he realizes he said too much. Llyr tips his head to the side, smiling slightly. "You're messing with his head now, Celena, and you need to stop."

"I—"

"*Yes*, you are. Stop messing with Phorcys, because it's also messing with your boyfriend."

"But it's working—"

"I'm aware of that, *princess*, but you need to have a conversation with him because from what I can tell, you haven't talked to him since all this happened."

"When exactly would I have had time for that, Llyr?" I roll my eyes at him as a school of fish catches my eye, nearly distracting me from my subtle insult.

Llyr wraps his hands around my elbows, willing me to listen to him.

"Celena, please. I'm looking out for both of you here. If I had to *lose you* to someone," he grins, joking, "I'm glad it was Merrick, but you two are my best friends, and if you hurt each other, I'll give you to the humans myself."

He releases me and swims away, leaving me floating outside the cave. After a moment, Merrick's arm settles across my back, just over my tail as he clutches my hip.

"You know I'm just trying to mess with the sirens," I say, turning into him.

He opens his arms, pulling me to him.

"I know." He nods, but his eyes are dark.

"Merrick," I sigh, reaching up to brush back his blue bangs.

Why does he have to be so darn cute?

I don't finish. Instead, I reach a hand around his neck, resting my forearm on his shoulder, my other hand on his collarbone. I pull his face toward me, kissing him.

It's slow and tender as he gently reassures me of his affection for me. I'm freer to use my hands than he is, not restrained by having to avoid any injuries like the ones covering my back—he has to be careful of where he touches me. He doesn't seem to mind as my hands roam from the base of his skull, down his shoulders and back, learning his curves and planes in a whole new way.

He tugs my hair back, tipping my head up to him as he stares at me, looking amused.

"Apparently, I'm jealous," he murmurs.

"I noticed." I smirk. "But I'm going to do what I need to in order to defeat the sirens, and if that means throwing Phorcys off his game—"

"I know." He sighs deeply, dropping his shoulder back.

"What is this?" a voice gasps.

As fast as the sharks running from the sirens when they pull out the scent of a dead shark to scare a live one off, Merrick takes off, whipping me around to face the threat as he propels us out of its path.

Dylana stares back, looking horrified.

"Merrick." I tap on his arm, trying to get him to slow. He whips around, releasing me to float on my own, holding his trident out to my cousin.

"Oh," he admits his mistake with the simple word. "Sorry."

I blink, trying not to laugh. Dylana is definitely *not* the enemy.

She swims over to us, raising her hand in front of herself, using her body to block her motion from the others. She points between us and smirks.

The others follow behind her, overtaking the cave when I point.

"So this is new." Dylana grins wildly.

Merrick wraps his arm around me in response as Dylana's eyebrows shoot up. She purses her lips, trying not to laugh.

"Admittedly, I didn't think you two would ever get around to this." She turns to me. "I was definitely going to force you to date—"

"Stop," I interrupt, cutting her off before she can mention the guard she wanted to set me up with before.

"Fine, but I was." She bobs her head victoriously. "I like this better though. Now, tell me what's going on."

"Nir's alive," I inform her, making her face fall.

"How?"

"I don't know, but he is. We just left him. His tail is damaged, so the sirens are carrying him around on some throne-type creation," I reply. "Tarni is with them, but we have Phorcys and a few of the others."

"Phorcys?" Her eyebrows are up again.

"Long hair," I say, motioning behind me as if I were brushing hair back off my shoulder. "Orange tail."

"Ah."

"There's something else you should know," Merrick adds, spinning me.

"Celena!" Dylana shrieks as she sees my injuries. The water shifts around me as she rushes up to examine me.

"I'm fine," I insist, trying to turn. She doesn't let me.

"*Hardly.*"

"How is Morgen?" I try to change the subject.

"Recovering," she rushes. "What is this?"

"They made her swim through a giant bloom of jelly-fish to retrieve a necklace that belonged to Nir's mother," Merrick supplies.

"Celena," her voice comes out as a lecture.

"We have bigger problems, cousin." I stop her. "The sirens need us. Royal lines have stronger sirening voices. They want all of us so they can force us to control the humans and destroy them—they didn't just want the palace."

"Perfect," Dylana grumbles, finally letting me turn back around.

"It gets worse. They made me siren the humans already—not all of them, just some of the sailors. I had to send them to the western shores to get their royals and return here for the battle."

"Royals? As in…?"

"Jarek's line, I assume."

"Oh, beautiful. Not only do we have to take on Chantay's lines, but now we get Jarek's too. It's like we crossed the barrier and swam back in time to Kaliania and Aila's lives."

"Except Ebba's line got fierce." I laugh ruefully.

"Oh. One point for *us*." She rolls her eyes.

"When will the others be here?" Merrick interrupts our moment.

"We left an hour before them to scout and make sure it was safe," Dylana brushes her hair back as it floats in front of her. "They'll be here soon."

"Good, because we're going to need all the reinforcements we can get."

"Gaspar should have handled Chantay when he had the chance," Dylana growls, turning to face the cave. "I'm done with this nonsense."

"Dylana," I call her back. "How is Morgen?"

"He'll be fine." She gives into my persistence. "They're moving him to Metten, which I'm worried about, but he'll survive. They're just going slow and protecting him."

"Your mother?"

"She's okay, but she's on her way. I forced your

mother to stay with her though—she wasn't happy about that."

"I imagine not," I reply.

"That would be like telling the two of *you* not to get involved in something," Merrick adds, pulling me closer to his side. I nestle under his arm, feeling every breath he takes.

"Are *you* okay, cousin?"

"Better than you from what I can see," Dylana remarks. "Merrick, go inside. I need a word with my cousin."

Merrick hesitates, looking to me for confirmation. I nod, and he flicks his navy tail to give us space.

"I figured you wouldn't say everything in front of him." The princess turns back to me, and I quickly explain everything that's happened.

"Caves made of skulls, lovely." She glares into the distance.

"It's a shame Morgen isn't here to see it—he'd appreciate the history in it," I offer her a sad smile. "Dylana, you know what we have to do, right?"

"Move the humans?" she surmises.

"They aren't a part of this war. This started under the water, and now we have to finish it. The sirens have been murdering humans for a century—it ends now."

"And is your plan to take everyone with us for this?"

"Do you think it should be?" I ask, unsure of how I would answer.

"I...I don't know," she admits. "If you and I can move them on our own, we can protect the collection. We still have to fight the sirens whether we move the humans or not and if the humans hurt our mer while we're trying to relocate them than the sirens will overpower us."

"So we do this alone?" I ask.

"I think so. Are you ready for that?" She bites the bottom of her lip as she waits for my answer. Unlike the princess, I've been sirening humans for the last week and a half—this will be her first experience, and she's unsure she can do it. It will be her first time face-to-face with humans too—a terrifying experience.

"I'm ready," I say confidently, trying to encourage her.

"And, if I die, there's always Morgen."She shrugs casually, as if it's unimportant. I shake my head at her. "Do you have a weapon?"

I glance down at the knife on my hip.

"If I go back in to get a trident, they'll know," I murmur. Dylana grimaces but nods.

"Let's go," she sets our plan in motion.

"Where are you two going?" Natale asks, swimming up behind us as we try to sneak away.

Dylana and I glance at each other.

"I'm coming too." Natale sighs. She swims quietly

beside us, trident in hand. When we're far enough away, we inform her of our plan.

"You realize you had three other royal voices in that cave, don't you? You think the two of you—the most powerful and irreplaceable two—should be doing this alone?" she argues, clearly annoyed.

"You said *we're* the most powerful," I retort.

"You're also covered in injuries, cousin. Just how did you plan on protecting the princess?"

"*Still here*," Dylana jumps in.

"That was a stupid plan, and you know it," Natale finishes. "Don't leave me out of things next time—I've already proven that I can help."

She spins in the water as she swims, her mossy green tail sparkling in the light. For as much as I overlooked my cousin, she was always one of the more stunning royal descendants with her neutral colored tail and brilliant brown locks.

"Isn't this something?" Dylana remarks. "Kaliania, Aila, and Ebba—off to war again."

"And *Chantay*—back as the sea monster she always was," I add.

"Time hasn't served her well—I hear she used to be quite the beauty," Dylana smirks.

"How are we playing this?" Natale asks, focused on the mission.

"We have to get the humans to move away from

where we can reach them—they have to move inland. We don't know where the sirens are, so at least one of us needs to watch for them," I reply. "I did well sirening them yesterday—the sailors all left the docks and went to find their royals."

"So maybe you should do the sirening, and we'll protect you," Dylana replies, looking to both of us. "Then if you need help, one of us can assist you."

"You," Natale interjects. "I'll hold off the sirens, and you can help her."

Dylana nods, sending her dark pink hair waving behind her in the water as we swim around a sea turtle that decided to cross our path.

"How long do you think we have before the boys notice we're gone?" I wonder out loud.

"Based on the way Merrick was looking at you, I only give it a few minutes," Dylana says matter-of-factly.

"It isn't *that* bad."

"Yes, it is," both of my cousins reply.

"You've seen us together for all of two seconds—you know nothing," I pretend to snap.

"*Sure*," Dylana teases.

"Even *I* noticed, and I don't even spend time with you," Natale adds.

"Wonderful, so I'm the only dense one." My mind floats back to the brine pool and how the density of the saline held it down in the water—I'd need to warn them about that soon.

I point out everything possible as we swim, noting where different locations are for my cousins. They grimace when I describe the Ropes to them and point out the general direction for the cave of skulls, informing them of the weapons I left there.

"Guess we don't have time to go get those first, do we?" Natale grumbles.

"Not if we want to handle this without getting caught," Dylana answers.

"We'll be fine."

"We'd better be." Natale frowns, letting her hands sink behind her.

"We're about to find out," I reply. "We're here."

CHAPTER 11

The docks are just as I left them—tall and dangerous. Sailors walk out along the boards, preparing their ships, moving cargo, and fighting with each other.

"And we're sure we want to save them?" Natale asks as we watch a sailor slam his fist into another's face, nearly knocking him off the dock.

"I'm sure we want one less enemy to fight with," Dylana says, chin just above the water.

The sailors haven't noticed us yet, though I'm not sure how—Dylana and I both have pink hair— a stark contrast to the blue waves. The fight seems to be distracting them.

Natale pops back under the water, checking for any oncoming problems.

"Are you ready for this?" The princess sounds nervous.

"I'll be fine. If you have to help me, just sing your instructions—don't get fancy about it—I learned that the hard way. Tell them what to do and move on—or repeat yourself."

"And you really think they'll follow our commands after they're out of range?"

"They seem to." I shrug, bouncing the water around me.

"Did you both decide to siren, or…?" Natale pops out of the water.

"No," Dylana shakes her head. "I'm coming. Good luck, Celena. I'm right here if you need me."

My cousins dip below the surface, tridents in hand. I pull my knife out of my makeshift belt just to be safe.

Swimming forward, I approach the docks. A giant ship rests near one of them, and I take great care to avoid it. Ropes dangle down into the water. A net falls carelessly near the back of one of the small ships, partially in the water.

A cry rises up as a few of the sailors notice me—it's now or never.

I lift myself out of the water higher, allowing my shoulders and chest to be seen enough to confirm that I am indeed someone in the water. The sailors call to me, assuming that I'm no human in need of rescue.

"Here, dearie," an older man with a scruffy beard calls. "Come here and we'll help you."

He reaches a hand toward me far enough that if the breeze kicks up, it will likely knock him over into the water. From that height, I don't know what kind of damage the surface of the water will do to his face. If it's anything like what I experienced when I fell off that boat outside Scylla, it will be painful.

"Hello, little mermaid," another calls over the first. He's younger and stronger looking. Dirt covers his pants and shirt, and his greasy hair hangs down in his eyes as he crouches on the dock.

"Pretty mermaid," another says, trying to stroke my ego as if all mermaids cared about their looks and sit about preening all day. "Why are you so far from home?"

I silently continue toward them as they watch me, calling out to me. I can see how sirens use this to fascinate men—they track my every move.

One sailor runs onto a boat. His footsteps fall heavy as he darts across the ship to the side closest to me. He grabs a rope hanging from the boom and leans out off the ship, dangling over the water.

"Hello, beautiful," he calls down to me. I have to fight to avoid glaring at him. "Pretty pink girl, look up here."

"Oy, lads," one of the more sensible sailors cries out. "Get back! She be the reason all the other lads disappeared!"

He confirms that the sailors I sirened yesterday really had obeyed.

"You said they abandoned their posts, Cap!" another man challenges him.

"Aye, but I didn't know *she* was around. She'll kill you dead if you don't get back boys—*get back* I say!"

I raise a hand, catching all of their attention. They fall silent as I wave a hand in the air, bringing it back down to the water's surface gently as I move the ocean in front of me. They watch as if I'm mesmerizing them.

Once they're silent, I open my mouth to sing. They all rock back on their feet, waiting for something horrible to happen.

I spin a song about danger coming toward them and the need for them to find an escape. When I'm sure they're all listening, I test my power over them, having them all return to the sand to face the water.

Swimming closer feels like a mistake, but I have to ensure that they can hear me and will follow my requests. It's a scary thing to float forward, getting so near to the shallow depths that a human might be able to swim down to the bottom and linger there on a single breath before returning—I'm too close to them.

I send them through a few tests, making their collection look ridiculous as they squat down and stand back up—Merrick would appreciate my inventiveness.

The men obey when I instruct them to return to their families, get their wives and children, and the other people in all of the nearby towns, and flee the city, traveling inland for the next year. I hope I've given enough time to end the war—assuming it doesn't end later today—though I'm unsure my sireny will last more than a few hours.

"We have a problem," Dylana slices through the water, nearly overshooting me as she surfaces in her haste to reach me. I lurch forward in the water, frightened by her appearance, voice warbling. "They're here."

"Who?" I ask, already knowing the answer.

"The sirens."

I screech at the top of my lungs, enforcing my earlier commands. The humans turn, ready to walk away.

Dylana disappears under the water. I duck, looking to see where she and Natale are. I can't leave my post yet—I have to make sure the humans are gone—but I need to know where to go once I can return to the water.

Through the choppy waves, I can see a blur of color as Dylana swims toward a figure I assume is Natale. I risk a moment away from the humans, sticking my face under the water so I can get a clear view of my cousins and enemies.

Dylana and Natale prepare to engage with a small collection of angry-looking sirens. They need my help, but if I leave, I can't ensure the humans will escape the shores.

When I lift my head out of the water, my long bangs fall over my face, impeding my vision. I struggled to pull it away, silently lecturing myself for forgetting to control my hair when I ducked under the water.

I'm more startled than I should be when I hear another voice. Her icy blue song captivates the humans —*my* humans—and calls them back to the sea.

The sailors start walking into the water, drenching their boots. The ocean laps at their feet, splashing high each time they break the surface with their feet.

Her white hair nearly looks pearlescent in the sun with the waves writhing about her shoulders. The sailors are mystified by her beauty as she sings to them. She occasionally rises out of the water to hold her long, slender arms out to them, beckoning the men to her embrace.

Anger washes over me as she tries stealing the men I've already sirened. Once again, she and I plan on attempting to best the other.

She glances at me, serene face breaking into a coy smile. She dramatically turns back to the sailors walking toward her and dips into the water, hands out to them. The blue siren calls them to her side, promising them love and riches for all eternity.

I could use my knife and gut her now, slicing open the exposed part of her abdomen just over her tail. I could do it and rid the ocean of her forever.

But that would take time away from saving the

humans and sending them as far from the bays of Hontan as possible.

Instead, I grip my knife at my side and turn back toward the shore. I consider swimming farther in again, but I won't risk getting beached. The blue siren doesn't seem to mind—she floats toward the sailors, welcoming them with open arms.

I sing, sirening them away. A few of the men start to twitch, turning their attention to me. The blue siren glances over, frustration overtaking her.

Her voice screeches as she commands a small group to drag me out of the water. I hold my place, refusing to put any more distance between us—her voice can't over-power mine.

"Celena!" Dylana screams to me, too far away for me to reach if I needed to. "We have to go!"

The blue siren's smile is eerily calm as she deftly moves just enough to see me out of the corner of her eye.

"Not yet," I call back.

Behind me, I can hear my cousins clashing outside of the water with the sirens. Their tridents slam into each other—metal against metal—as they fight to protect me while I struggle to win the humans back.

"Celena!" Natale calls.

My song spills out of me as I win more of the sailors back. They turn, rushing to the shore as I command them to take their families and leave, following my earlier instructions.

The siren's fists pound against the surface of the water as she loses control of more sailors to my song. She bares her teeth at me, turning.

The majority of the sailors are racing away, far out of reach of our voices, though a few still linger, hanging between our commands. The blue siren works tirelessly in her attempts to win them back. She demands they murder me—though she knows it won't come to that. *She* couldn't kill me even if she wanted to—Nir's orders say otherwise.

She splashes toward me until something under the water catches her attention.

I duck under the surface too, where I discover Marilla and my mother have arrived. They swim quickly toward Nir, his back toward them.

The siren screeches under the water, warning him. His small collection—the same ones I saw yesterday— turns, staring down a matching collection of mer lead by our mothers. The group must have been out scouting.

I don't have time to wonder where the rest of the mer and siren collections are—the blue siren lifts her head back out of the waves, hair arching strikingly in the air as bits of water fly off in all different directions.

My hair hangs down plastered against the sides of my face and shoulders again. The remnant of the two-siren lead war-on-land stares back at us. I direct the men further back, sending them to the left toward the docks.

The blue siren reaches me, pushing me under the water. I struggle against her as she tangles her hands in my hair, forcing me to stay down. The siren knocks the knife from my hand before I can plunge it into her scales to free myself.

Instead, I push at her with my hands, raking my nails down the side of her. She cringes away, accidentally giving me enough space to wriggle out of reach.

I whip my hair out of the way as I exit the water this time, keeping my face clear of my locks so that I can fight back with my song. A fish pops up out of the water at the same time as it attempts to eat something, making it look like we planned the exit.

The blue siren has coerced the remaining sailors onto a boat. They hang over the edge on ropes like the greasy one did earlier, reaching toward us.

The men lower a net into the water as the blue siren swims to them. I stare in horror for a moment, wondering why she would risk getting close to them. She aims herself directly toward the net.

She's a few lengths away when I figure out her plan— she's going to have them drag her up into the boat so she can direct them. I can't let that happen.

Diving under the water, I race toward her. Dylana and Natale follow a few lengths behind.

"What are you doing?" Natale shrieks, swimming wide as she tries to catch me.

"We can't let her on that boat!"

"What?" Dylana snaps, realizing what's happening.

I reach the siren first just as she grabs hold of the fishing net. The men lift her out of the water, droplets falling to the ocean surface in streams as she rises into the air.

With no other choice, I throw myself at her, catching her tail. The wind kicks up, whipping against my tail as it's exposed to the air. Dylana grabs on to my waist as Natale latches on to the net by the siren.

"Hold on," Dylana says through gritted teeth as she attempts to drag herself up my body to the net.

Once her hands are secure, I fight against the siren. She thrashes against me, angry that we've spoiled her plan. Slapping her with my tail throws her off balance, and I use the opportunity to pry her hands off the netting.

She slashes at my arm, missing. Her hand catches the net as I free the other one just in time to catch herself. Dylana delivers a powerful blow with her tail from the side, sending the blue siren careening down into the water.

"*Cassidia!*" a siren shouts from the water as she splashes below the surface—I hope it hurts as much as it hurt when I fell from the deck of a ship because of her.

The humans start to snap out of their trance, and I realize both siren songs have stopped. They drag the net up greedily.

"Don't let go," I command, knowing it won't do us any good to injure ourselves. "Sing with me."

The mermaids pause, listening to the first lines of my instructions to the humans. After a moment, they pick up the words with me, helping me to enchant the sailors into doing our bidding. They look like they're going through shock as the men swing us over the deck of the boat, gently setting us down on the wood in desperate need of a cleaning.

I look around as I continue to keep the men at bay, looking for anything that might help us in the fight below. A cannon sits on each side of the cargo ship to fend off unwanted company, but sending a cannonball into the bay could easily mean the death of a mer instead of a siren. I've held a cannonball before under the sea—I don't want to risk the kind of damage I know it can cause.

The blue siren screams in the water below us. There's no way she could keep her serene face calm and still sound like that, but I can't peek over the edge to see how her features have twisted.

"What do we do?" Dylana asks, pausing her melody for a moment.

She picks it back up so I can answer.

"We have to move the boat."

"Move it where?" Natale asks, the last part of the word morphing into the notes she sings.

"West. We have to stop the humans from coming back here with the prince. We need to block them from returning from the western shore."

"But our mothers—"

"Will lead everyone here," I cut Dylana off. "There's nothing we can do to help at this point."

"She's right," Natale stops singing again. "This is our best shot at stopping this and prevent more death."

Dylana nods, not bothering to pause her vocals.

I use my hands to turn myself on the dock of the ship. The net grinds under me uncomfortably. I locate the old man—the one they called Cap—and instruct him to set sail.

The boat lurches forward. We sail away from the dock. Dylana's eyes grow wide as she pulls herself to the side of the ship.

"She's mad," the princess reports back on the state of the blue siren. "We haven't seen the last of her—unless our mothers kill her. She'll be out for our blood when we return.

"We'll have a new plan by then," I remark, allowing Natale to continue singing while I rest my vocal chords for a moment. "And, apparently, a ship. Keep going, Natale—I'm going to see what else is here."

A man standing nearby eyes me curiously even in his trance. Lowering my voice, I call him over to me as I once did to a cabin boy on the last ship I visited. He stoops down and slides his dirt-covered hands under my tail, supporting my back painfully as he lifts me up.

I wrap an arm around his shoulders and neck for extra support should something happen. Quietly, like a whisper, I instruct him to carry me around the ship.

I glance at his face as we walk from one end of the boat to the other and I picture the skulls in the cave piled on top of each other. I could shudder as I picture it, but I hold myself together.

Trying to wipe the image from my memory, I focus on his skin. It's light, but dark at the same time. I've read in books about how sailors have different skin than most from working outside all day and night, but I hadn't thought it would be like this. His hands are rough, full of calluses.

The sailor's hair is longer, resting a bit above his shoulders. The collar of his shirt is off-center and smudged with dirt and blood. Hair pokes out on his chin and cheeks curiously, looking brittle.

Much like us, his chest rises and falls under the work-load of carrying a mermaid across the length of the ship. A heart beats somewhere in his chest just enough for me to feel it.

The men are quiet, only producing noise when they

move heavy objects as they handle the mechanics of directing the ship, giving the boat a sullen mood.

I direct the man to place me at the front of the ship on a raised area where I can see everything that is happening, then send him back for my cousins. They look as nervous as Coralie as he lifts them one at a time, but knowing it is per my instructions, they allow him to carry them across the deck.

I had searched the deck twice before choosing this location to stay in for the remainder of our trip, finding nothing helpful. Piles of rope and nets sit everywhere, cluttering the space, but unless we decide to tie the sailors up, I doubt that will be useful to us.

Dylana turns, facing the front of the ship while Natale and I stare at the sailors under our command. The princess looks for the men I sent away yesterday and oncoming threats, while Natale watches the waters behind us and to the sides. I watch over the sailors as we each take turns singing to protect our vocal chords.

When we feel dried out, I instruct several of the men to haul buckets of ocean water to pour over our tails, cooling us down as we sit in the sun that looks perfect, but scorches the deck of the fishing vessel.

We pass the area where the skull cave is located, and I point it out to my tiny collection of mermaids so they know where to find it should they need it. We sail beyond it as the sun rises higher in the sky.

I pick up singing as Natale taps my tail, passing off the responsibility of maintaining our captives for a while. I sing softly, testing to see if there's any change in the men. I consider pausing all together to see if they'll continue doing our bidding, but decide the middle of the ocean with no help in sight probably isn't the best time to test the waters.

"There," Dylana points. "There they are."

I turn without meaning to. Along the base of the cliff, a row of men march in a line toward the main docks in Hontan, a young prince and princess in their possession being held against their will.

CHAPTER 12

"I'D LIKE TO SAY I DON'T MIND SEEING HUMANS IN CHAINS, but that's just depressing," Natale murmurs.

"I didn't tell them to do that." I stare blankly at the sailors dragging their royals along in chains.

The prince struggles against the chains, keeping a careful eye on the princess in her ornate dress. She looks nervous and too young to fight back. She reminds me of Coralie, but my sister is far more capable than the young girl on the cliff surrounded by brutish sailors.

"Turn the boat to the cliff," I sing, instructing the humans to change directions.

"It just seems wrong going to all this trouble for them after what they did to our ancestors," Dylana sighs. "I get it—we don't need to make the situation worse—but we're on a human boat, sailing toward the enemy to…turn them around? What is our plan here?"

A sailor with light brown hair carefully pours a bucket of water over our tails, dousing us in a tiny bit of the sea. I run my hand over my scales, moving the water around to cover the spots it missed.

"Yes, we'll turn them around. I'm sure they'll wake up and restore their *prince* to whatever throne they plucked him from."

My tail twitches as I speak.

"She doesn't look happy," Natale comments, mimicking my motions to spread the water around on her tail.

"Would you be if you were chained and being dragged along?" I reply thinking of the last few days.

"Sorry." She cringes, realizing.

"Let's have them unchain her," I look to Dylana. "It's the least we can do after forcing them to drag her out here. *He* can stay chained though."

I have no remorse for Jarek's great-great-grandson—I assume it's his descendant anyway. From here I can't see any similarities, but we're too far away to really see anything.

"He doesn't look like the picture in Aila's locket," Dylana frowns, reading my mind.

"We don't know that was Aila's," I protest, "and the only thing we can make out from here is that his hair color is different. You and *your* mother don't have the same hair, so they might not either."

"True," Dylana concedes. "Still, I'd like to know if

that's what we're facing."

"We're not getting close enough to find out," Natale points out. "We're staying on this boat until we can't anymore."

"How long *are* we staying on this boat?" Dylana asks. "If we're sending these men away, are we planning on swimming back?"

"Oh, umm," I stumble over my words. "I'm not sure."

Suddenly, the boat shudders beneath us, pitching us forward. I topple into the deck, nearly slamming my jaw into it.

"Everyone okay?" Natale yelps.

"What was that?" Dyalan gasps, pushing the entirety of her hair back over her head.

"We hit something, I think."

I turn, singing a man to my side. I command him to explain. Just as I thought, we hit a sandbar, running the boat ashore.

"We sing from here, I guess," I shrug.

Opening my mouth, I call out to the men on the side of the cliff. They stop to listen to the haunting refrain. My cousins join me, instructing the men to free the princess and return the royals.

My heart stops when they misinterpret our song. They unwind the bindings from the princess' waist, leaving them on her wrists, and throw her into the sea while the prince screams on the cliff, miraculously immune to our song. The sailors hold him back and prepare to march away, back the way they came.

The girl crashes through the air, slamming into the water. We all crawl forward on the boat to see if she comes back up.

She doesn't.

The prince thrashes against the sailors as they restrain him. He elbows a man in his attempts to escape and save his sister, but they hold fast, refusing to relinquish their grip on him despite their bloodied faces.

"We can't let her drown." I scramble to the edge of the ship.

"You're not going over the side, are you?" Dylana shrieks.

"Yes, follow in the net. Natale, you come too, but keep singing."

I dive off the edge of the ship, feeling the pain course through my body before I even hit the water. The water surrounds me as I point my fingers up, changing my direction to propel me toward where the girl crashed into the water.

Looking around, I desperately search for her. When I find her, she's struggling to swim, not knowing which way is up.

I reach her before I hear Dylana yell that she's on her way. Dragging the girl up is difficult, as her dress blossoms in the water around her, tangling with my tail. We push through the surface, choking.

I attempt to throw my hair back before desperately wiping her long, dark locks away from her mouth and nose so she can breathe. The girl panics, flailing even though I'm holding her up.

"Are you okay?" Dylana asks. The human princess' eyes grow wide.

Up close, I can see that she has a tiny nose and high cheekbones. Her dark brown hair is matted against her face and shoulders. Her lip trembles, partly out of shock, partly out of fear.

"You're okay," I assure her. She doesn't look convinced.

Noise rings out low on the cliff as the prince escapes. A rowboat sits on the small shoreline and he throws himself in it, ripping something off that was wrapped around his head—maybe a blindfold or something to keep him from overhearing the sailors' plans. He paddles as hard as he can toward us. The prince keeps checking over his shoulder, threatening us as he steers the boat in our direction.

"You'll be fine," I tell the girl as her brother hurls vicious words at us. "Your brother will be here soon."

I nod to Dylana.

"Get back."

She shakes her head, worried over leaving me alone

with the humans.

"I've got this, just get back."

Dylana hesitates again.

"You can come help if I need you, but for now, just get back, princess." I use her official title, hoping to get her to realize that she needs to protect herself for the sake of the kingdom.

The human girl's eyes dart toward Dylana as she shrinks back in the water, disappearing before the girl's brother arrives.

The prince glides up next to us quickly, his face twisted in anger.

"She's safe," I inform him. *"She's safe."*

He glares at me but slows the boat so he can retrieve his sister.

Reaching down, he grabs the chains between her wrists, tugging her away from me. The young royal drags her to the rowboat, his sandy brown hair flopping in his face with the motion.

I slowly approach, wanting to assist.

"Stay back," he yells, grabbing an oar to swing in my direction.

"Let me help you get her in the boat," I say, trying to calm him.

He locks eyes with his sister, and though they don't say a word, she convinces him to stand down.

"I'm just going to push her up while you pull and then

I'll leave," I say, hoping to avoid trouble. Though, I think if he had a weapon, he would have already used it.

The prince moves slowly, watching me as I swim toward his sister. I don't make sudden movements so as not to upset him.

"Ready," I announce, giving him a moment to prepare himself to pull his sister up.

I attempt to lift her by the waist as he hauls her up. She topples into the boat as I flop backward in the water. The rowboat rocks viciously as the two fall inside it, nearly tipping over.

My hand darts out before I can stop it to steady the contraption—swimming is so much easier than flailing around in a boat—and I calm it in the waters. The prince's head pops up over the side, glaring down at me while my hand still rests gently on the side, fingers spread out as I stabilize their transportation.

I pull back quickly, recoiling as if he were about to cut my hand off while still attached to the boat. He looks as if he's about to lash out but takes a deep breath and quiets himself as he stares at me.

I move back in the water, lowering myself until only my face is above it. Just as I'm about to submerge myself, he speaks.

"Thank you."

His hair frames his face as he leans forward in the boat. His sister works to right herself beside him, but he doesn't notice her struggling. His fingers wrap over the edge of the boat.

Up close, he shares Jarek's eyes from the portrait, but his nose and chin are all his own.

"You're not safe here," I warn him in a small voice.

My words force him out of whatever strange state he's in, and he pulls back, jerking away like I bit him. He grabs the oars, commanding his sister to sit as he jerks the rowboat into motion.

I watch for a moment as he steers them away. When I duck below the water, I wonder if I've done the right thing.

He rows his sister away from the sailors, deciding to stay on the water rather than risk losing her to the sailors again—probably a dangerous choice if the sirens manage to find him this far away.

Natale continues singing to the crew of the ship beached on the sandbar in the water of the bay. Dylana joins me, and we swim to finish our mission with the sailors.

Together, we convinced them to return to the western shore. We stop singing for a moment to ensure they'll follow through even when we're gone. The men respect our wishes, and we feel free enough to escape under the water.

The swim back is short-lived. We barely make it to the cave full of skulls before we discover the war has come to us.

Both the sirens and mer have gathered reinforcements, clashing along the shallow waters of Hontan's coast. Several sirens appear to be hovering above the surface, calling to humans that aren't there.

Much like a pod of dolphins, the three of us jump out of the water, raising our heads above the waves just enough to spy on the sirens. They call to the land, but no one is close enough to hear their cries. Under the water, I check their tail colors only to discover that the blue siren —Cassidia—isn't among them.

Sirens attempt to wrap netting and ropes around mermaids and mermen, trying to drag them to the surface. A boat sits on top of the water, the humans under siren control as they help pull the mer from the waves. Our collection fights back, trying to drive the sirens away from the boat they are protecting so the humans will stop obeying them.

Nir directs the sirens nearby in a net at the surface. He holds on with one hand, wielding a trident in the other. A magnificent crown sits on his head—the detailing would make any royal jealous. He raises and lowers himself on the net, giving instructions in dual locations. Cassidia hovers near him, reinforcing his words while she sirens the humans for him.

"Looks like we're going siren hunting," I mutter.

A line of sirens blocks the fighting from extending to Nir, only allowing sirens with captive mer to pass by just long enough to drop their victims off to be taken onto the boat—they planned this well.

In the distance, Marillia is surrounded by her guards as they attempt to fend off a nasty-looking group of Nir's mermen. If their goal is to capture the royals, Marilla will likely be their most sought-after target. The king is by her side, taking on as many sirens as he can.

"Mother," Dylana whispers.

"We have other things to worry about, cousin," Natale says, grabbing the princess' arm.

"Who should we take out—Nir or the blue siren?"

"Cassidia," I reply, moving to dive around the ship. "She's controlling them all for Nir."

"But Nir is the royal—his voice is stronger." Dylana's eyes dart between us, looking for an answer.

"It's going to take all of us to hurt Nir." My fingers move with the current, nearly dipping me in the water. "The boys tried to take him on, and they had trouble. If we try to take him on, Cassidia could rally the humans. We need to get rid of her first."

"The princess!"

We turn, searching for the voice. A siren points up in the water as we try to quietly make our way around the boat where Nir and Cassidia can't see our approach. The sirens surrounding them swing around to face us as one tugs on Nir's tail.

He lowers his face below the waves, spotting us.

"Get them," he instructs, not even bothering to stay below the surface long enough to watch. We must not be that much of a concern to him.

Dylana and Natale block for me, swimming in front of me. They use their tridents to attempt to fend off the sirens while I use my knife to defend myself.

A merman tries to collide with me, working to knock me off course. My knife digs into his forearm, making him yell as blood blooms around him, dissipating into the water. He jerks forward, trying to hit my tail with his trident.

I feel a second siren approaching behind me, prohibiting me from escaping that way. Taking hold of the trident, I wrestle for it, clawing at his hands to force him to release his grasp.

He pokes the weapon at me again, but with my hands on the metal, he can't angle it enough to reach me. Twisting, I duck under it, changing the trajectory of his assault. The trident slams into the other siren, piercing him in the stomach.

Horror washes over the first siren just long enough that I succeed in taking his weapon. Having no other choice, I rip it out of his friend's abdomen, pull back, and lash out at him, striking his tail.

The merman flinches, roaring in pain after he realizes what happened. I pull it back, taking several of his scales along with it. When he sees me prepare to go after him again, he hurries back in the water using his arms to propel him since his tail is now damaged.

"Celena, behind you!" Dylana calls, tucked around where I can't see her.

Whipping around in the water, I discover Cassidia has taken notice of my arrival. She slowly wraps her hands around sirens' forearms as she glides through the water, allowing Nir to do her job while she does his.

"You didn't bring my ship back," she says quietly, for the first time speaking to me rather than singing or hissing.

"They had somewhere else to be," I reply.

"So do you—a grave."

Her hair floats around her ethereally. White strands fill the ocean, surrounding her as she gently moves toward me. Her presence alone is so overwhelming that I see why Nir selected her as his lead siren.

She holds her weapon in her hands next to her chest, but she and I are too similar for me not to realize what she's doing—she's attempting to trick me into thinking she's not as much of a threat as she really is.

Beyond the siren, in the foreground, I see several figures swimming toward us.

Caspian and Llyr angrily handle the line of sirens

blocking us from the rest of our collection while Merrick rushes toward us. I try to conceal his approach by making grand motions to keep Cassidia's attention. Her eyes are fixed on me as I move forward to strike.

Before I can reach her, Merrick swims up behind her, slamming into the back of her skull with the flat end of his trident so hard that I'm positive everyone on the ship can hear it. Sensing trouble, Nir reappears in the ocean.

"I just can't kill you, can I?" Nir bellows.

The mermen must have been looking for us after we disappeared because they aren't coming from the main part of the fighting.

"Do you *really* think the sirens want a king who can't kill their enemies *and* can no longer swim?" Merrick taunts. He grins at me, throwing an overly-dramatic wink and kiss.

I have every intention of slapping him later for the theatrics—the last thing I want right now is for him to make himself a target. Isn't it enough that Dylana and I are where the sirens are focusing?

Behind his taunting, I can see the frustration in his eyes before he tears his gaze away. I'm sure he's upset that we swam off without any warning.

"You're very confident that you're going to live through this, *mer*," Nir sneers at him.

"I have a feeling only *one* of us will," Merrick retorts. He shrugs casually.

Llyr suddenly darts away from the siren he's fighting, racing past us in the water. His tail moves as quickly as a kelp forest during a storm as he rushes by us. Beyond me, I hear Dylana and assume he's on his way to help her and Natale.

"I actually need your princess, *mer,* but I can hurt her in other ways—like you, for example. If you die in front of her, she still lives long enough to do what I need her to do, but…"

He leers at us in a failed attempt to scare us.

"I'm pretty sure even if you let go of that net *right now,* Nir, you still wouldn't be able to reach him. Why is that?" I taunt him, attempting to torment him in any way I can. "Oh, yes, because he speared your tail. How is that going, by the way?"

Tipping my head casually to the side, I smile sweetly, waiting for an answer.

Nir smiles back, pausing just long enough to make my blood go icy to the point that I wonder if I was magically transported to the kingdom of Keldori in the north. He leans forward, still holding the netting.

"About as good as this." He shrugs quickly before launching himself away from the net and swimming as quickly as he can toward me, suddenly able to use his tail.

I scream.

CHAPTER 13

NIR HAD FOOLED US. WHILE STILL INJURED, THE GIANT merman is still able to swim, having recovered remarkably fast for his injuries in the week since it happened.

He slices through the water so fast that I barely have time to react before he's within an arm's length of my body. I flick my tail, trying to move before he can reach me.

Nir grabs hold of me, clutching me to his chest as he twists in the water. We spin as if he's attempting to drown me by forcing me deep under the waves. Each time I move, he moves with me, propelling us forward.

I cling to my trident—though it's useless to me with my arms pinned against my sides. His trident rests in his hand, running parallel to my tail.

The welts against my back collide with the muscles in his abdomen and chest, but flinching isn't an option.

Using my tail, I intentionally try to get in his way, slowing him down as he spins us away from the other sirens.

He grunts as he moves, but doesn't have the ability to speak easily while he's busy trying to kill us both.

Llyr flashes by me again as I move. I barely see him start to come after us when we spin by him and Dylana.

When Nir finally stops twisting around, he pushes his tail as hard as he can to move me away from the boat. As easily as if he were holding my tail, he forces me through the open water without much resistance.

He's prepared for me to bite him this time, jerking his hand out of the way only to move it back, grabbing my chin. He pinches my jaw bone, forcing his fingers to poke my cheek between both rows of my teeth painfully. My mouth is forced open so I'm unable to close it. His fingers are gripping me so tightly that I wonder if he will break through the skin and touch my teeth.

"Don't," he commands.

After a painful moment, I nod, hoping it will alleviate the pressure. He pushes hard on my jaw before releasing me.

Merrick and Llyr call out after me, and I realize just how fast Nir was actually swimming. It will take a moment for the mermen to reach me.

I consider flipping my trident around but worry I

might hit my own tail by mistake. The only thing I can do is wait for help.

Nir slows, starting to tire. He pants as he swims, but refuses to loosen his grasp on me.

"Nir, let her go!" Merrick calls, catching up to us.

"I'd rather have my cousin by my side for this," Nir calls over his shoulder. The muscles in his torso shift dramatically as he turns to call over his shoulder.

We continue slowing down—Nir is unable to keep up the breakneck pace with his injuries, even if he has healed a bit. I shift, trying to work my hair out from between us in hopes that it will block his vision and slow us even more.

"Len, careful!" Merrick yells just a breath before Nir and I go careening toward the ocean floor.

Nir relinquishes control, needing his arms to guide where he swims. I twist, looking up to see Merrick turning over his trident—he had struck Nir's tail with the end of it to knock us off course.

Realizing my mistake in pausing, I quickly use my arms to course correct and attempt to swim away. Nir is fast, grabbing on to the end of my tail. Before his fingers can close around it all the way, I flip it powerfully, slamming through his fingers into his face. He reels back as I dart away.

Merrick catches me as I throw myself into his arms, attempting to grab his waist to spin myself behind him until I can get my bearings. Instead of letting me slip past him, he wraps an arm around me, and I bury myself in his chest for a moment.

When he doesn't scoop me behind him, I turn to see what we're facing. Nir swims away from us, joined by two of the other sirens. They slip under his arms and help him swim through the water, as he finally starts to suffer for swimming before he should be.

His tail slips up high, revealing the front of his scales as he moves. His injury looks like it may have ripped open, but it's hard to tell.

"We can't let him get away." Keone swims up behind us, not stopping to wait. Llyr takes after him, Dylana close behind.

Natale puts her hand on my arm, questioning if I'm okay as she swims with Merrick and me through the open waters away from the boat and fighting.

Nir and his sirens swim toward the caves, darting into a small kelp forest to try to lose us. We stay to the edge, looking from the outside. When they exit, assuming we've haven't found them, we aren't far behind.

We lose sight of the battle, dropping behind a coral reef to track the sirens as they flee. The waters shift, and the colorful fish quickly disappear from sight as the light starts to retreat—a storm is taking over the early evening.

"He can't escape again." Llyr sounds frustrated as he

rakes his hands through his seafoam green hair. "We can't keep this war up."

"We'll find him." Dylana's words are determined.

Tarni screeches at us not too far away, trying to get our attention in an effort to save her cousin—she found us. We have to choose which one to chase—the king or the princess who started this mess.

"It's going to take all of us to stop him," Merrick decides for us. "Someone else will take care of Tarni."

When we turn back from her outburst, Nir is gone, hidden somewhere in the caves. Tarni sees us leaving and takes off after our collection, a small group of sirens trailing behind her as she attempts to stop us.

"Let's move," Llyr says, speeding up. "If we're going to stop him, we need to reach him before Tarni catches up."

We dive low in the water, swimming along the ocean floor, avoiding the storm brewing above the surface. Rain pelts the ocean's waves, mixing with the movement of the turbulent water.

"Which one?" Keone asks, matching Natale's movements closely.

"We have to check them all," Merrick announces, looking at the different caves. "We can't risk it."

"Can we afford to stop that long?" Natale asks, picking up speed.

"I guess we'll find out," I comment, tipping my fingers

ahead of me so that my body swerves and cuts them off. "First stop."

I don't slow until I reach the side of the cave. Merrick, Llyr, and Natale are right behind me while Dylana and Keone watch Tarni's approach, prepared to warn us if she advances too far.

I take the lead, prepared to strike if Nir is hiding around the corner. Leaning around the corner, I find the cave empty. Merrick and I sweep the cave quickly, confirming it's the wrong one.

The collection darts out, racing to the next cave several boat lengths away. We follow the same pattern, sweeping the cave. When we exit, Tarni is drawing near, but the light is so muted that we can barely see her racing toward us like an angry swordfish.

"She's too close," Natale proclaims. "We need to do something."

"Come on, I have a plan," I say, intentionally skipping the next cave.

"Celena, where are you going? We need to check that —" Merrick starts to argue as I set a course for the second cave ahead.

"That's the skull cave, it has weapons and shoulder armor," I reply. "And better than that, it has a secret."

The others look skeptical, but follow my lead, pulling around the next cave. The darkness envelops my friends and I, making it nearly impossible to see the sirens behind us—a perfect covering for our escape.

I dip low, as if we were going to rush into the cave we're really darting around just in case Tarni has better vision than I do. I careen around the edges of the cavern, hiding behind it so that it blocks us from view.

Quietly, I guide my collection into the skull-covered cave. When we surface, it still glows. The others look around, taking in the sight of the skulls ground into the walls and floors.

"I need you to trust me," I say, surfacing. "We have to go up there. That's where the secret tunnel is."

"*Excuse* me?" Natale asks.

"Come on." I fling myself as high as I can go, dragging my body up the rest of the way. "Watch your scales."

I pull myself along the ledge, making my way over to the secret compartment where I left the weapons. The others start to follow and I point to the tunnel to the right.

"Merrick, go first," I encourage him, knowing he'll protect us best if he takes the lead, leaving Llyr to protect the end of the collection while traveling through whatever we might find inside the tunnel.

When I turn to Llyr to tell him my plan, I notice lines of water running along the ledge from where we dragged ourselves.

"Llyr, splash water up here, we have to cover our tracks."

He looks at me quizzically for a moment before realizing what he needs to do. As he and Keone shower seawater over the entirety of the ledge, I tuck myself along the wall as Dylana and Natale slide past. Thrusting my hand inside the compartment, I pull out everything I had left behind the day before.

"Time to go, princess," Llyr addresses me as he and Keone arrive at my side.

"Got it." I hold up the armor, passing the knives off to Keone to help move.

We maneuver ourselves toward the exit, sliding as quickly as possible across the ledge's rocky surface. I will never get used to the feel of sand gritting between my scales and the rock beneath me.

The tunnel is dark and echoes strangely as we slip through it. I wish on all the starfish that this leads us somewhere safe where Tarni and her sirens won't find us.

The lapping water of the cave fades away as we continue to drag ourselves down the tunnel. I can only see flashes of Dylana as she rounds corners—Merrick and Natale are too far ahead to see.

Occasional streams of water grace the walls of the tunnels, tricking down in the darkness. My eyes begin to adjust to the difference in the light the deeper into the tunnel we crawl.

When we reach the second turn, I hear Tarni in the main part of the cave, yelling to the others, and I'm grateful we slipped into the tunnel when we did. Keone and Llyr speed up, remaining as silent as possible as I lead us to where I last saw Dylana ahead of me.

We follow every bend in the tunnel until it starts to get brighter. The dripping sound gives way to the lapping of water once again—I assume it's about to open up into the sea once again judging by the coloring of the light.

Instead, I take the last corner and promptly drop straight down.

I grit my teeth together as I fall, trying not to make any noise that the sirens might hear, though I doubt they can be heard clearly from this distance. I crash into the water, nearly losing my grip on my trident and the shoulder armor I'm carrying.

The second I go under, I propel myself back up, trying to warn Keone to be careful. He sits on the edge, staring at me.

"I'm aware," he smirks. I relax my lips, having twisted them up to inform him of the drop. Keone leans forward on his tail—knives in hand as he watches me.

"Len?" Merrick asks behind me.

I turn and see an incredible cavern dancing with cool colored lights reflecting off the water. Steam fills the room, and I'm suddenly aware that the water is warmer than what I left in the main part of the cave—I hadn't realized it since I was still catching my breath from the fall.

"A hand?" Keone draws my attention back.

I pass the shoulder armor and trident off to Merrick and back up enough that Keone can drop the knives into the water one at a time, blade up. Once it begins to sink, I catch it and balance it in the crook of my arm until I've collected them all. After I move away, Keone drops into the water.

Llyr follows, and we all press ourselves up against the wall under the drop in case we have any unexpected visitors. On the far side of the cave sits another ledge—this one without a tunnel.

When we finally feel comfortable enough that we believe Tarni has moved on, we spread out, dipping below the steam. We sink to the bottom, resting on the ground of the shallow pool.

"Now what?" Keone asks, setting his trident down.

Examining the shoulder armor, I pass it off to Dylana and Natale—its more important that they have it during battle than the rest of us since Dylana has to survive and Natale will be the one to ensure that she does.

Merrick tips his head back against the cave wall, his blue hair dipping down in front of his eye for a moment before swaying back up into place. I scoot over and curl against him, resting my head on his shoulder.

"Ow." Llyr rubs the back of his head, leaning forward. "What is this?"

He turns making us all perk up. His hands run over the wall, examining something.

"Well," he mumbles as if it's an answer.

I watch him curiously. He pulls back, revealing a hidden door.

"Is everything a secret around here?" I blurt out.

"Everything but your relationship," Llyr mutters making Keone snort.

"Careful," I warn him—*I know things too.*

He quickly clams up, not wanting me to reveal his secrets.

"Looks like this will take us back into the sea," Llyr murmurs, examining the door.

"Tomorrow," Dylana says. "We need to rest first. We're safe here."

Llyr shuts the door, turning to rest against it once more. He offers Dylana a small smile as she nestles onto the floor beside him.

"We can take turns keeping watch," Merrick offers.

"You just want us all to sleep so you can kiss your girl-friend," Llyr teases. Once again, he stops talking when I eye him.

"Is that a problem?" Merrick asks, wrapping an arm around my shoulder.

"No, she and I already had a conversation about this,"

he teases.

"*Sleep*, Llyr," I command, rolling my eyes.

I can't help myself as my eyes drift shut and I fall asleep on Merrick's shoulder, his fingers brushing against the skin on my arm, lulling me into rest.

When I wake up, Merrick is resting his head against mine, sleeping quietly. My hand is wrapped around his arm uncomfortably, and it takes a moment for me to untangle our limbs.

My movements jostle his head, luring him out of sleeping.

"Go back to sleep," I whisper, hoping he can drift off again. He blinks twice before yawning.

"Never," he whispers, eyes still closed.

I bite back my smile and lean onto his chest. My head rises and falls as he breathes.

"How are you feeling?" he asks quietly, stroking my hair.

"I'm pretty sure I'll survive long enough to end this with Nir and Tarni, and that will be the end for me," I reply dramatically.

"You're just going to leave me after all this?" he jokes.

"Well, I mean, a couple of good kisses don't—"

"Excuse me, *good*?" His eyebrows shoot up in shock

and offense. "Those were nothing short of incredible, *princess.*"

"Fine, incredible kisses—"

"Which we need to repeat," Merrick smirks.

"Sure," I reply, deadpan. "But I—"

"Talk too much?" Merrick interrupts playfully again. He reaches up, brushing back my hair.

"You know the second we do this, one of them will wake up," I whisper, leaning in, tempting him.

Natale moves in her sleep and I jerk back, biting my lip in annoyance. I point to her as if to prove my point.

Merrick sighs, disappointed. He settles back against the wall, beckoning me to return my head to his shoulder.

I slowly move toward him, acting like I'm following his lead. My hand reaches up, grabbing his chin while he's busy watching me smile and I surprise him. I pull Merrick's face to mine and taste his lips, making him smile.

He shifts, making it easier to reach me. Merrick's hand settles on my hip, and I shift all of my weight onto my hands and locked elbows as I lean on the ocean floor between us.

Slow kissing Merrick is just as incredible as our original kiss. He holds still, letting me do most of the work— if he doesn't, his hands will be in my hair, and staying unnoticed by our friends won't be an option.

We keep our hands mostly to ourselves as I support my weight between us and he casually rests his hands on the top part of my scales. Merrick tips his head to avoid hitting my nose as I control the rest of our kiss.

"See?" he asks when we pull back. "*Incredible.*"

Merrick licks his lips quickly before grinning, half of his face stretching toward his ear in a smoldering half-smile. He's always been good at getting attention by being flirty, but it's entirely different when it's focused on me and not meant as a joke.

"Putting that spy training to good use, I see," he murmurs in my ear. "I didn't see that one coming."

"Did you mind?" I slowly close my eyelashes once, opening them back up to a rather intense look.

"Not at all," he says softly.

"And if you two are done now…" Llyr snickers.

Merrick groans, rolling his head away as he puts some space between us.

"*You* clam up, Llyr, or I'll tell her—"

Just then, the rest of the group starts to stir, and *I* clam up, not wanting them to catch on to my threat.

"Llyr, check outside," Dylana instructs, sitting up to stretch. "We need to get moving."

"Looks like the storm died down," he answers, closing the door back over after checking. "It was a nightmare last night. I'm glad we weren't swimming in that."

"We need to get going," Dylana presses. "We don't

know what the others have been through, but we need to get back."

"So, Celena... Where would Nir be?" Natale looks to me.

"I have no idea."

'You've been here longer than any of us. You've seen more of the area. Where would they be?"

"Well, he wasn't in the caves we checked." I try to think through where he might be. "He could be in the one we skipped. It's possible some of the caves have hidden places like this."

"So should we go back and check all the caves?" Keone questions.

"I'm going to check..." I point up, not bothering to finish as the group discusses our next move.

I quietly slip up through the water, leaving them to sit on the floor of the heat spring. The world above is suffocating as I emerge into the steam. I feel like I'm choking on the moisture that clings to my face.

Backing down a bit, I propel myself through the water, launching into the air as I grab for the entryway I fell out of last night. My ribs slam into it, and I cling on to the rock, trying to listen for voices.

Climbing through the tunnel won't do anything but give me scratches from the sand against my tail, so after a moment, I drop back down. A cloud of bubbles floats around me, trickling to the surface quickly.

"Nothing." I shake my head as I settle back on the ground.

"Don't get comfortable," Llyr informs me. "We're headed out."

I nod, floating up to follow.

Llyr leads the way, this time leaving Merrick to bring up the tail of the group. I follow out after Keone, my cousins in my wake.

The water is clear and blue as ever. There are no sirens or mer in sight. We loop around, deciding to check the cave that we skipped before moving on with our search. We cautiously enter and find nothing helpful.

We turn to leave, but Merrick darts back in the water, arm stretched out to prevent us from continuing. I reach behind me, stopping the rest of the collection as I bump into Merrick's arm.

I push my hair back, preventing it from floating out of the cave as I peek around him. Tarni and her collection swim through the water, just past the cave.

Nir is nowhere in sight.

"He had to have gone back, right?"

"I don't know where else he would be," Tarni replies. "We looked everywhere."

She sounds exhausted as they swim a little slower than they would typically swim. I glance at a starfish crawling along the ocean floor and silently wish on it that

Tarni is too tired to fight well once she returns to the battle.

We hold still until they're far enough away that we're sure they can't hear us.

"Do we honestly think he went back?" Merrick asks the group.

"Here," Dylana grabs my hand, slapping something into it. I look down to find an oyster in my hand. "We're not prepared for today. If we keep going like this, we're going to look like Tarni, and then we'll be no help to anyone."

Her focus is always two steps ahead, but Dylana has always liked to take care of her collection. She motions to me, insisting I eat something.

"She's right, we need to eat," Llyr adds. He darts around the cave, picking up a few shells with breakfast inside.

We eat quickly. As soon as we're done, the mermen move behind us and wrangle our hair back into simple braids so that our hair isn't in the way as we enter the battle again.

Merrick tolerates me as I move around the cave while he's working, stretching to collect broken shell pieces to weave into our hair. He still manages to finish my braid before Llyr and Keone finish with my cousins. My hair is sharp to the touch—perfect for throwing my head into Nir's face the next time he tries to catch me.

I almost hope he tries, just so I can do a little damage.

Merrick's fingers drag along my neck before we separate, swimming to the entrance of the cave. I shudder, rolling my head back toward my shoulder to control it as my shoulder rises up to my ear.

"I feel more prepared now," Dylana announces, shaking her head from side to side to ensure her braid is sitting comfortably on her back.

"Good," Merrick says, glancing back in the cave over his shoulder. "Because it's time to face Nir."

The siren king has arrived.

I'm suddenly extra grateful for the broken shells wrapped in my hair. I raise my trident to my chest before glancing down to ensure my knife is still resting on my hip.

Merrick holds his hand up to signal us. We wait for Nir and the two mermen to swim by the cave. Once Merrick's hand drops, we silently dart out in the open water behind the sirens.

Nir's arms are looped over the mermen again, accepting help for the swim, probably trying to save his strength for when he returns to the fighting.

Llyr and Merrick dart forward, grabbing Nir's tail, and pull him back while we prepare to take on the other sirens.

Nir turns, roaring as he attacks our mermen.

CHAPTER 14

THE SIRENS TURN AROUND TO FACE US AS THEIR KING IS ripped away from them. Angry scowls quickly fill their features as they glare at us, flipping in the water to attack.

Phorcys dives at me—I hadn't realized he was one of the sirens that helped Nir escape last night in the darkened light of the sea. How did he escape? His hair waves around him brilliantly just before the merman lurches forward in the water, pinning it back as he moves.

He nearly crashes into me, but I use my trident to collide with his, setting him off balance.

"How did you get out?" I demand, preparing to crash into him again.

He whips around in the water, facing me once more.

"I have my ways, *mermaid*," he glowers, curling his lip.

"You were under our watch, how did you escape?"

"I didn't." He grins. "It was a rescue. Your mermen are

dead. Good thing for you, your little sister and your annoying brother got out right before it happened."

Marilla will be heartbroken when she hears of this. I'm sure Dylana is seething too, assuming she overheard.

"Great, we'll add you to the body count," Natale says, attempting to stab at Phorcys' tail.

Phorcys turns, catching Natale's arm with his trident. It rips her skin back as he pulls, making her cry out.

I return the favor, slamming my trident into him enough that it punctures his forearm, poking out the other side. I twist it before pulling it out, adding a little extra pain for what he did to the guards.

He turns on me, ready to fight. I don't have time to watch the other sirens or consider helping the rest of my collection—my job is to take Phorcys out of the game.

Something flashes across his face before he squints at me, but I can't quite read it. He grits his teeth, and I follow suit as we both flick our tails in the water, preparing to engage.

At the last second, he swerves away from me, dipping in the water until he slams into Merrick. Before I can say anything, Nir turns on me. Llyr attempts to stop him, but Nir rushes past him, slamming into his shoulder so that his flips around in the water.

Llyr turns back, rushing after the siren king as he attempts to slow him. I use the opportunity to swim, getting the siren king to chase me.

There's only one way I can win this, and I know exactly what I need to do.

Darting through the water, I guide us away from the collection while Merrick handles Phorcys, and my cousins deal with the other siren. Glancing back, I can see that Keone is chasing after Llyr as he follows us in our race to the skull cave.

I rush inside, Nir right behind me. Before I can enact my plan, Nir catches my tail, forcing me to a halt. He pulls cruelly on my tail, propelling me back into the wall.

A skull crumbles under the force of my head slamming into it. A chunk of the bone bounces down in the water, pinging off the side of the wall until tiny fragments of bone fall into my hair as part of the forehead drops into my lap. I pick it up, tossing it aside.

Nir grabs my shoulders, slamming me again into the wall. Llyr and Keone tug on him, attempting to remove him from pinning me against the cave. I shout for them to use their tridents, but once again, they don't want to risk hitting me. If they damage my tail, I'll be of no help to anyone.

As another skull crumbles above me, I use the rounded piece of shattered bone that falls between us to slash at Nir. I cut his cheek, leaving a nasty gash on his face. He reels back just enough for Llyr to latch onto his shoulder, pulling the siren king away from me.

I struggle out of his hold, nearly hurting myself as he lets go and turns on Keone and Llyr.

"Go!" Llyr instructs, trying to get me to leave the cave.

"No!" I shout back, unable to tell him about my plan without giving it away. "I won't leave you!"

"Celena, go!" Keone yells, fighting to hold back Nir's thick arm when the siren turns on me.

As they struggle, I notice the necklace around Nir's neck that I retrieved three days ago. He must have put it on as soon as Tarni gave it to him yesterday.

For my plan to work, I had to get the mermen to release Nir.

Llyr and Keone work together to slam Nir against the wall, making more of the skulls cave in on themselves, crumbling down the side of the rock. Nir shakes his head, trying to recover.

He slips his arm away from Keone just as yelling fills the water outside. I do a backflip, darting outside to make sure everyone is okay. The boys allow Nir to follow me, likely because it's wise not to be trapped in a tight space with a sea monster.

Phorcys and Merrick collide, their tridents slamming into each other as a school of fish angle themselves to swim around the mermen. Once I see that Merrick and my cousins are still alive, I do the stupidest thing I can think of to do—I swim over Nir's head and race back into the cave.

He tears himself away from Keone and Llyr, pushing past them roughly, and follows me back into the cave, threatening me.

"Len!" Merrick calls.

When I look back, Nir is gaining on me, but Merrick is nearly close enough to latch onto the siren's tail. I swim faster, pushing myself through the water—I only have one chance at this.

I lift my hands in front of me as I swim, slicing through the ocean as I prepare to lift myself out of the water. Like a dolphin, I arch myself out of the water. Slamming into the ledge knocks the breath out of me, but I don't stop.

I scramble across the ledge, dragging myself through the gritty dirt on top of the rock. Pebbles grind into my scales and poke into the flesh on my hands as I scurry away from Nir.

He follows me without hesitation, launching himself onto the ledge. Without being able to use his injured tail to propel himself out of the water like I had, he has to resort to using his arms to drag himself up, slowing him down just enough to give me a lead.

Merrick follows behind him, but Nir evades him by the width of a piece of kelp. I slip into the tunnel as Merrick calls a warning to me. I don't stop.

Turning around, I face Nir, moving myself backward through the cave. I use my tail to push me along, while my arms pull me. He struggles to keep up, not used to his weight above the water. Nir grunts, growling horrifying things as he chases me.

I look over my shoulder frequently to guide myself so that I make the corners and don't slam into the walls. Intentionally looking panicked, I let him believe he's cornered me.

"You will die here today," he warns. "You'll pay for what Aila did."

"You've really got to let that go," I throw my words back at him like a weapon. "They were our great-great-grandparents. They've been dead for years."

"You're right. We'll all move on from this after today… once you're dead."

I drop my trident, leaving it behind. Nir drags himself over it, unable to avoid it as we move quickly. He cringes as the barbs hit his scales, but he keeps coming toward me.

Merrick, following behind, slows enough to move around the trident. When he looks up, he catches my eyes and figures out my plan, realization creeping over his face. He nods, yelling at Nir to keep up the charade.

"I won't let you hurt her!"

"You can't stop me," Nir shouts, finding a new depth to his rage. He turns, trying to wrap his hands around Merrick's throat. "Especially since you'll be dead. You'll be a good lesson for anyone that tries to take me on in the future."

I scream a battle cry, launching myself at Nir. Wrapping my arm around his neck, I pull back in an attempt to stop him. Merrick manages to get his trident back far enough to slam it into Nir's shoulder—the tunnel only has so much room and clearly wasn't designed for fighting.

Nir roars in pain, reaching around to flip me over his head. My hair drags across his skull, the shells cutting into his face as he pulls me upside down into his lap—I barely avoid crashing my face into the floor as I slide.

Merrick grabs at me, trying to get me upright before Nir can react. I slap Nir with my tail and he bats at me, eyes closed. His face twitches as the sting from my slap starts to burn into his skin, taking him a moment to notice. He holds a hand to his face.

"Wrong move, cousin." He bares his teeth, trying to launch himself at me.

There's nowhere for him to go though—I'm too close for him to get any speed. His chest bumps into me as his arms reach around my waist. I duck my head, allowing the underside of his chin to crunch against my hair.

I snicker as the broken shell pieces in my hair cause more damage.

"Fine, you were right," Merrick sighs, pretending to

have lost an argument we never actually had. "It was worth following you around this morning."

"I'm always right," I remind him as I toss my head back, colliding with Nir again.

My head throbs from the collision, but that doesn't stop me. I angle myself to do it again, but Nir pulls back, adding space between us.

I take Merrick's trident and jab it at Nir. He lurches back, trying to put more space between us as Merrick turns to retrieve the weapon I had discarded a few moments ago.

Able to move faster than the giant siren king, I crawl toward him menacingly. The edge of my trident strikes the ends of his fins, tearing little holes as he struggles to avoid me.

"Come back, Nir," I say in a gentle voice. "We're not done with our reunion yet."

"You're insane," Nir replies, still dragging himself back. He bumps into the wall, but I give him a moment to collect himself, turning to move down the hall.

Each time he reaches forward to try to spear me, I slam the barbs on my trident into his fins. He doesn't have much left of his tail to use, but shredding his fins really could be the end of him.

Realizing that he's allowing me to control the situation, he sits up, stopping his retreat. Using his trident, he throws it toward me, catching the end of it at the last second so he doesn't lose the only weapon he has. I slash at him with mine, barely managing to deflect the blow.

Merrick's trident flies over my head, sinking into nearly the same place he had already hit. Blood pours from Nir's shoulder. It cascades down his chest, over each of his muscles, forming a river much harsher than the ones trickling down the sides of the tunnel as it drips onto the floor.

All we need is one more turn and we'll be near the end of the tunnel. If we can get him back far enough, we can push him over into the hot spring, and if we don't give him enough time to look around, he won't find the hidden door to escape.

"Don't let him back there!" Llyr's voice fills the tunnel as he follows behind us. He must have caught on to the plan.

"Go get help," Merrick instructs, playing along to get Llyr out of the cave to block the hidden door while simultaneously getting Nir to go exactly where we want him.

"Clam up!" I shout, sounding even angrier than I meant to. "Don't move, Nir."

Nir takes another jab at me, but Merrick grabs the trident from my left hand, deflecting Nir's attack, while I reach out and rip the trident from Nir's shoulder.

The tridents collide next to me, and Nir whips his arm around, knocking Merrick's trident into the wall. He nearly loses his grip but hangs onto it enough that he can regain his hold.

Nir moves toward the last part of the tunnel, and I act flustered, which only encourages him. Merrick pushes me behind him, acting as if he's trying to protect me—I'm sure he actually is.

The siren king hovers near the edge of the tunnel, taking the last turn as he teeters on the edge. Instead of falling in, he reaches forward, grabbing Merrick. He lifts him into the air, throwing the merman over his head.

Merrick careens through the air, arms waving as he tries to catch himself even though nothing is there to save him.

"Merrick!" I screech. My hands fly to my mouth, knowing I shouldn't have called out, but I can't take my eyes away from him.

Nir had twisted around at some point to see Merrick's flight. His movement to turn back to me catches my attention, giving me just enough time to take advantage of the situation. Using my tail, I kick as powerfully as I can against his hip.

He falls over the edge, crashing into the hot spring below. The slapping sound he creates fills the space, echoing off the walls as the steam rises around him.

Beyond him, Merrick lays on the edge, having skidded across the rock. It looks painful to breathe, but

I'm hoping that's because of the shock of the collision and not because it caused any real damage.

"Merrick?" I scream as Nir hovers under the water, not moving.

Merrick flinches, trying to prop himself up on his elbow. His back is to me and the muscles in his side ripple as he shifts his weight.

"I'm okay," he grunts, obviously in pain.

The sharkskin on Nir's shoulder armor rises out of the water before the rest of him does. The steam swirls around him as he lifts his body up on the ledge. The siren pushes up on his hands, rising out of the hot spring, moving toward Merrick.

"Behind you!" I shout.

Merrick turns just as Nir grabs his tail, pulling the merman toward him. Nir picks up the trident that Merrick dropped on the ledge as he fell and flings it into the water where Merrick can't get it. His own trident lays a few feet away.

The siren latches on to Merrick's wrist, dragging him close enough to dig his nails into Merrick's shoulder. The movement makes Nir's wound bleed profusely, dripping onto the ledge.

Merrick tries to fend him off, slamming his fist into the side of Nir's head. The siren reels but doesn't relent. He forces Merrick back, crashing him backward onto the ground.

I suck in a deep breath before I push off the ledge, dropping into the water with my trident in hand. Diving to the bottom, I pull Merrick's weapon off of the hot spring floor.

I'm louder than I think when I surface. Nir hears me, whipping around. He crawls toward me dangerously, eyes locked on mine.

"Celena!" Merrick shouts. "Get out!"

"Not a chance," I mutter quietly as the steam rises around me.

Nir crashes down on top of me, bent on destroying me however he can. He doesn't care that we're stuck in a small hot spring from which we seemingly can't escape. It doesn't matter that Merrick could come after us in an attempt to defend me—the only thing that matters is that he has me cornered.

"Sing, siren," he mocks me when the water clears. His hands are on my shoulders, forcing me down in the water.

"I have yet to sing for you, Nir," I reply, digging my nails into the back of his hands. "Aila wouldn't let Persephone get away with her treachery and I won't let you get away with yours."

"Too late, little mermaid. I've already won. My sirens have already taken your family hostage. They'll siren the humans whether I'm there or not—Cassidia will see to that. We will wipe them out and own the seas—they'll never work against us again. The ones we leave alive will live to serve us."

"You're really okay with dying for all this?" I snarl.

"To fulfill my family's wishes? Yes. Tarni will carry our legacy on once we've repaid Jarek and Aila for what they did."

"Well, good news. I think we can help you with the dying part."

I flip my tail, wriggling away from him as Merrick crashes into the water. He carries the trident I left for him on the ledge, driving it into Nir. The siren whips my weapon away, but I grab for my knife.

Nir's trident jerks through the water, knicking my side as it slams into the warm walls of the hot spring. I claw at him as I swim to the side, out of reach.

"Go!" Merrick instructs as the two grapple for control of the trident.

I race to the door, trying to open it—it's stuck.

"Llyr!" I scream, banging against it. After several attempts, the door loosens. I throw it open.

"Celena?" he gasps, looking through the unassuming exit.

Merrick yells for backup, and I flip in the water, swimming toward them. I crash against them, driving both mermen into the wall.

Nir makes a strangled noise, and I realize Merrick's trident is still protruding from his back—when I slammed into them, I wedged it between him and the wall.

He holds my gaze as he slips away, sinking in the water.

Merrick grabs my waist, moving me back until he's sure the siren is dead. His eyes flutter open and shut, hovering between life and death.

"Come on," Merrick whispers to me as he pulls Nir by the tail.

We exit, the bottom of the trident scraping along the ocean floor as we move the fallen siren king. Llyr's face is pulled taught, eyes wide with surprise as I pull the trident out of Nir's body.

"Nir?" Phorcys' voice rings out in the water. He has apparently followed Llyr around the cave, as have the others.

Nir bucks, blinking.

We all lurch back in the water—Nir isn't dead yet.

Phorcys and the other siren rush toward us as I skirt the half-dead siren to take them on.

CHAPTER 15

OVERCOME WITH RAGE, PHORCYS ATTACKS, TRYING TO injure me. The mer collection spaces themselves out, each taking on different opponents as Nir lets out several strangled cries, trying desperately to cling to life—or take one of us into death with him.

Knowing their king is dying, the other siren attacks mercilessly in revenge.

Phorcys and I collide, tangling in a frantic battle. He uses his trident to sweep my tail out from under me, turning me upside down just long enough for me to do the same to him, pulling out his tail from under him.

I flip around crashing the broad end of my weapon against his arm, not nearly strong enough to force him to drop his trident. He reaches around, yanking my hair only to discover the shells. He pulls back, angry.

I can see Nir bucking out of the corner of my eye as

Phorcys growls at me, clashing against my trident once more.

The waters grow still despite the fighting—Nir is dead.

Furious, Phorcys raises his trident in both hands, preparing to hit me with the long end in an attempt to force me to drop my weapon. At the last second, I release one of my hands, blocking his strike with my trident as I grab my knife with my dominant hand. Turning it quickly in my hand as I dart through the water, I plunge it into Phorcys' side.

His eyes grow wide as his head jerks forward. His jaw looks like it may fall, but shock quickly overtakes him. Still holding the trident in place, he glances down at his side as I pull my weapon from his flesh.

For a moment, I feel terrible when he looks at me—he looks so helpless. He breathes in a shuddering breath before he starts to sink.

With my hand still on my trident, I free three of my fingers and quickly snatch his weapon away, holding them both awkwardly in one hand. He doesn't fight me.

I pass the tridents off to Dylana. In the distance, the siren she was fighting swims off—the only one to escape.

I help Phorcys to the ground. Natale joins us while the mermen check Nir to make sure he really is gone. My cousins strategically block their view of me as I help Phorcys.

His long hair moves in the water gently as he holds a hand to his wound. His eyes hold accusation, but more than anything, he looks surprised.

"I told you not to fight me, Phorcys." I instantly regret saying it. "I didn't want to hurt you."

"Of course you did." His voice cracks as he grimaces. "You've wanted me dead since the brine pool."

"You shouldn't have hurt my sister."

"I didn't, if you'll remember. That was Roni," he points out.

"She'll pay for that, too," I assure him. "And I won't go easy on her like I did with you."

"I helped you."

"If you mean carrying me back from the jellyfish attack, you didn't have a choice." I cross my arms in front of my chest, covering my *iluse.*

"I could have let you swim." He blinks in pain.

"I wouldn't have made it. I was slowing you down, that's why you did it."

He looks like he wants to say more. When he doesn't, I continue.

"I can't tell how bad it is."

"Bad enough," he mumbles as I try to lean around him to see how badly he's bleeding.

He reaches up as I stretch over him, grabbing my waist. Phorcys pulls me to his chest, inches from his face. I push back, trying to hold myself away from him.

The merman stares at me without speaking.

"And now we leave him to die alone," Natale says loudly, burying the end of her trident forcefully in the sand.

The siren lets go of me, and I struggle to push away.

"I doubt he'll make it." Dylana motions to the injury she can see better from her side of the conversation. "And even if he did, we'd have to kill him for that little stunt."

"You couldn't have me if you tried, Princess," Phorcys addresses Dylana. "Don't be jealous."

Dylana makes a face, but I can tell it's forced. Under other circumstances, she might actually develop a crush on the merman—too bad he's slaughtered far too many people she cares about.

"I have a feeling I'm going to like you better dead anyway," Dylana snips. I'm overwhelmingly proud of her insult—she's usually so nice.

Phorcys cringes, folding in on himself as a wave of pain washes over him. I touch his arm, trying to get a better look at his injuries as he gasps.

"Just go," he begs. "Just let us die."

"He's already dead," Natale points out, motioning behind her to where Nir is stretched out on the ocean floor. "He's not coming back."

"Just let us be," Phorcys requests again, tail folding up toward his chest as he coughs. He latches on to one of his necklaces as he moves, running his finger over it. "I don't want you here for this."

He makes eye contact with me, pleading with me to remove my collection so he can die alone. I hate the idea of anyone dying alone, but I also understand not wanting to be surrounded by enemies when the time comes.

"We should go." I nod, looking up to my cousins. "We can give him this. He made sure I made it back in time to save Coralie from Roni, so I can offer him this much."

Natale and Dylana grumble as I start to float up, but they turn to tell the mermen it's time to go. Phorcys catches my wrist once they aren't looking.

"I really wasn't trying to hurt you," he murmurs.

"Could have fooled me, Phorcys."

"I'm sorry about your sister." He sighs.

"So am I."

I'm not going to give him the satisfaction of letting him know I care that he's in pain. Despite everything we've been through, he's right—he did help me a little, even when he didn't have to.

"I hope you don't suffer," I tell him, swimming over him. "Much."

He snorts, and I turn to find him stretching himself out on the sand, arm reaching toward his king. His eyes lock on the merman's body, and he mumbles an apology before closing his eyes.

His chest still rises and falls with shallow breaths,

assuring me that while the end is near, it hasn't arrived yet.

Merrick holds his arm out to me.

"She would have been better with me," Phorcys calls, finding some semblance of strength to speak.

Merrick flinches, turning toward the dying merman, but doesn't say anything.

We swim away, leaving Phorcys to die by his king.

Nir's body looks just as imposing in death as he did in life. His dark hair and darker tail shimmer in the light streaming down through the water. The fish, already curious, hover near him.

I point to the merman, motioning that they should take the necklace from around his neck as proof of his death. They covertly follow my instructions.

If Nir's mother hadn't died, Nir would have made the perfect shadow spy—something I've said since the moment I met him—as he worked for the siren's cause. There are days I almost wish I could trade my pink hair and purple scales to be able to conceal myself better when working for the queen, but seeing him lie there on the ocean floor makes me grateful I have something a little more dazzling for when people look on me after I'm gone—I don't want to stay hidden in mystery forever.

"Are you okay?" I ask harshly as Merrick wraps his arm around me, leaning heavily on my shoulders.

"I'll be fine, Len." His voice is hushed. "He did a number on you too, are you all right?"

"I don't know at this point," I admit. "We need to get back though, it sounded like Nir has a plan in case anything happened to him, and Tarni and Cassidia are probably enacting it already."

"Cassidia?" His eyebrows dip down as he asks.

"The blue siren."

"Oh." Merrick's eyes widen, smoothing out the little lines between them from his frown. "Great, we got rid of Nir, but we still have to deal with Tarni and her friend."

"It could be worse," I remind him. "Tiko could be roaming free."

"Considering everyone else seems to have gotten themselves free," he grumbles.

We spend the swim back trying to come up with a plan.

We swim around the coral only to find the fighting has moved. A trail of bodies leads the way closer to Antaire—perhaps this really *will* end where it all began.

"If the fighting has moved toward Jarek's kingdom, that also means it's closer to Metten." Dylana's worry invades the waters, trailing out to each of us. "We sent everyone there to be safe—now the fighting is coming to them *again.*"

"This time, we might not be able to protect them," Merrick mutters.

"Oh!" I gasp as I see one of my neighbors lying on the ocean floor beneath us. His body is marred with gashes. He lays randomly on the ocean floor—proof of the vicious fight.

"Don't look." Merrick tries to stop me from seeing the carnage.

"If our families are down there, we have to know, Merrick," I whisper.

It isn't too much longer until we come across another body. It's getting difficult to tell mer apart from siren.

We pause, stopping to collect armor from the fallen sirens, covered in pieces of sharkskin for the boys to wear. It's strange to see them wearing siren attire, but as long as it keeps them safe, we don't invest much time worrying about it.

The closer we swim toward Antaire, the more the feeling in my stomach transforms into something hard, convincing me I'm part shellfish and producing a pearl inside of me. Merrick squeezes my hand, alleviating some of the dread.

"Metten is over there," Llyr points. "What should we do?"

We turn to Dylana—the highest-ranking royal we have.

"What would you do, cousin?" she addresses me.

I take a deep breath. My head swings back and forth between the human kingdom and the mer one.

"I would go to Antaire. Tarni's mission now is to end the humans—she already has all the royals she needs here in the battle, so unless our mothers somehow snuck to Metten, they're here somewhere. And if they *did* sneak off to Metten, then our collection there has already been warned and are making plans to survive any possible attack."

"I was thinking that too." Dylana nods.

"As was I. We need to stop this war now and we can't do that from Metten," Natale joins the conversation.

"Halt!"

We whip around to face a small collection of mermaids and mermen. They hold their weapons out to us, ready for a fight.

"Wait…Celena?" one of them questions. "You're Celena, right? And you're…"

The mermaid trails off, catching herself.

"What is your name?" She stiffens—trying not to give away too much information without getting some in return—and nod at Dylana.

"Dylana, princess of Scylla and Metten, daughter of

Queen Marilla," Dylana answers, straightening her shoulders.

The mermaid breathes a sigh of relief.

"Good. I'm glad we found you."

"Who are you?" I demand.

"I'm Larina," she replies, resting her weapon at her side. "We're from Ambra. We came to help as soon as we got your mother's message."

Dylana raises her eyebrows.

"There's a whole collection of us here," one of the mermen says. "I'm Quilo, by the way. We were just with your families."

"Your sister told us about you, Celena," Larnia informs me. "I recognized you and the princess because of your hair. It's amazing you're still functioning after everything you've been through the last few days—I guess you really *are* as strong as she said you were."

"Where are they?" I snap, fingers flying to my grandmother's necklace. "Are they safe?"

Their faces grow dark, and my body goes cold. Merrick takes my hand, preparing for the worst.

"Coralie is fine, she's with your father," Larina informs me, her hair floating in front of her. "But the sirens have your brother and mother. We think they're going to try to use them against the humans."

"That's *exactly* what they're planning," I reply.

"What about *my* family?" Dylana interjects.

"The queen and king are safe—or at least they were when we left."

"The mer outnumber the sirens now that the collection from Ambra has arrived," Quilo says. "It's just a matter of time now, assuming they don't get to the humans first."

"The blue siren is leading them, isn't she?" Merrick looks for confirmation.

"Yes, and that other mermaid siren," one of the Ambra mermaids says from the back. Her hair and tail are striking.

"Where are *you* all going?" Llyr asks skeptically.

"The fight swam through this area pretty fast. The fighting has tapered off a bit now that the sirens control Almenna and Caspian, and everyone separated to regroup." I cringe as she says my mother's name wrong. I bite back the urge to correct her as she continues. "They sent us to come look for survivors, just in case the collection missed any during the battle."

It's logical that Marilla would send part of the collection from Ambra to look for survivors—she wanted to protect the mer that selflessly came to assist us, even when they didn't have to.

"You should hurry," Quilo announces, looking at me. "They're planning what to do about your mother and brother—at this point, the only royal left that can help is the queen."

Dylana, Natale, and I are the only other royals that can handle taking on the sirens and humans with our voices—aside from Natale's mother. I hadn't considered it yet, but it would make sense for her to be as skilled as her daughter is. Perhaps she's secretly launching a counter attack as we speak—assuming she's still alive.

I wonder what's become of Merrick's parents and siblings, and Llyr's father. I realize I don't know that much about Keone's family, but I know he has one that I'm sure he's worried about too. We need to find everyone's family when we return.

"Will you be okay?" Llyr asks, making sure we remain friendly with the group.

"We'll be fine," Larina replies. "You should hurry though. Did you see anyone alive on your way through?"

"No, none that we saw," I reply, itching to go.

"Okay, you go ahead. We'll finish checking back to where we left off, and then we'll be back. Keep a careful eye out—we hear there are sirens hiding in caves."

"We haven't seen any yet, but just be aware as you travel," Larina adds.

We thank them, swimming away quickly.

"We'll get them back, Len," Merrick assures me, not bothering to mention his worries about his own family. A bruise is starting to form on his ribs where he slammed into the ledge—it looks painful.

A pod of dolphins swims overhead as if the world

below isn't falling apart. A turtle glides through the water, swimming past a small fever of stingrays. The ocean faces death every day and holds no remorse for us as it continues on in the wake of our destruction.

The trip doesn't seem to take as long as I think it really does, but that's because I'm lost in my head, already formulating a plan to rescue Casp and my mother. I keep Merrick in my peripheral vision, letting him guide me as we swim. My eyes are focused somewhere ahead of me, but by the time we arrive, I have no idea what we passed or where we had been.

We hurry through the collection, looking for the queen. When we find her, Dylana rushes forward. She quickly pulls back after hugging her mother, requesting an update.

"Celena," my father's voice erupts behind me. "Where have you been?"

I spin in the water and rush to him.

"We were chasing the siren king. He's dead."

"Nir is dead?" Marilla's voice is high-pitched as she faces me.

"He's dead," Dylana confirms. "We left his body and came straight here."

"Which just means we have to deal with Tarni and Cassidia."

Marilla shakes her head, waiting for an explanation as I release my father.

"Nir's cousin—the weak one," I inform my father. "Cassidia is the blue siren Nir has been using to control the humans."

"How is that mermaid controlling the humans? She's not related to us, is she?" Marilla ponders out loud.

"Not that we can tell—Nir was his mothers only child and the last of Chantay's line. As far as we know, she's just a siren who practiced really, really hard over the years. We don't know more than that," I reply.

Coralie reaches around my father, grabbing my hand. She clamps down on me but knows it's not her place to interrupt while I'm speaking to Marilla.

"They have your mother," Marilla informs me quietly.

"They took Caspian while he was trying to stop them." Coralie sounds like she's going to cry.

"We'll get them back, Cor." I swim around my father to scoop her into my arms.

"Celena!" Marilla sounds horrified as she sees my back. My father's jaw tightens, but he doesn't say anything.

"Where did they take them?" I inquire, still holding on to my little sister. She rests her head on my shoulders.

"Toward Antaire." Marilla points toward the distance. "There's a line of sirens we'll have to get by first in order to reach them."

"There has to be a way around them." My eyes dart around, looking for an answer so far over the horizon that I can't see it, even if it *does* exist. "The caves maybe. The one we were in had a secondary entrance. Maybe there's one hidden that we don't know about."

Between us and the horizon, mer swim back and forth, preparing for the next stage of the battle. They all look anxious as they speak, working out a plan.

A mermaid catches my eye, holding my gaze for a moment before flicking her mauve tail to propel herself back into action. Her light brown hair picks up hints of copper as the light catches it and for a moment, I'm jealous of her beautiful color combination. She glances back at me, reminding me of how worried I should be.

"You really think we wouldn't know about that if one existed?" Marilla reproaches me. "Lanika worked exquisitely hard to create all of our maps—"

"*After* King Gaspar moved everyone to Scylla. Her maps of Scylla are flawless, but she had to design the Metten maps from memory, and she wasn't one of the ones who would know the area so well. Aila or Kalania would have been better suited for that."

"What makes you think they didn't help?"

"Maybe they did," I relent. "But that still doesn't mean they might not have missed something. Right now, it's our best shot."

"She's right, Mother." Dylana comes to my defense. "We should go."

"Absolutely not." Marilla rises up in the water. "We'll

send a collection out to search, but you two are staying here."

"There's no way I'm waiting here," I protest, horrified at the thought.

"If you go out there and get caught, they can use you against the humans. It's too risky. The others will get Almetta and your brother back."

"I'm not leaving my mother and brother out there in the hands of the sirens when I can do something about it. I'm the one who's had the most experience with the sirens—especially Tarni and Cassidia. I nearly got Murdoch on our side while we were with them—"

"And she basically sirened Phorcys like Tarni did to Murdoch," Dylana adds, cringing the moment she says it.

"*Excuse me?*" My father's voice is the last one I want to hear right now.

"Of everyone here, I'm the best one to take them on," I continue. "I've already proven that I can overpower Cassidia, and Tarni has yet to do me in."

"Celena, I forbid you." Marilla crosses her arms. Her crown sits at an angle as if it had been knocked off balance during the fight and she forgot to adjust it.

"You know she'll just sneak out while you're not look-ing," Natale pipes in. "You might as well send her with a team so at least she has a fighting chance."

Marilla looks conflicted, opening her mouth several times to speak before she actually does.

"Take Marrick and Llyr." She sighs angrily. "Do not get caught."

She motions for a decent-sized collection of mer to join us. They quickly prepare themselves to go.

"They'll be fine," I promise Coralie. "Just stay safe until we get back."

I hug her and my father goodbye.

"*No*," Marilla raises her voice to her daughter when Dylana tries to join me. "You and Natale are staying here. We can't risk it."

I swim up to Dylana and hug her quickly.

"Be careful," I warn her. "I'll be back soon."

"Take this," Marilla insists, pulling her armor off.

"I can't—" I start to protest, knowing the queen shouldn't be exposed to attack.

"I'll only be without for a few minutes—we have extra. Go before you lose any more time."

I quickly shrug into the armor, long pieces covering my arms as it trails off my shoulders. Coralie double-checks it for me, hugging me before I go.

Dylana and I share a look before I swim off with Merrick, Llyr and our back up in my wake.

CHAPTER 16

THE CAVES ARE QUIET—THEY ALMOST FEEL FORBIDDEN to enter.

Skulls line some of them—many still intact in their original, unbroken state. The mer guards with us look horrified for the first few caves we check, but they quickly grow accustomed to the sight.

The first three caves we check are simple caves with no possible hidden exits, but the fourth holds the promise of more. We check several times before leaving, not locating any hidden panels to escape from the cave.

"Are we sure this is the right idea?" one of Marilla's mermen asks. "We're getting awfully close to the sirens, and if they catch us, our plan is over. Should we start searching for another way to get around them—a distraction maybe?"

I consider his words as a school of fish moves around

our collection, darting by us in a flash of red before we angle off to check the next cavern.

"A few more," I instruct, taking the lead. He sighs, following behind me.

This cavern has a ledge much like the one in the skull cave. Merrick and Llyr perk up on either side of me.

"Promising," Llyr mutters.

"I'll go," I say, preparing to launch myself out of the water again.

"I—"

"No, Merrick, you are not doing this one. Ledges didn't work so well for you last time," I try to joke.

"Nope," Llyr cuts in, grabbing my arm. "You're not throwing yourself out of the water this time, princess—I'll help you."

I let my hand sink back down to my side while I close my mouth—I had been prepared to argue, but he wasn't telling me I couldn't be the one to go—he was volunteering to help.

Llyr puts his hands around my waist, and we both swim up. With the combined force of our tails, I pop out of the water, and he boosts me up so that I'm sitting on the ledge.

Not slamming into a flat rock is the highlight of my day.

"You okay?" Merrick asks, floating above the water. The other mermen look nervous.

"We've been doing this for days, it's fine," I tell them. "I'm going to look around."

The mermen float in the water, watching over me. We leave one merman down below to monitor the entrance, so there are no surprises.

I crawl around on the rocks, searching along the walls. There are no tunnels in this cave, but that doesn't stop me from checking every inch.

"Merrick, check below."

He hesitates, but follows my orders, diving below to check along the wall.

"Is there a particular reason you sent him and not me?" Llyr asks.

"I just thought staying under the water might be good for him." I shrug. "He's already injured enough—I don't need the air drying him out or something."

"You think the air will dry him out in five minutes?" He speaks as if it's preposterous.

"I don't know, Llyr," I snipe back, running my hands down a crevice in the wall. "I'm just worried. I'd do the same to you if *you* had collided with a rock."

Something clicks under my fingers.

"What was that?" Llyr splashes up in the water to see. His hand taps on the surface, indicating that Merrick should come back up.

The water separates as Merrick breaks the surface.

The waves lap along the edge of the rocks, slapping softly.

I work my fingers into the tiny line in the wall I have created, feeling gently for another lever to open it fully. After a moment, I find it.

"Well, well, boys, what do we have here?" I grin as I speak.

The door opens up, revealing a small tunnel—this one just big enough to swim through horizontally.

"What is it?" Merrick shouts.

"You're not going to like it," I call back. "It's a tunnel, but it's tiny. We should all be able to fit through it, but it's going to be slow going because we won't be able to move our tails very far."

The tunnel immediately dips down, leaving only a hand's width dry at the top. We'll have to slip down into it and then pull ourselves through the space.

"Can you see the end of it?" Llyr sounds skeptical.

"Barely, but yes. It looks like it goes right back out into the ocean—not a hot spring this time."

"All right, boys, you heard the lady. Time to move," Merrick directs.

Merrick turns around to help the others up on the ledge while Llyr comes to examine the tiny tunnel. I wish he wouldn't push himself like that—he's already injured enough.

"I'm going to check it out, block for me," I whisper.

"Celena," he tries to discourage me.

"One of us has to, Llyr. I'm the least likely to get stuck, and I'll have the easiest time coming back if I need to. Besides, do you really think you mermen can flip around in there? You're not nearly flexible enough. I'm the only one who has any hope of getting back up here, so let me do this."

Without waiting, I turn and dive into the tunnel.

The water splashes around me as I drag myself through the tunnel. I was right to think there wouldn't be much space for flipping my tail to move me forward—the mermen will have an even worse time.

It's uncomfortable crawling through the exit, but after a moment, I reach the end of it. I hover near the opening, pausing long enough to get my bearings.

"Len?" Merrick whispers loud enough for me to hear, obviously having discovered my plan. His tone tells me we'll be talking about this later.

I slide out into the ocean, finding it empty. Double-checking, I give it a moment before calling up to tell the boys to follow me.

I guard the exit as the mermen work their way down the tunnel. Llyr appears first, apparently having convinced Merrick that he was in a better condition to help me if I needed it.

"Good luck handling this one later," he mumbles, taking a place beside me.

Once everyone is free of the tunnel, we set out toward Antaire—the site of Marceline's original sireny that prompted the human-mer treaty, *and* the place where Persephone and her mother destroyed it. Nerves wash over me as I realize what's at stake.

We swim up to one of the caves, and a few of us peer around it. In the distance floats a line of sirens—we've passed them. Llyr nods to me, commending me for a job well done.

We stay shielded behind anything we can find—coral, kelp, caves. Occasionally we find small siren collections swimming our way, and we hide until they pass by us. Engaging them now will only lead to us being found out before we reach Tarni and the others.

I glance over at Merrick, noting he's no longer having trouble swimming. While most wouldn't notice it, I did—I would be a terrible partner if I didn't.

He catches me staring and offers a smile that makes me blush every shade of coral under the sea.

"So I assume this doesn't count as our first date?" His smirk makes me forget to breathe for a moment, and I have to turn away to conceal my next large breath, using my hair to block it from him so he doesn't tease me. It's remarkably hard to hide behind my hair while it's braided back so beautifully, but I manage.

When I turn back, he's still watching me. Llyr peers around him, grinning smugly at me.

"Your hair looks nice, Celena," he compliments, even though he's been with me since Merrick braided it back.

"It's sharp," I reply, tossing my braid playfully.

"Looks like you did a number on Nir's face with it…"

"I assume so." I forgot to look—I was so busy dealing with Phorcys.

"It looked like that other guy gave you some trouble," Llyr guides the conversation. "Want to talk about it?"

I realize that this is the first time any of us have stopped talking about defeating the sirens long enough to have a conversation about anything else that has happened.

"I don't." *What was I going to say?*

"He seemed pretty bent on harassing you until the death," Llyr surmises. "Merrick too."

"Seemed that way."

"He really is dead, right? It's not like he's going to come back to haunt us…" Merrick's voice trails off.

"I don't see how he could have survived, I stabbed him in the abdomen. I'm pretty sure he has to be gone by now. We should have ended him before we left though."

If by some miracle, he survived, it would be my fault. I instantly run through every scenario where Phorcys could have lived—if another siren found him, if a mer found him and took pity on him, if a jellyfish drifted over and zapped him back to life. This line of reasoning is ridiculous, but it lingers at the forefront of my mind as we travel.

"Come back to us, Len," Merrick murmurs after a while. "Everything will be okay. You need to focus on fighting Tarni and Cassidia now."

"Now that Nir is gone, does that make Tarni their queen?" I try to focus on other questions to get Phorcys' death out of my mind.

"I don't know, I suppose we don't know much about how the siren's hierarchy is structured. Chantay wanted to be in charge, so I'm sure they put measures in place to make sure her reign lasted." Merrick brushes his hair back as he speaks. "It would make sense that if something happened to her direct line, any other connected living sirens would be eligible to take over."

"Tarni *was* running the show with Nir, and Nir definitely protected his cousin—she was like a sister to him—so I would imagine Tarni is in charge unless someone else swam in and took power from her," Llyr adds.

"Do you think Cassidia would try to take power away from her?" I ask as we duck behind coral, peeking out as we check for sirens.

"Do we know anything about her?" Llyr questions quietly. "I haven't been close enough to get a read on her."

"She's incredibly calm—unless she's not," I answer. "When I slammed into her while they had Coralie and I, she barely flinched, but when I steal the humans away from her, she actually hisses at me like a sea monster."

"She *hisses?*" Merrick checks to see if he heard correctly.

The light bounces down through the waves, shifting in the water as the sun rests high overhead. It sparkles off the fish swimming by, and for a moment, I want to rise to the surface and bounce through the waves like a dolphin.

"Every single time she's angry, she bares her teeth at me, hisses, and comes after me," I confirm. "If it weren't so strange, it might actually be funny."

"Maybe we can get her to focus that rage on Tarni and let her take the siren out *for* us," Merrick jokes. He gives me a sympathetic look.

"Splitting them up doesn't sound like a bad idea," Llyr remarks, adjusting the shoulder armor that's slightly too big. He cringes when he accidentally touches the sharkskin.

"How would we turn them against each other though?"

"Tell her Nir told you the blue one would be in charge," one of the guards behind us interjects—I had forgotten we weren't alone. "If she thinks Tarni is taking a job away from her that Nir meant for her to have, I doubt she'll take kindly to that."

"That's brilliant." I sound more surprised than I meant to. I rush to speak, trying to cover it up. "If we make her think Nir meant for her to be his heir and she confronts Tarni about it, there's bound to be some kind of fight.

"And," I pause dramatically, "I know just how to make that happen.

I nod to Merrick's hip. He looks at me quizzically for a moment before his face brightens. Reaching around, he pulls the necklace out.

"We were the last ones to see Nir alive—what's to say he didn't tell us as he was dying that Cassidia would take over for him and destroy us in his name? She'll have no idea, and if we do it strategically, she won't even know we're planting a fight between them."

"How do you plan on doing that?" the same guard asks.

"By engaging in battle with her." I turn back to look at him while speaking. "I'll wear the necklace so she can *accidentally* see it and then while we're fighting, I'll make some flippant comment about how Nir was wrong and how she can't defeat us. She'll force me to explain myself and I'll let the whole story slip."

"If it's in front of Tarni, all the better," Merrick adds. "That makes it easier to ensure Cassidia will actually tell Tarni and not just murder her when she isn't looking."

"Do you honestly think Cassidia would do that?" I'm shocked at the idea, but it wouldn't actually surprise me, especially when I consider her past behavior—after all, she *did* murder all those humans. If Tarni is seen as a threat, she might be considered the enemy.

"I think she's one of the most capable sirens we've faced—yes, I think she would consider it."

"I do too at this point," Llyr adds his opinion to the conversation. "Whatever they do, we're just the catalyst for it—we didn't cause it. They make their own decisions, just like we make our own decisions. Our goal is to divide them."

"We can't take it on ourselves if something else happens."

I'd still feel guilty, but that's not going to stop me from ending this war. I don't think Tarni is strong enough to hurt Cassidia in any way. I wouldn't put it past Cassidia to offer Tarni to the humans though. I'll just have to try to keep my eye on her when the time comes in case I can prevent it. I don't mind seeing her suffer, but I'd rather not have her filleted on the deck of a boat.

I reach out to take the necklace from Merrick. He drops it into my hand, carefully avoiding touching me. He raises an eyebrow, pulling his hand back.

Pretending not to notice his attempts at flirting, I turn back, reaching around to clasp the necklace behind my neck. A piece of my hair gets caught in the clasp, and I struggle to untangle it—usually, it would just slide right out, and I could try again, but with my hair in a braid, there's nowhere to slide it.

"Want some help there, princess?" Merrick smirks, delighted to have a reason to come to my rescue.

I struggle for another moment, unable to work it out of my hair.

I sigh, allowing him to swim over and lift my braid, reaching under to set me free from the clasp. He works it through my hair, flipping my braid over his arm so he can use both hands to disconnect it.

After a moment, the necklace comes loose, and Merrick dips it down in the water so he can get a better grasp on both ends. I reach up, holding the medallion in my hand so it doesn't fall while he fiddles with the clasp.

Quietly, he clips the necklace around my neck and lets the chain fall against my skin where it can be clearly seen round my other necklace. He lingers for a moment before taking my braid off of his arm and replaces it on my back as we continue to swim.

"Thanks," I mutter.

"You're welcome," he replies, swimming back to his position between Llyr and me.

"*Adorable,*" Llyr sings. "Now when we get there, are you two going to *cute* them to death, or...?"

"*Clam up,* Llyr," we both say at the same time, nearly identical in tone.

"We probably *all* should—it looks like we're here."

In the distance, we see the under side of the ship Llyr is pointing to. It sits in the water next to a wall of rocks that almost looks like the underside of an island formation, not too far away from the shore that somehow snuck up on us. Several other ships bob in the water too —mostly larger ships, but various rowboats litter the water as well.

"Wait, is that—?"

"It is," I breathe. "It's the steps. We've reached the castle."

CHAPTER 17

ANTAIRE IS AN INCREDIBLE SIGHT FROM UNDER THE OCEAN. I imagine it's even more beautiful above the waves. Aila's stories always mentioned the opalescent castle she would sit under as she rested on the steps that cascaded down into the ocean when she spent time with Prince Jarek and her cousin, Persephone.

If I can get above the waves far enough away to have time to look, there is said to have been the most magnificent light in the highest window of the palace. I'd love to see it, especially if this is my only chance.

"Metten is a short swim from here," I remind everyone. "We have to be careful. If anything goes wrong, we need to warn them, but we also have to be sure the sirens don't follow us."

"Do we know anything useful about this place?" Merrick asks.

"Aila passed down stories about the human palace, but they were mostly about its grandeur. I know about the queen and the prince, and what the palace looked like from the steps, but nothing about the waters below, aside from the cave Persephone sirened Jarek in, and the fact that they were able to chain her to the shore until they arrived to rescue her."

"Any chance the cave could help us?" Llyr huddles with us, but we turn to make sure everyone is involved in the conversation.

"I don't think so. Jarek was able to run out on the ledge, so it sounds like the tunnels would only lead to land, which wouldn't help us in this case."

"So we're on our own…" Llyr trails off, looking over his shoulder at the boats.

"It looks that way," I agree.

"Okay, so what's our plan?" Merrick defers to me.

"Find Tarni and Cassidia. We need to get me in front of one—or both—of them so I can show them the necklace. That means one of *you* will have to be in charge of rescuing my family." I look directly at Merrick. He grits his teeth but nods at my instructions. "Llyr you will help him—he's in no condition to be doing this alone right now. The rest of you will split up between supporting us."

I motion with my hand, dividing the group in two. They separate slightly, indicating that they know whom they're going to be following into battle.

"I think it would be wise for the three of us to go in first—they already know we were traveling together, so they might not expect us to have found reinforcements on the way here."

Everyone nods, agreeing with my assessment. The mermen and mermaids keep a careful watch over my shoulder as I speak.

"Let us swim in first to see if we can learn anything quietly before revealing ourselves. Just stay close and pay attention to what we're doing. If it looks like we need help, give it another two minutes, and then join us if it still looks bad."

They grimace at my words, but I know they'll follow through. They hover behind us as we swim toward the boats in the water, pausing far enough away that they might not be noticed as they watch us.

"We stay together until we can't," Merrick commands.

"Agreed."

"No arguments here," Llyr responds, gripping his trident harder.

The face of the rocks holding up the palace drops straight down into the water. The staircase extends from the rocky land out into the water, making it easy for mermaids to crawl up them to socialize with the human royalty we had first befriended two centuries ago.

The boats grow in size as we approach, taking up more

of the waters than I'd like. Unlike most of the boats I've seen, these do not have nets in the water. Suddenly, the boats start to move in the water as if they're about to go out to sea.

"What are they doing?" I whisper to myself.

"Are they sending the ships out?" Llyr voices my concern louder.

"I think so."

"That can't be good." Merrick glances at me, knowing we can't save everyone. If the ships are headed to their death, we don't have the ability to stop them right now, but we *can* help the human collection standing on the shores, surrounding the steps.

"Is that Caspian?" Llyr points in the water where a blue tail appears to be struggling.

"I can't tell from here," I say nervously. I don't want to expose our position too early and risk not finding Caspain and my mother.

"I think *that's* your mother." Merrick points in a different direction. "And that looks like Cassidia's tail next to her. If that's Almetta, than *that* has to be Casp over there."

"Which means they aren't together. That changes the plan."

"We'll get Casp, you get your mother." Merrick decides for me. "We'll go at the same time."

"How do we plan on getting past the guards up there?"

I ask, nodding to the sirens doing a terrible job at keep watch for us.

"By causing a distraction." Llyr grins, pointing up as a pod of dolphins swims our way. "You good on your own, Merrick?"

"Go." Merrick grins back, releasing Llyr to be our distraction.

He shoots up in the water, mixing with the pod of dolphins before steering one toward the sirens. The dolphin dives in the water, taking Llyr with him.

They swing by the sirens as Llyr acts like he doesn't have control of the creature. The sirens shoot up in the water, chasing after him, but they're no match for the dolphin's speed.

As soon as they're facing away, we turn, swimming toward the surface where my family is being held captive. I wave our backup forward, encouraging them to get on this side of the siren wall while they still can. They find places to hide behind large rocks on the ocean floor.

Merrick and I split off—he goes to the left to help Caspian, while I go to the right to save my mother from Cassidia. The blue siren is singing to the humans, trying to force my mother to do it *for* her.

Tarni holds a knife to Caspian's throat. She sees me, but Merrick is nowhere in sight.

"I'll kill him if you don't," Tarni shouts to my mother, ignoring me.

"You need him just as much as you need me, Tarni," my mother calls back.

"I'll kill your daughter too!" Tarni amends her threat.

Cassidia whips her head around, locating me. My mother's eyes grow wide when she sees me. I lock eyes with Cassidia, making sure the necklace is on full display, but I don't point it out yet.

My mother recognizes Marilla's armor, giving me a brief nod but I don't acknowledge her. I need to keep the focus on me, not what my mother is quietly doing while Cassidia isn't paying as close of attention as she should be.

The ships start to leave the area, clearing the waters for a greater war. Cassidia opens her mouth again, instructing the humans to enter the water. The first group splashes in and quickly disappear under the water as the sirens pull them down, just as Chantay and Persephone once drowned Jarek's guards a century ago in this very place.

Foam laps along the rock wall each time the water crashes against it. It jumps along the shore, leaving the off-white film to skitter across the grass and rocks. Pieces tumble along in the breeze. Miraculously, the foam avoids the steps.

"Do you honestly think you can control the palace, Cassidia?" I point to the palace that is just as opalescent as Aila described it to be, though dingy with age.

"We will, though there won't be much left when we're done, I'm afraid." She smiles. "We were so lucky your brother fought so hard to save your mother back in Hontan—we might have left him behind."

"You left my sister though," I remind her. "I guess you really *don't* have what it takes."

I finger the necklace resting on my chest under my grandmother's necklace just long enough to draw her attention to it.

"What's your plan, Cassidia—take over as the reigning siren queen?"

"Nir will be here soon," Tarni yells. She screams as we hear a loud splash. Cassidia's face goes white, and I whip around to see what happened.

Caspian is no longer in her grasp, and Tarni looks shocked. She ducks under the water where Merrick has pulled Caspian to safety. I see their outlines through the waves and assume they're safe.

"Are you really trusting *her* as your right hand?" I turn back to Cassidia, mocking her choice for council. "I thought Nir had trained you better."

Tarni pops back up in the water, swimming toward me.

"What happened, Tarni?" I ask in my most innocent voice. "Lose something?"

"You're boyfriend pulled your brother away, but don't

worry, my sirens are getting them back. Good thing we only need *one* of them alive."

I'd quake if her threats scared me at all—we've survived the sirens this long.

"Honestly, it's not them I'd be worried about though—it's you. This time, we're going to kill you."

She pulls out her knife, prepared to take a chunk out of my tail. Tarni arches her back, leaping out of the water in an arc before she dives down in front of me, bent on cutting my scales.

I dip under the water, pulling my own knife as she swims toward me. I jerk my tail to the side and Tarni swipes at the water where I had been.

"I only pulled off one scale last time, Celena—time to take them all," she growls.

Above us, Cassidia's tail thrashes in the water as my mother tries to escape to help me. When neither appears under the waves, I assume Cassidia has the upper hand in the situation.

A tidal wave of humans pours into the water, jumping off the side of the palace grounds. They swim over us, covering the waters, blocking out much of the light. The men surround my mother and Cassidia, but don't appear to be hurting them.

Tarni slashes at me, barely missing. I drag my own knife across the top of her wrist, cutting her with a shallow motion—I should have tried harder, but I was hoping to avoid detaching her hand from her arm. She moves quickly in retaliation. Blood bubbles up on the top of my hand, but she doesn't do enough damage to deter me from fighting.

The light shifts as the humans swim above us. Their bodies hover above us, occasionally dipping down into the water. A boot nearly kicks me in the head as a man moves over us. I push it away, shoving him roughly—he barely notices under Cassidia's trance.

Suddenly, the entire group of humans plunge beneath the waves. Their heads dart around as they search for something. The men's eyes lock on us—on *me*—and the entire collection of humans turns to try to attack me.

Tarni grins wildly as she realizes what is happening. She swims up, double-checking that Cassidia has only sent them after me. The men swim by her as if she's not even there. As soon as she's free, she surfaces.

Having no choice, I attempt to siren the men as they swim toward me. In between hands and feet groping the water to get to me, I see my mother's face under the water. Cassidia's hand grips her hair as she fights to get her above the waves.

My mother's voice fills the water as she tries to assist me. Caspian and Merrick nearly collide into me as I swim to the ocean floor.

"Sing!" I command.

Caspian looks unsure, but he follows my lead, his

voice blending with mine. Merrick makes a move to swim under the humans, trying to get around them to reach my mother while my twin and I attempt to move the humans away from the area.

Hands touch my sides, brushing against my waist and hips as the humans surround me. They shove Caspian aside, desperately trying to drag me to the surface.

I push at them, trying to beat their hands away—they drag me toward the waves anyway. My tail flips against them, trying to remove the people from me. When I can't pull away, I use my knife, trying to avoid doing any major damage.

A man reels back at the touch of the blade, but only long enough to display that instinctual reaction before the sireny takes back over. He continues swiping his hands toward me, attempting to follow orders.

Slowly, the men in the water stop, latching on to our siren song. Caspian filled in the gaps as I paused to attack the men coming after me, and between us, the men have turned to listen. They slowly swim to the surface and move back toward the land.

"No!" Tarni screams as we surface. She wheels around to face Cassidia. "Do something."

Cassidia attempts to sway them back, now forcing my mother's head under the water so she can't lend us her voice above the waves.

"Separate them," Cassidia says between lines. She nods at us.

Tarni turns, choosing to take on Caspian. She races at him, slamming into his chest. Murdoch would be furious if he saw the way she threw herself at my twin.

Where is *Murdoch?*

Caspian and Tarni disappear under the water. Cassidia holds my mother's tail in her hands, preparing to slice off her fins.

"He said you wouldn't flinch if it came to that." I raise an eyebrow, trying to act casually. I nod to my mother's tail. "I supposed *that's* why."

"Why *what?*" Her voice is low and dangerous as her hand twitches near my mother's fins.

"Why he left you in charge instead of his cousin."

She quirks her head at me, studying me as I float in the water.

The water breaks as Tarni surfaces without Caspian.

"You have more friends, I see," she snips at me, swimming over.

I ignore her, turning back to face the blue siren.

"I'd like to say you're going to live to see your days as queen, but I'm not convinced you're going to survive *today.*"

"Queen?" Tarni sounds offended. "Nir isn't taking a wife anytime soon."

"And it certainly wouldn't be *me*," Cassidia adds, taken back by Tarni's words.

I allow my eyes to widen, mimicking shock.

"You don't know?"

Cassidia squints her eyes at me, leaning forward as she temporarily forgets she's holding my mother's tail.

"Know what?" Tarni growls.

"Cassidia is queen now." I have to fight my smile.

"What do you mean?" Cassidia hisses at me, lurching forward as she bumps into my mother.

In the water behind her, I see the shadow of Merrick's blue hair slipping through the water under the surface—I have to keep Cassidia distracted.

"He left you in charge," I reply, reaching for the necklace.

"How did you get that?" Tarni seethes in the water a few lengths from me—I have both of their attention.

"I took it to bring it back as proof."

"Proof of what?" Tarni shrieks, hair flopping in front of her she slams her hand on the surface of the water.

Behind the sirens, the humans are climbing into small boats and are rowing back toward us, no longer under anyone's siren spell. For now, I have to deal with one problem at a time—and I still have a few minutes before the humans reach us again as they row back from the palace steps Caspian and I sent them to.

"Nir is dead, and Cassidia is the queen," I inform her.

"He can't be dead!" Tarni gasps, preparing herself to wail over the loss of her cousin.

"He's gone, Tarni," Cassidia says quietly as if she has confirmation of it.

"We were just as shocked as you are that he would pass the crown to Cassidia and not you, Tarni," Llyr calls as he swims over to us. He and Caspian slow their crashing approach, releasing the dolphins he has apparently used to rescue Casp from Tarni's grasp—which also explains why she surfaced without him.

When they turn to look at them, Cassidia is pulled beneath the waves. I dart forward, grabbing onto her wrists, squeezing so hard that she releases my mother's tail.

Merrick drags her down in the water so quickly that she can't fight back. I dart up, telling my mother to swim. Llyr smacks the water, directing a dolphin to my mother.

"Go! Don't stop—we'll catch up. Find the guards!"

She grabs onto the dolphin's dorsal fin, letting it carry her away to get reinforcements. I imagine her tail is quite sore from being pulled on like that. I can't be sure, but she might have had a small encounter with Cassidia's knife as they were pulled under—I hope they didn't split her fin like they did to mine.

I careen back into the water in search of Merrick, but Tarni is on top of me, trying to rip my hair back.

"Give me that necklace, you eel!" Her shout is overtaken by the pain she feels when she latches onto my braid and rakes her hands across the shells Merrick wove into it.

"Nir said the exact same thing," I yell back. "Only it was his face, not his hands!"

I laugh cruelly as I taunt her, trying to throw her off focus.

"I will murder you," she screams, unable to come up with a more creative threat in the moment.

"Not going to let the humans handle it this time?" I throw back over my shoulder. "They're coming for us, you know."

I point up as I swim, noting the humans are drawing closer. I hear her startle behind me, gasping at the sight of the small boats coming for us.

"You'll pay for this!"

"I'm sure I will," I mutter as I continue to dive toward Cassidia. She and Merrick are locked in battle—she somehow freed herself of his grasp. They circle each other, knives in hand.

"Come to watch your boyfriend die?" Cassidia calls, noticing me.

"Go handle the humans, Celena," Merrick says without looking at me. The two continue to spin in a wide arch, waiting for the other to strike first.

"Tarni, do not let her get control of them," Cassidia instructs. "Go to the surface."

"You're not queen yet, Cassidia. I'm the next in line for the throne, and I'm staying to kill this *mermaid.*" She spits the word out like it's toxic.

"We have to work together, Tarni," Cassidia calls. "If Nir's plan is going to succeed, we need them all under our control. I'll kill both of them, and then join you so we can start the ceremony."

"What ceremony is—?" My words are cut off as Tarni screams again, this time in agony.

Tarni is jerked through the water, a harpoon extending out of her arm. Blood clouds behind her as the humans pull her toward their boat. She screams, knowing her fate if they catch her.

The siren princess attempts to rip her arm away, but the barbs at the end of the spear prevent her from ripping it from her arm. They pull her so quickly that she doesn't have time to free herself anyway.

Cassidia races away from Merrick, attempting to help her princess as the sailors drag Tarni into their rowboat. Their tiny boat shifts under their weight. Several humans move to the opposite side to balance it out while two men haul Tarni out of the water.

"Help me!" Cassidia shrieks before she reaches the surface. She pulls herself out of the water, slamming into the side of the boat as she reaches for her friend.

"We can't let them kill her." Without any logical reason, I race toward the surface to help save her.

The air feels heavier when I surface as if everything is weighing me down. Screams sound overhead as creatures move in the sky above us. I ignore them as I make my way to the boat where Cassidia is attempting to siren the humans as she claws for Tarni.

The siren princess sits in the center of the boat as the men attempt to bind her, wrapping ropes around her arms to pin them to her sides. One of the men breaks the harpoon, pulling it from her arm as she cries out.

Cassidia's song drops as she screams for Tarni, only fragments of notes escaping her lips as she bounces between trying to siren the men and direct the princess. I open my mouth to sing, but something hits me in the back of the head, sending me pitching forward. My face slams into the water but I bob right back up, knife in hand.

A man glares at me, ready to hit me again.

"We won't let you siren *us*, you sea witch," he sneers.

I duck under the water, darting toward the boat in an attempt to tip it. It's heavier than it looks and I only manage to rock it as I collide with the underside of the vessel. The oar dips back into the water behind me, and I turn, pulling as hard as I can, flipping the man into the water.

I swim away, trying to return to save Tarni. On the surface, I start singing, attempting to sway the sailors into leaving. The men shout directions to each other, passing along orders from closer to the shore.

A figure stands on the top of the steps leading to the palace in the distance—he looks like he's giving the orders. If I can get the men over there, they could silence him.

I lurch forward as a boat collides with me, striking the middle of my back enough to toss me forward again. Arms reach around me, lifting me out of the water.

CHAPTER 18

THE EDGE OF THE BOAT SCRAPES OVER MY SCALES painfully as the men haul me into the rowboat. I fight against them, looking for Merrick, but he's nowhere to be found.

Several boats over, I see Llyr grappling with a human in the water. Caspian is a few lengths away, trying to turn a boat away from coming to help the humans with Tarni and me. Cassidia pummels the boat, darting away each time they reach for her.

Tarni's cries turn to pleas for mercy as they go after her scales.

"Leave her alone!" I scream before bursting into song in an attempt to free myself.

One of the men pulls at my arm, forcing it over my head as I'm positioned to lay flat against their knees as they hold me between them. I try to pull my hands back as his knife dances over them, taunting me.

"We're taking you to his majesty," the man informs me. "Hold still, so we don't have to take you in pieces."

I sing louder, finally latching into their consciousness. The men slow, starting to fall under my song. I order the man to throw his knife into the sea, and he releases it quickly—I hope it doesn't hit anyone on the way down.

At my insistence, they gently lift me into the air, leaning over the side of the boat to set me in the water. When Cassidia sees me, she calms, trying to gather herself enough to siren the humans.

Cassidia is a smart mermaid—she knows Tarni is next in line for the crown, and if the princess is gone, there's nothing stopping the bigger, more brutish sirens from moving in and disposing of *her* so *they* can rule. She's wise to keep Tarni alive as the only siren that has a possible claim to the crown—it's written all over her face. She could care less about Tarni, but her safety and position are at stake.

I glance over while they're moving me. Tarni is in tatters, her tail being slowly shredded. They pull at her scales, each wanting one as a prize. One man takes a knife to her fins, slicing them into strips.

Tarni passes out from the pain, quieting as they rip her apart. My voice jumps an octave as I throw my words at them, stilling their hands.

The men set me in the water, allowing me to float on my own. I stretch my arms out to the side, continuing to lean back to stay in the same position, preventing my song from breaking or changing while I'm sirening the men with Tarni.

"Tarni!" Murdoch's voice is clear and strong above the yelling of the humans from the other boats as they attempt to catch more mer and sirens.

He rushes toward the boat, bent on saving her. I have no idea where he's been all this time. Cassidia blocks his path, holding a hand up.

"We have to save her!" He tries to counter the blue siren's moves.

"She is," Cassidia says calmly, looking at me.

From the corner of my eye, I can see Murdoch still, watching me. I carefully direct the men to pick Tarni up, and Murdoch raises himself up in the water, nostrils flaring as he prepares to murder me if I do anything to his precious siren.

The men in the rowboat lower the broken siren into the water. Her blood washes away as the water claims her body back from the human world.

"Take her." I slip the words into my song. "And don't ever come after the mer again or I'll give you all to the humans. The war is over."

Cassidia takes Tarni's unconscious body and dips

below the surface. Murdoch hovers, and I lower my voice so I can hear him over my notes.

"Why did you save her?"

"No one should die like that," I tell him, adding a few notes to keep the humans at bay. "I tried to save Durdania too."

"They said Nir is dead."

"He is. I killed him."

"You killed Nir, but not Tarni?" He swims as close as he dares to me.

"Nir attacked me. I couldn't save him even if I tried. Tarni attacked me too, but I wasn't going to let her die at the hands of the humans—but so help me, Murdoch, if I *ever* see you, Tarni, or any of those sirens again, I will personally feed you to the human king and his family."

I sing quickly, my anger nearly rousing the men out of my trance. Calming, I sing lower, lulling them back under my command.

"So we're free to go?"

"Assuming you can get past the mer, yes. I'm sure they've arrived by now."

"They have—it's a bloodbath."

"Then might I suggest finding an alternative route?" I'm not sure why I'm telling him how to escape the wrath of the mer queen after all he and Tarni have done to us. I don't think they'll ever come after us again after we killed their king and rescued their—temporary queen?

"Thank you, Celena." He ducks his head, not looking at me as I right myself in the water. "I'm sorry for what I did to you."

"Just go, Murdoch."

He starts to turn away but spins back around.

"Relo didn't know. I know he stood up for me during your trial, but he didn't know what was going on. He just trusted me when he shouldn't have."

"Relo won't be punished for your mistakes," I promise him. "Now leave before I change my mind."

"I don't think there are many sirens left at this point, Celena. I think it's between the mer and the humans now."

He dips under the water, rushing away to find Tarni and Cassidia and extricate them from the situation before my collection finds them—bad things would happen if they did. I shake my head as they go.

If the sirens are disbanded, that leaves the mer to clean up their mess. I wonder if we could escape back into the sea and live another hundred years without the humans finding us.

I doubt that the humans will allow us to remain in the ocean at this point—they'll probably do everything in their power to hunt us down.

"Celena!" Caspian calls, searching for me around the boats.

"*Here,* Casp!"

I start turning the boats toward the shore. If I drowned them all now, I'd know for sure these men wouldn't come after my collection today.

"Celena, the collection is here," Caspian informs me, swimming up to me and grabbing my hands. He pulls me into a protective hug.

"I know, Murdoch told me."

Caspian's face grows cold.

"Where is he?" His whisper sounds vicious and deadly.

"I let him go." I hold a hand up between us as his eyebrows shoot up. "Tarni is practically dead—though I don't think Murdoch realizes that yet—I caught a look at her side before Cassidia took her away. Cassidia isn't planning to lead their collection, and Murdoch told me that there aren't many left anyway. They'll wander, but I don't think they'll be a problem. Murdoch knows I'll kill him if they are."

"That was stupid."

"Probably," I reply, smiling as he purses his lips in understanding annoyance.

"Llyr is bringing the dolphins back around. The humans frightened them off, but they didn't get too far. Where is Merrick?"

Merrick.

"He was right behind me." My eyes grow wide again, and I'm convinced my face is going to start thinking it belongs that way. I whip around, searching for Merrick in the water. Caspian shouts for him as I duck under the waves, quickly searching for him.

"Casp!" I shout, surfacing. "*Phorcys* has him."

"*What?*"

I stare at him for a moment, gaping.

"Do sirens *never* die?" Caspian throws his hands in the air.

"Apparently not, because he's down there." Tears spring to my eyes, leaking out. They drip down my face, causing a tickling sensation—I don't like it.

The inside of my nose feels heavy as the tears drip off my cheeks. Caspian looks horrified.

"Is that what those look like?" He mutters under his breath before grabbing my shoulders. "We have to stop Phorcys."

"Phorcys?" Llyr splashes us as he races by on a dolphin. He looks at me like I've lost my mind.

"He's alive," I tell him. "He has Merrick."

"Let's go." He motions to the pod before diving under the water and racing toward where Phorcys is dragging Merrick back in the water. He's so far away, I can only tell it's my boyfriend by his brilliantly blue hair and the way he's struggling to get free—Phorcys must have knocked him out to have bound him like that. Merrick bucks against the restraints tying his wrists to his tail.

I hold onto a dolphin as we dart through the water,

leaving the humans to their own devices on the surface. We slice through the water, rapidly approaching Merrick and Phorcys.

Merrick shakes his head violently, trying to warn us off.

Llyr motions next to me and a dolphin breaks away from the pod, headed straight for the mermen ahead of us. It slams into Phorcys, knocking him off balance. Another dolphin counters, also striking Phorcys as we arrive.

I don't know how Phorcys is moving, let alone controlling this situation. But then, Nir surprised me as well. I flash back to when we left the two sirens for dead—Phorcys has a necklace. Maybe it was like the one I'm wearing from Grandmother Tama and holds secrets that he used to survive. I doubt I'll ever know though—I'm going to kill him before I have a chance to ask.

I urge my dolphin not to stop, mimicking its friends' attack on the siren. We slam into him, and I use the opportunity to pull Merrick out of the siren's reach. I don't have time to remove the gag.

"You shouldn't have left me alone," Phorcys taunts. "The smart ones never die, Celena."

"How did you manage to fix that injury?" I angle myself between Merrick and Phorcys, hoping one of the boys will untie the blue-haired merman behind me. His body rests against the small of my back as he struggles to free himself.

"You're not the only one with friends, Celena." He refuses to say more. The way his eyes narrow in a challenge, I can tell there's something to this story that I don't know yet.

It doesn't matter though—the entire mer collection—or what's left of them—swims up behind us. Our reinforcements form a wall Phorcys can't escape. He looks around for a moment before pushing himself to swim up in the water, headed toward the surface. His wound looks incredibly painful.

The collection starts to follow him, ready to take him back to Metten with us for question. I spot Marilla with my mother near the middle of the group. My father and Coralie swim nearby until the nets descend.

I've already started swimming when I notice the ropes. I'm two lengths away from the surface as I try to flip in the water and go back to help. I call out, but it's too late. The nets start scooping up mer.

They swim away, collectively trying to escape. The boats above rock as the mer pull against the ropes.

I'm stopped short, tangled in a net. It pulls me up—something I'm growing accustomed to now. I fight against it, attempting to cut the ropes so I can slip out.

I bump against the side of the boat as I snap the last rope I need to create a hole big enough to wriggle out of it. Merrick races toward me—now free—Llyr and Caspian behind him. I throw myself into his arms.

The mer that escape rush to the surface. I sing, trying to stop the madness while they surround the rowboats and larger ships that arrived from somewhere while we were under the water, attempting to free our friends and sink the ships intent on harming us.

Phorcys flops in one of the boats as the men try to subdue him. The larger boats approach—some huge, towering above the water, some just long enough that we couldn't capsize it if we tried.

My voice stops the men again as I command them to return any stolen mer to the waters below their ships. My hold over them lasts long enough to drop most of the collection to the ocean, including Phorcys. His wound bleeds as they move him—I'm still not sure how he's able to move with an injury so deep. The siren flounders in the water, trying to get away, but he's functioning about as well as a fish with one fin.

"Coralie!" Caspian yells, rushing past me.

I turn to find Coralie in a boat far enough away that I must not be reaching the men with my siren song from where I am. She's tangled in a net as my father tries to reach her. The men beat him back as he tips their rowboat in the water, desperately trying to pull Cor out of their grasp.

One man raises some kind of weapon to my father,

preparing to strike him. I shriek as I race through the water, unable to duck below the waves where it will be faster because the men will fall out of my sireny.

The man looks to me as I slice through the water toward them. His expression is cold as he moves his shoulders back, building up momentum to hit my father.

Whatever the weapon is, it's effective.

It slams into his face, producing the most horrific sound I've ever heard. He crumples under the blow, sinking against the edge of the boat before driting down in the water.

The men turn back to Coralie, and I can see them prepare to fight for pieces of her like they did with Tarni. Caspian pushes ahead of me, determined to rescue our sister. I push as hard as I can, but I can't keep up.

They raise a knife to my sister, preparing to cut her.

I won't let them.

They will never touch my precious little sister.

I stop in the water, freezing on the spot. The entire collection of humans turns to look at why I suddenly halted. I open my mouth and without hesitation, I command the human with the knife to plunge it into his own heart.

He does, toppling over onto the side of the rowboat.

Caspian turns around, horrified. He shakes his head to clear his thoughts, spinning around to get Coralie while I systematically command the men in her ship to throw themselves into the water and swim to the bottom. If they make it, perhaps they'll have enough time to swim back up. If they don't.

The men take turns leaping out of the rowboat, rocking it so hard that Coralie is nearly pitched out into Caspian's arms.

He reaches her, throwing himself as far into the nearly empty boat as he can get. My twin scoops Coralie up, pulling her back into the water. The body of the dead sailor rocks in the boat. His head tips over the back edge of the boat, dangling in above the water, head lolling back —the sight is horrifying.

Caspian nods when he turns back to me, telling me I did the right thing. I don't have time to consider it either way—the humans are still attacking.

Whipping around, I continue sirening the men as I try to get them back to land. If I can separate them from us, we can disappear into the ocean and figure out how to proceed.

Caspian darts below the waves to hand Coralie off and, hopefully, find my father and see if he's still alive.

Merrick had attempted sirening the humans while I was saving Coralie—he managed to keep them under his control, but it took a great deal of effort, even with others joining in. I raise my voice up, commanding the men in the boats far easier than he had.

The vessels turn, heading back to land. For a moment,

I consider having them tear down the steps leading to the sea with their bare hands, but I'm not willing to risk losing any time—they need to abandon their posts here in Antaire and flee for the country further inland, far enough away that they can't hurt the mer.

The man on the steps shouts, oblivious to my siren call—*something isn't right.*

I swim closer, hoping it's just the distance between us. More men rush from the shore, carrying small rowboats over their heads. They splash into the water, rowing toward the mer collection, clashing with their fellow humans as they try to take them away from my control.

"Fall back!" I shout, realizing something is wrong.

"What's the matter?" a human calls to me from a boat to my left. It drifts dangerously close as all of the men eye me.

They watch me thoughtfully, clearly not under my control.

"Oh, that's right," he shouts loudly. He points to his ear. "We can't hear you."

CHAPTER 19

THE MAN GRINS AS HE REACHES FOR ME.

"Fall back!" I scream again, realizing that I can't siren the humans if they block out my voice.

I lose control of the situation quickly.

Weapons are raised, maiming and killing my collection. Bodies float in the water—both human and mer—almost instantly.

Llyr clashes with the men in the boat next to me. They use their weapons to try to injure him, jabbing at his shoulder. He ducks under a harpoon aimed at him, and it slices through the water. Llyr reaches up, grabbing hold of the weapon the man next to him is holding and flips the human into the water.

"They can't hear me!" I shout, frantically searching for another way to fix the situation.

"I got that!" Llyr yells back.

All around me words swirl from the humans, blaming us for the deaths of their family, friends, and the men they work with every day. They scream obscenities at us —at least I assume that's what those words are by the way they're saying them—as they blame us for the destruction of the seas.

They speak to each other with their hands, waving them wildly and pointing because they aren't able to hear each other either—they must have something in their ears to stop the noise from entering. The men are surprisingly good at reading each other's lips—probably from being out at sea and needing to know what people are instructing them to do from across the ship or over the roar of waves and storms. Merrick and I have become good at doing this too while we're on missions.

"We have to stop their leader," I murmur.

"What?" Merrick asks, arm flinging out in front of me to stop an oar from hitting me while I turned to look toward the palace. The impact jars me out of my thoughts. I whip around to face him, face slack with shock as I realized I wasn't paying attention.

"Merrick, we have to take out their leader—he's on the steps." I point to the distant steps leading into the ocean. The man still stands on the top step, as far from the water as possible. More boats launch into the water, traveling toward us.

"Llyr, get them back!"

I swim toward the boats coming for us.

"Celena, do *not* go over there!" Llyr shouts, starting to follow me as he splashes loudly through the water.

"She's right, we have to stop the man leading them. Get the rest of the collection back to Metten, Llyr. You have to," Merrick insists.

"Can you do this by yourselves?" Llyr hesitates, still following us.

"We'll join you as soon as we can."

Ahead of us, Keone ducks under the water, swimming in the same direction we are.

"We'll help them!" Natale shouts, waving for Llyr to take charge of reaching Marilla and getting the collection back to Metten before we flee for Scylla and make plans on how to escape the wrath of the humans.

A few mer stay with us, willing to fight to help us escape the humans. It's incredible how many mer are willing to die to protect the others.

Llyr turns, diving under the sea as he races back to Dylana and her mother. We could use his help, but the collection needs him more. Besides, if we don't survive this, Marilla will still need trained spies to keep the collection safe—at least Llyr will be there to support them.

I dive under the water, trying to avoid the fighting until I can make my way to the steps. If I can gain enough speed, I can dive out of the water and land halfway up the steps. Crawling fast enough, I could potentially reach the man giving direction and pull him into the water with me. All I need to do is silence his commands, and his people won't know what to do—they're under his siren spell just as much as they were once under mine.

A leader is nothing more than a siren with intentions of good or bad outcomes and all those that hear their directions fall under their command, whether it is desired or not.

Their human siren stands on the palace steps ordering our deaths.

He looks even more imposing as I draw near. Still, several boat lengths away, I can start to make out more than his basic shape as his arms fly from his sides, shouting orders to the men under his siren call's control.

Looking up, I find the men in a rowboat motioning to a group of sailors in a longer boat sailing up alongside of them. They're pointing to their ears.

Not all of them are blocking us out yet—they're trying to warn them.

"Merrick, up!"

He follows my lead and we swim to the surface. As soon as I'm free of the water, I start singing. The men start to turn toward me, falling under my song, but the ones trying to warn them quickly catch on. They turn to me, prepared to end my control over the other sailors.

"Get down," I warn Merrick. "I have to stay above the

surface, but if they reach me, you'll need to save me, and they can't know you're here."

My point rings true, and he scowls as he darts below the water, moving far enough away that they can't easily see him once they approach. I work as hard as I can to force the men under my control to stop those that blocked out my voice, but it isn't enough.

I swim quickly, making my way toward the steps as the boats not under my siren song chase me. Seeing what I'm doing, they work to block me. I can't swim under them while sirening, so I have to swim around, taking me on a strange path through the water to reach their leader on the steps.

Someone figures out what my course is and moves the figure—a man I assume is their king— off of the step to higher ground. As I continue, determined to take him away from them, they rush the king back into the palace. Running off, he looks exactly as Aila described Jarek running off after his mother rescued him from Persephone's sireny when she attempted to drown him.

Inside the palace, I know there is no way to reach him, but I have accomplished my goal—the human sireny has been stopped for the moment—he no longer controls the men in the boats.

Another man *does* though. He's tall as he stands on the deck of a boat that's long enough that we couldn't tip it if we tried but low enough to the ocean's surface that if he lowered himself over the edge and I dove out of the water, perhaps I could pull him in.

I have to stop him.

Swimming quickly, I make my way back to his boat, darting around bodies in the water and gliding past boats under my control as they float in my way.

All I have time for is to keep the men at bay—I cannot use them to help me, nor can I siren them out of my way. My only mission is to get them to listen and stay motionless in the water.

Water laps in my face as I sink lower in the ocean, trying to blend in, even though all eyes are on me. My mouth hovers above the waves just enough so the crests don't block my words.

Just as I reach the boat, I feel Merrick tug on my tail below me. Before I can see what he wants, a giant net snaps around me as the humans catch me. It had been hidden closely along the side of the ship, waiting for me —Merrick's warning had been too late, and I was too busy locking eyes with the prince I met yesterday as he stares at me from where he commands his subjects on the long boat.

His face is stony as I struggle against the net, but his men leave me dangling in the water. He walks forward, examining me. The prince kneels down, balancing between the toe of one foot and his other knee.

The young prince places a hand on the side of the

boat as he studies my movements. The man behind him looks worried, staying close to his side. He looks to be about the prince's age.

"Do you know who I am?" he asks, not shouting like the others.

"The prince," I reply. I can feel Merrick struggling with the net below me.

"If you try to siren me, I'll have you killed immediately, and it won't be pleasant."

The man behind him leans forward, something in his hands—he's holding something that will block out my voice. The same thing sticks out of his own ears—he's safely protected from my words and his job is to also protect the prince should I try anything.

The prince has nothing blocking his ears at this point so that he can speak with me, but his friend can easily fix that if I try to siren the royal.

"We knew you were coming," the prince explains. "We left the ocean a century ago, but our men couldn't leave—the ocean is our way of life. It's out survival. The fishing trade is what allows us to survive. When your kind started attacking more frequently, we knew it was only a matter of time."

He glares at me as if I was the cause of all his problems.

"My sister and I weren't supposed to be here—we stayed inland while my father came to oversee the battle

—but you dragged us here. We were supposed to be safe, but you sent sirened men to capture us and bring us to you."

When I sent the man to fetch the human royals, they took the prince instead of the king because they weren't in the same location—I should have been more specific. Then again, how could I have possibly known what the royal family looked like now.

A sailor raises his spear, prepared to plunge it into my skull while the prince watches. I struggle against the ropes wrapped around me. Terror controls my body as I jerk to escape.

"Please don't do this," I plead with him. "We didn't hurt your men, the sirens we were fighting were. They're gone now. Please!"

The guard behind him leans forward, ready to protect him if I try to siren his prince. The prince waves his hand.

"I can't trust you. Your kind have killed our people for generations."

"It wasn't us," I promise, fighting against the ropes. "We've lived in the middle of the ocean, as far away from you as we could get since Persephone tried to siren Prince Jarek. I'm from Aila's line—she tried to help your prince."

He lurches back at Jarek's name. I push forward, trying to convince him to leave us in peace.

"Please, we haven't done anything but try to avoid you for years. It's Persephone's followers that did this to you."

"You're all like them. I haven't seen a single mermaid not act out against us." I open my mouth to protest, but he cuts me off. "*You're* not innocent, *mermaid,* I've watched you try to control us twice now."

He has a point.

"I've only sirened to protect us from you," I shout. "I saved your sister."

He pulls back at my words again, contemplating what to say next.

"I haven't figured that out yet—*it doesn't make sense*—but just because you rescued Analia doesn't mean I trust you. I'll never trust you—I saw you hurt all these sailors. I saw you force a man to plunge a knife into his heart."

"To save a thirteen-year-old mermaid they were bent on ripping to pieces!" My shrieks are in vain—the prince has no intention of saving me.

The noise dies down around us as the mer collection tries to escape, disappearing under the waves as Llyr forces them away, leaving only the remaining warriors to help us fight—I'm not sure many of them have survived this long. Merrick works quietly below me, snapping the net around me as I block him from sight with my tail.

The moment the net breaks, Merrick pulls me down, but the men are ready—they throw ropes around my torso. Most catch around my arms, but one loops grace-fully around my neck.

I slam my hand into the water, making Merrick stop before the men snap my neck. Merrick freezes, following my commands. His hand presses against the bottom of my tail as he realizes what is happening. He pushes me up in the water enough that the rope loosens, putting slack into the line.

"I told you, we're prepared for you," the prince informs me, rocking back on his heels as he balances on one knee. "We've known you were coming for us since your sea witch tried to drown my great-great-grandfa-ther. We were smart enough not to come back to the sea until now, but now that you've dragged us back here, you're going to pay for what you've done to our men over the generations."

I shake my head, not daring to speak.

A rumble races across the group of humans as they yell instructions to each other—*kill the sirens...kill them all.*

The boat jerks, knocking a few of the men off their feet. The rope around my neck tightens as they move. I force my eyes shut, trying not to gasp.

Everything pauses for a moment. The men stare at the water as if a dangerous predator might appear, creeping out of the depths of the ocean—too bad none of them had seen Nir—they'd be terrified.

They lean over the edge of the boat, looking into the water.

Natale's mother launches herself out of the water in a brazen attack against the men holding me. She twists in the air, lashing out as the men ready their weapons to use against her.

I had assumed Merrick had caused the boat to lurch—though I don't know why since he hasn't let go of me in all this time—instead, I discover it was Natale's mother.

Natale appears, throwing a knife at a human near the prince. It sinks into his chest, knocking him back. The prince looks horrified as he darts back in the boat to avoid being hurt.

"Pull her up," the prince instructs. "Pull her up *now* and don't hurt her!"

Merrick wraps his arms around my waist, still trying to remove the ropes. The men lift us out of the water. Miraculously, the one with the rope around my neck lets go, preventing me from being strangled as they lift us.

"Merrick, please," I beg. Attempting to remove his fingers from around me is an impossible task as I try to drop him back into the ocean like he had once done to me when I tried to rescue him from being dragged onto a ship.

"Celena, I will *not* leave you," he growls viciously, fingers biting into my waist so hard that I think I might break.

A human raises a spear to us, preparing to kill the blue-haired merman attached to their captive.

"Merrick!" I scream, unable to say or do anything else.

"Take them both," the prince instructs, holding up a hand.

The men swing us onto the boat and drop us *hard*. We collide with the deck painfully. I land partially on top of Merrick, and he instantly pulls me into his arms, trying to free me.

I know this merman, and I know he's going to try to rip the ropes off of me and push me into the water, fully prepared to pay the price for setting me free.

It doesn't matter though—the men are on us before Merrick can even attempt to remove the ropes.

Natale's mother launches herself out of the water again as the humans bind Merrick. She screeches as they spear her. Twisting, she convulses violently in the air. It's nearly as terrifying as watching Coralie in the brine pool had been. She collides with the water, disappearing from sight as Natale dips below to help her.

Merrick attempts to sing, hoping we can siren the men, but one of the guards slams into his skull with an oar, knocking him out. He flops onto the boat deck. All I can do is scoot closer to him and nestle against his head with mine—my hands are tied behind me making it difficult to even push myself to sit upright. My braid flops over him, and I carefully angle it to ensure the broken shells won't hurt him.

"Back to shore," the prince commands. "We're going to study these two."

A loud commotion sounds from the far side of the medium-sized vessel.

"Three, sire," a man informs him.

I turn to see which other mer they caught. My chest tightens when they drop Phorcys onto the deck. He struggles against them, but it's a losing battle with his injuries getting the better of him.

"I tried," he murmurs when he makes eye contact with me just before passing out from the strain on his injuries.

I look up into the eyes of the prince as he puts something into his ears to block noise out.

I can't turn as I hear the voices, but I can clearly hear Caspian and Llyr screaming that they'll find us and rescue us in the distance—they must have returned to assist in the fight and were too late.

"Time to see the palace you were so intent on ruling, *mermaid*. I'm sure you'll find it rather interesting."

They row us back to the steps. Men on the shore hold the boat in place as the guards pick us up—four sets of uncomfortable hands on each of us—and lift us out of the boat.

They carry us up the steps Aila and Persephone once sat on with Jarek before our worlds were divided. The men take the bumpiest course possible as they walk up the path.

The palace shimmers in the setting sun. The light glares off the opal-colored walls—a fierce, blinding orange color. It towers over us, both beautiful and terrifying.

A tear leaks out of my eye and down my cheek as the giant doors open. Merrick and Phorcys are still unconscious in the arms of rough, angry sailors working for the prince.

Our war with the sirens is over, but it was nothing compared to the one we face with the humans. This battle has only just entered into our lives, and it has no intention of releasing us until one side or the other is destroyed completely.

The king stands inside, appraising the situation, hands behind his back—he looks like the picture of Jarek in Aila's locket. He's terrifying as he points, directing the guards.

The palace doors slam shut behind us, trapping us within the human walls.

Acknowledgements

You are a completely fabulous person for sticking with me on this journey! I love, love, love Celena's tale (tail?) and the fact that I got to go darker in this one and really explore a lot of different themes is just such a gift for me.

I feel like a lot of this particular story has to do with family—specifically with siblings. As an older sister myself, a lot of my experiences with my little sister influenced Celena and Coralie in this story, though, to be fair, the mermaids aren't based off of my sister or I in any way. But that protective spirit Celena has is definitely something I've experienced with my sister.

I'm *so* excited for you to see what happens next in the Siren Wars, and while we're wrapping up Celena's story in the next book, you actually met some characters in Darker Depths that you're going to want to remember… because the spin-offs are in the planing stages! I can't wait!

Special thanks to Elle for all of your support and

guidance while I was knocking out this series—you're amazing.

Thanks to Jess for all the effort you put into helping me flourish in this industry—I'd be lost without you!

Thank you to Yentl for being the fabulous person that you are—you make the dramatic times far more fun than they have any right to be!

Thanks to Susie for being my little sister so I could create this awesome relationship between Celena, Caspian, and Coralie!

Thanks to Julie for always being there to encourage and support me on my trips down the rabbit hole (oh, the jokes) on this series.

Extra special thanks to the aquarium cams I had in the bottom of my computer screen while I wrote this series—I appreciate the visuals which I immediately wrote into the story whenever I saw something cool out of the corner of my eye.

Most of all, thank you to YOU, oh fabulous reader! You are the most epic, awesome, lovely person and I'm truly grateful to get to hang out with you through these pages.

I'll see you in the final book in Celena's story (but not the final in the Siren Wars Saga) soon—be sure to check out the blurb on the next page and then the first chapter after that!

Stay inspired!
-K.M. Robinson

BEYOND THE SHORES

Inside the human palace, Celena is faced with a choice—cooperate or die. Separated from Merrick and the other mer, her only choice is to sway the human prince into befriending her *despite* his father's resistance to create a new treaty with the mer.

When her twin and the collection find Celena and Merrick, they create a plan to escape, but dangerous advances from above threaten to destroy their chance at survival.

Celena and her friends find themselves thrust into a new side of the war—one where they have to side with the humans and work to help save them before it's too late for *anyone* to survive this new battle. She may be fighting for her enemy's safety, but the royal humans might kill her anyway.

One way or another, the Siren Wars will finally end.

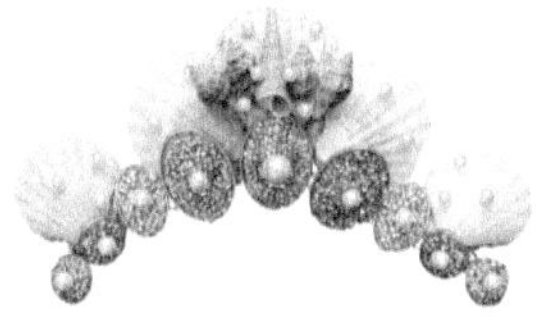

Get your copy at
beyondtheshoresinfo.kmrobinsonbooks.com

Read the first chapter on the next page!

BEYOND THE SHORES-CHAPTER 1

IN THE DARKEST HOURS—THOSE WHERE EVERYTHING SEEMS lost and hopeless—we often find our redemption.

This is where I have learned to survive, even as my world falls apart.

Noises are something I've always identified my life by —the sound of my little sister's breathing when she snuck into my bed in the middle of the night as a mer child, the noise a dolphin makes when it glides through the palace hallways, the atmosphere of a kelp forest during a brewing storm—no matter where I am or what I'm doing, when I hear those noises, I'm taken right back to the first time those noises made an impression on me.

The sound of the palace door slamming behind me is one that will haunt me for the rest of my life.

Phorcys starts to stir as the humans carry us through

the halls of the palace. I know better than to speak and upset our captors, but I try *willing* the siren to look at me.

His head lolls back, but he takes in the sights around us, quickly becoming alert. He attempts to sit up, but the humans forbid it. When Phorcys connects with me—upside down as he's pushed back—I shake my head quickly.

Like it or not, the siren is in this with us, and we're going to need to work together to save ourselves.

Merrick wakes but holds deadly still. I've seen him pretend to sleep enough times to know he is alert and listening to everything happening to us. His eyelids twitch, confirming that he knows what's happening and that he's taking advantage of the situation. I let out a quick breath of air from my nose, louder than the rest to assure him that I'm still with him.

The palace glides by me as easily as the ocean does. We slice through the hallways, flipping around corners in the air as the men carry us, doing all the work on our behalf.

Perhaps Nir had it right when he forced his sirens to carry him around the ocean on a makeshift throne. Then again, Nir is dead, so perhaps he's not the best merman to get ideas from at this point.

The hallways are an internal representation of the outside walls, casting an opalescent shine onto the floor as the light bounces off of them. The harsh sunset makes everything glow orange as light streams in through the window.

The chandelier my great-great-grandmother, Aila, had told our family about is even more stunning in person. I look up as we pass under it. Aila had never seen it up close—only through the window from the ocean outside the palace—but I imagine she would have loved this. If I were in the sea, I would swim up and touch the crystals.

I check on Merrick again as he continues to pretend to be knocked out. His breathing is steady, and he doesn't look to be in any more pain than the last time I saw him before the sailors hit him on the head with that oar when they pulled us into the boat, but I'm not entirely sure considering the beatings we've been taking the last few days.

"Let go," Phorcys insists, shattering the quiet. The men threaten him, hoping it will silence his rant. When it doesn't, they move to gag him.

"Phorcys," I say in a hushed voice, trying to still him. If the humans get too close to his face, I'm positive he will try to bite them, and there's no telling what they'll do in retaliation.

He bucks a few times but remains quiet.

Large tapestries fill the halls, dangling from the roof nearly to the floor in shades of gold. Fine, white sand appears to be covering each of them, though it looks like some of it has been swiped away by someone brushing against it, revealing a more brilliant shade of whatever gold it is made out of—perhaps threads of spun gold from the books I once read.

We walk by a throne room, and I peek inside as we brush past the door. The thrones are covered in jewels that sparkle as the sunlight glints off of them, entering through a high window positioned perfectly to bathe them in light. We rush by so quickly that I can't see anything else in the room.

We wind down a set of stairs, and for the first time ever in my life, the stairs I'm encountering are actually *needed*. It's uncomfortable as the men bump down the stairs, jostling me with each step.

"Over there." A man with a sharp nose points down a hallway. "Take her over there."

He points to the right, scribbling on a piece of paper in his hand.

He's separating us.

"Merrick!" I react without thinking it through.

His eyes fly open as he tries to sit up. Merrick reaches for me, his blue hair flopping in his eyes. It's amazing how quickly his hair dried, while *mine* is still mercilessly dripping down my sting-covered back.

"Don't take her," he begs, stretching as far as he can. The men cling to him, refusing to let him reach me.

"Merrick!" I lean toward him, trying to grab his hand.

"Celena!" He struggles against them.

"Please, just let us stay together," I try to negotiate with them. "We'll do as you ask, just let us stay together."

The guards pull us apart. Merrick and I shout to each other as he and Phorcys are taken down the opposite hallway.

"Shut up!" one of the guards orders, lifting a hand as though he might strike me.

I cower, letting them think I'm more scared than I am—much like Tarni spent her entire life doing until her cousin became king and she came out of hiding. The humans don't need to know I'm capable of killing them *before I actually do it.*

Little things stick out of their ears, blocking the sound of my siren song—not that I'm attempting to siren them right now. It looks like maybe they used pieces of rolled up fabric to block me out, but I can't be sure.

I'm close enough that I could reach up and pull whatever it is out of two of the guards' ears. I could siren them quickly enough to disrupt their plan, but at least two would be impervious to my song, and retribution would be swift.

They carry me down another set of steps and around a wall that doesn't reach the ceiling of the room. When we round the corner, an oval-shaped wall sits in the middle of the room with water in it.

I'm dropped into water that's barely big enough for

me to do a flip in. I could sit on the bottom and be fully submerged, but this contraption is designed to keep me where they can get to me. If a human were to crawl in, they could stand and their heads would easily be above the surface.

The water is still—I've never seen the surface of any water so calm in my life. It ripples when I move or when the men tap on it to get my attention. They leer at me as I assess my situation.

"Like your new home, pretty?" one of them asks.

"Do not taunt the siren, you fool," a man who has clearly worked for the king his whole life addresses the grubby sailor. His voice is more proper than the sailor's, as is his ensemble.

I look at him, pleading with my face, afraid that if I open my mouth, he'll take it as an attack and hurt me.

He wrinkles his nose in disgust and backs away. Motioning for the others to follow, they leave the room. I'm alone.

I try to climb over the wall, but there's nowhere for me to go. The floor is massive. By the time I crawl to the stairs where the men brought me in, I'll be discovered— or dead from the exhaustion of dragging myself across the stone. Even if I made it to the stairs, I'd have to climb up them.

There is no escape from this room.

I dart around the water, checking every angle and

side. When I find nothing useful above the water, I lower myself under—*unable to dive*—and search the walls for an escape, hidden message, or anything that can help me. Finding nothing, I return to the surface.

This room is different than the others. The walls are a bright white color but hold no opalescent shine to them. The floor looks like smooth rocks have been positioned to create intricate designs, though the entire floor is a solid white, sculpted only by the shape of the flat stones. It swirls around the room.

A window sits high above me, nearly reaching the ceiling. I can see bits of the pink sky as it fades into night, but the ocean is out of my sight. Soon the stars will be out—I might even be able to catch a glimpse of the moon one last time before my death.

The water bounces off the walls of my prison as I swim around in circles, trying to learn my limited surroundings. I grow to hate that sound.

The color fades from the sky, pulling all references to its hue from the room as it goes. The room grows dark until the moon appears, casting a pale glow through the opening. The light from the window bounces off the water of my prison and reflects on the ceiling and walls. It dances in eerie lines, shattering and moving as it consistently changes.

I breathe out, trying to slow my heart rate. Leaning against the wall, I wait for one of my captors to come fish me out of this place. Every so often, I dip under the water, cooling my skin and hair. I refuse to stay under long though—I don't want them sneaking up on me.

The toll of the last few days weighs heavily on me. I still haven't recovered from most of the trauma I've been through—the jellyfish stings, the beatings, the fights, even the brine pool—but as I'm forced to be still in the water, it all comes crashing down on me. My muscles scream, and I feel like bending in on myself to try to stop the agony. The welts on my back from the stings burn, even though they shouldn't at this point. My cuts pierce into my skin, a constant reminder of the war I was just ripped out of against my will.

I hurt, and I can't help myself to feel better.

Spreading my arms out over the top of the wall, I try to keep myself upright out of the water as I face the steps. I watch, waiting for them.

Eventually, exhaustion wins out, and I slip beneath the surface and curl up on the floor of the mini ocean as the moonlight dances over me.

I wake with a start. My eyes dart around the tiny space, checking the walls and surface above me before I lift myself out of the water. The room is still empty, but the moon is gone, replaced by the very first rays of morning.

The sun is still too low in the sky to be seen, but its pale reach graces the room. Not too much longer and the sunrise should appear, and I imagine, the room will be cast into many colors again.

"Well, well, look who is up."

I start at the voice, whipping around to face the steps as a figure rounds the corner. Last night I could hear men walking on the steps, but I was so focused on the window that I let my guard down, and he snuck up on me.

A second man follows the prince, much like he did yesterday on the boat. His ears are blocked once again, prepared to rescue the prince if he needs it. He scowls at me over the prince's shoulder.

I stay on the far side of the water—if he wants to reach me, he'll have to jump into the water or walk around to the other side, giving me time to change my location. I stay quiet as I watch him.

"If you try to siren me or any of my men, I will have them separate you from your tail, and no questions will be asked." He levels a cool gaze at me. "I haven't talked to your friends yet, but they're next, so don't make me angry."

He walks around the length of the wall, examining me. His servant follows along behind him. The prince pauses back where he started, leaning forward to rest his arms on the wall at an awkward angle as he leans toward the water.

"Who are you?"

"I am Celena, great-great-granddaughter of Princess Aila, daughter of King Gaspar."

"You're royalty?"

"Distantly, yes."

"So you don't rule the ocean?" One finger taps on the side of the wall as he tries to glean information.

"No, my cousins do."

"Why were you sirening my people?" He blinks through his sandy brown hair, dark eyes snapping at me.

"There is a war under the sea between sirens and mer—"

"You're all sirens," he snaps.

"What?" I ask after a moment, taken back by his outburst.

"There is no difference."

"We all have the ability to siren, yes, but some choose not to use it unless we have to—that's why we had the treaty."

"You broke the treaty."

The light shifts in the room as the sun starts to come up, tingeing everything yellow. The prince doesn't seem to notice.

"The treaty was broken." I nod my head in agreement. "But not by my grandmother. She tried to prevent that from happening."

"The mermaids tried to kill my great-great-grandfather."

"*Not* Aila. She and Jarek were friends," I insist.

"Do *not* speak the king's name," the prince growls at me.

"The royals from both of our kingdoms were once united in friendship. The king and my grandmother were friends, and when her cousin tried to hurt him, she saved him. She told us all about him—"

"What did she tell you?"

He looks angry, so it puzzles me that he's still talking to me. The prince watches me like I might leap across the water at any moment and attack him, but also like I'm a riddle to figure out.

"She told our family many stories that have been passed through the generations about how she, Persephone, and your grandfather used to sit on the steps outside and watch the waves together. He would pet their hair, and they'd tell him about life under the sea.

"Aila told us about the chandelier in the palace window that she always longed to see. She told us about Prince Jar—about the prince's mother, and how she was always looking out for him.

"She also told us *in great detail* about the destruction of the treaty, and what Persephone and her mother, Chantay, did to ensure there was a division between us."

He purses his lips, taking in the information, but doesn't look convinced.

"Aila said after she discovered that Persephone and the prince were together, she found them in a cave where Persephone was attempting to siren the prince. She convinced him to dive into the water, and Aila saved him from drowning.

"Your Highness," I begin. "After the human-mer treaty was dissolved, the mer split as well. Those that wanted to hurt you were banished, and the rest of us tried to avoid the humans' wrath. We moved far away from our home and never left our borders until now."

"And just why did you leave, *mermaid?*"

"The sirens—those that wanted to hurt you—also wanted to hurt us because of Chantay's banishment and Persephone's imprisonment. They've waited a century for revenge, and this was their last opportunity."

"Why is that?" The prince leans back, standing on his own.

The prince is looking for information, and I'll gladly give it to him. If I can be helpful, perhaps he will listen. If nothing else, I need to position myself to not seem like a threat to him and his people.

"The last of Chantay's line died without a female heir. Her son and husband were fulfilling her wishes to make both the humans and mer pay."

"That explains why *they* were here. Why were *you* here?"

This prince is nothing like what Aila told us Jarek was like in her stories. That boy was weak and passive—a dreamer. The prince before me looks like he will kill first and ask questions later.

His face has some similarities to Jarek's, but his hair and eyes are different. The prince's chin, cheekbones, and nose are close enough that I feel comfortable believing this is one of Jarek's descendants.

"They attacked us first," I explain, brushing back my hair as it floats in the water in front of me. "They tried to take over our palace and lost. They kidnapped my sister, and when I tried to save her, they took me too. My collection came after us to save us, but when we arrived, the rest of the siren collection was on their way, intent on using us to hurt the humans."

"I thought you said you didn't siren." His eyes narrow at me like I'm lying.

"The mer collection doesn't, but we still have the ability to. Most of our collection has lost it because it hasn't been used in a century, but those of royal blood have more powerful voices."

"And their royals are dead, so they wanted *yours*..." he murmurs.

He turns, starting to walk away, his servant rushing to keep up.

"Wait!" I call. Realizing I shouldn't have, I sink back against the wall, waiting to suffer for it.

The prince flinches but slowly turns.

"You're leaving?" I ask in a small voice, hoping to convince him that I'm not a threat.

He raises an eyebrow, turning again to walk out.

"What's going to happen to us?" I call, braver.

"Answer my questions and we'll see," he calls over his shoulder. His words echo around the room, setting my teeth on edge. The only time I've ever heard an echo was on the surface, and I don't like it. Even so, I can't let him walk away yet.

"Where are my friends?"

"They're in their own little pools," the prince answers.

My prison has a name.

"I need to know they're okay," I call. "Please!"

"They're fine...for now. We'll see how they cooperate." He turns to glance at me as he mounts the stairs. "If you behave, you'll live—for now. If you don't, we can make things very difficult here until we get the information we need and then we'll split you in half. Remember that, Celena."

"*Princess,*" I snap.

"What was that?" He takes a step back off the stairs.

"*Princess* Celena," I correct him.

He appraises me, considering my words.

"Very well, *Princess* Celena."

The prince nods before ascending the stairs once more.

"We'll see how long you last."

Their footsteps fall heavy as they finish climbing the long stairs, turning once they reach the landing, and exit the room as an overwhelming feeling of dread washes over my body. I sink back into the water, waiting.

Read the rest by grabbing your copy of Beyond The Shores at

beyondtheshoresinfo.kmrobinsonbooks.com

ORIGINS OF THE SIREN WARS

A CENTURY AGO, THE HUMAN-MER TREATY WAS established to protect the mer from the humans while they guided ships through storm-plagued waters. Now, Aila and her cousin, Persephone, act as representatives for their grandfather, King Gaspar, to the human world.

The mermaids share a close bond with the Prince Jarek, but when Aila catches Persephone trying to siren him into the waters, she must work to protect her friend from her cousin without hurting the human-mer relationship—something Persephone's mother won't tolerate.

War is brewing and Aila and Persephone are caught in the middle of a battle they never saw coming—one that will last for another century.

Get your copy at
originsinfo.kmrobinsonbooks.com

BONUS SCENES

Want to read a bonus scene from The Siren Wars? We're giving out an exclusive bonus scene over on the K.M. Robinson Facebook page!

Get it by sending the page a direct message at facebook.com/kmrobinsonbooks

We're also giving away Siren Wars freebies in the newsletter. Join for free books, excerpts, and more! newsletter.kmrobinsonbooks.com

We're constantly giving out additional bonus scenes for preorder swag, giveaways, and more, so watch the social media pages carefully for the next scene giveaway.

WORLD PORTALS

Ready to learn exclusive facts about The Siren Wars and other K.M. Robinson Series?

World Portals are now available on
www.kmrobinsonbooks.com

Learn behind the scenes facts, watch videos, play games, check out our book filters, find out where to get bonus scenes, view fan art, and get access to other secrets we've hidden away inside the World Portals on the website.

You can also see the map that we weren't able to add to this version of the story due to file size limits.

The World Portals are constantly changing and information is being taken away and added all the time, so check back frequently for new content!

BONUS FACEBOOK FILTERS

WANT TO GET YOUR HANDS ON SOME INCREDIBLE Facebook filters for Siren Wars? Now you have the ability to get filters for the story, characters, etc right inside your phone.

You can use these on your photos, profile pictures, videos, and live broadcasts. All you have to do is like my author page and they will automatically show up in your filters!

I've even taken these clips and put them on Instagram Stories by saving them to my phone and uploading them to Instagram.

Visit www.facebook.com/kmrobinsonbooks to grab these filters for your photos, videos, and broadcasts! Bonus points for tagging me @kmrobinsonbooks so I can see how you're supporting The Siren Wars.

K.M. Robinson is a storyteller who creates new worlds both in her writing and in her fine arts conceptual photography. She is a marketing, branding and social media strategy educator who is recognized at first sight by her very long hair. She is a creative who focuses on photography, videography, couture dress making, and writing to express the stories she needs to tell. She almost always has a camera within reach. Visit her at her website: www.kmrobinsonbooks.com

CONNECT ON SOCIAL MEDIA

facebook.com/kmrobinsonbooks

instagram.com/kmrobinsonbooks

twitter.com/kmrobinsonbooks

Get free books and excerpts of other K.M. Robinson
books at excerpt.kmrobinsonbooks.com

ALSO BY K.M. ROBINSON

The Siren Wars Saga

Book One: The Siren Wars

Book Two: Darker Depths

Book Three: Beyond The Shores (Coming July 2018)

Origins of the Siren Wars: Prequel Novella

The Jaded Duology

Book One: Jaded

Book Two: Risen

The Complete Series Boxset/Omnibus with exclusive epilogue
(Summer 2018)

The Golden Trilogy

Book One: Golden

Forged: A Golden Novella

Book Two: Locked

Book Three: Edge

The Complete Series Boxset/Omnibus with exclusive bonus novella, Tempered

The Legends Chronicles

Along Came A Spider: A Prequel Novelette

And They'll Come Home: A Prequel Novelette

The Revolution of Jack Frost (Coming November 2018)

Virtually Sleeping Beauty: A Novella Retelling

The Goose Girl and The Artificial: A Novella Retelling

The Sinking: A Novella Retelling

JADED: BOOK ONE OF THE JADED DUOLOGY

Her father failed in his mission to take control from the Commander, a defeat that has cost Jade her life. She will die as punishment. Now she belongs to the Commander's son—as his wife. Knowing his intent is to quietly kill her in revenge, Jade's every move is calculated to survive—until she learns her death ensures the safety of her father and her entire town.

Roan doesn't want to kill Jade, but once his family isolates her from her father and community, his only choice is to go through with the plan. Jade doesn't make it easy as she tries to sway him into falling for her. Each misstep makes him question his cause. Each moment makes every decision harder, but the Commander won't allow him to fail.

One chooses life. One chooses death. In the midst of the chaos, only one will succeed.

Now available!
Learn more about The Jaded Duology at
jadedinfo.kmrobinsonbooks.com

GOLDEN: BOOK ONE OF THE GOLDEN TRILOGY

Goldilocks was never naive. She was sent on a mission and Dov Baer is her new target.

When the girl with the golden hair betrays everyone, not even she has hope of surviving.

The stories say that Goldilocks was a naïve girl who wandered into a house one day. Those stories were wrong. She was never naïve. It was all a perfectly executed plan to get her into the Baers' group to destroy them.

Trained by her cousin, Lowell, and handler, Shadoe, Auluria's mission is to destroy the Baers by getting close to the youngest brother, Dov, his brother and sister-in-law and the leaders of the Baers' group.

When she realizes Dov isn't as evil as her cousin led her to believe, she must figure out how to play both sides or her deception will cause everyone in her world to burn.

If her allegiances are discovered, either side could destroy her...if the Society doesn't get her first.

Available now!
Learn more about The Golden Trilogy at
goldeninfo.kmrobinsonbooks.com

ALONG CAME A SPIDER: THE FIRST PREQUEL NOVELETTE TO THE LEGENDS CHRONICLES

Little Hacker Muffet
sat on her tuffet
destroying her cords and Way.
Along came a hacker named Spider,
who sat down beside her
and frightened his opponent away.

WHEN FET, ONE OF THE MOST SKILLED HACKERS IN THE Legends, discovers her best friend and leader of her group has been abducted and held for ransom, she must escape unnoticed and find Peep before it's too late.

When Spider, a new recruit training to join her hacker ring, slips out with her and claims to have a plan to save her friend, Fet is forced to bring him along. As she discovers he's not who he claims to be, she faces grave danger and learns just how deadly a spider bite can be.

Now available!
Learn more about The Legends Chronicles at
acasinfo.kmrobinsonbooks.com

VIRTUALLY SLEEPING BEAUTY

She may be doing battle in the virtual world, but in the real world, they can't wake her up…

All Rora wants is to help people as class president, give her time to local charities, and quietly earn her way to the top level of the virtual reality system that the entire country uses without anyone noticing she's the second best player in the game.

All Royce wants to do is level up as a knight inside the gaming system, slay dragons, and eventually play his way to controlling the palace as he takes the crown away from the reigning queen.

When his Aunt Perry calls him, hysterically screaming that her goddaughter, Rora, has been inside for more than the four hours the game allows, Royce rushes over to help.

Entering the game, Royce soon discovers that Rora is trapped inside the system after an encounter with an evil magician who can change forms inside the game and control the virtual world. If he and his friend can't help her beat the game, she might not be able to wake up in the real world at all.

When virtual knights and princesses meet to slay dragons and defeat evil rulers, there's nothing stopping them from suffering real-world consequences too.

To wake her up, he must enter the game and help her beat it.

Now available!
Learn more about Virtually Sleeping Beauty at
vsbinfo.kmrobinsonbooks.com

www.ingramcontent.com/pod-product-compliance
Lightning Source LLC
Chambersburg PA
CBHW030531190726
48283CB00006B/1857